Praise for *Flash Fiction In...*

"*Flash Fiction International* reminds me that the world is so very small and fragile . . . and yet contains an animal as muscular and fast as this wild horse of a book."   —Claudia Smith, *American Book Review*

"One of the most striking things this collection shows is how flash fiction can allow what has been suppressed to find a voice . . . to introduce readers to voices they may never have heard, and show that this penetrating form has found a niche nearly everywhere."

—*Economist* (UK)

"Flash feels very much like a phenomenon whose time has come. . . . [A] form well-suited to our fragmented, globally interconnected age."

—Roger Cox, *Scotsman*

Praise for *Flash Fiction Forward*

"Consistently swift and powerful, distilling the intricacies and flourish of short fiction into just a few pages. . . . Ranging in style from crisp, sober realism to outlandish surrealism, these [are] small treasures."

—*Publishers Weekly*, starred review

"Although the form is concise, the subjects broached tend to be substantial, and it is a particular pleasure to read these pared-to-the-bone stories that cover the spectrum from blithe to intense, funny to sad."

—*Booklist*

Praise for *Flash Fiction*

"These stories are not merely flashes in the pan; there's pay dirt here!"

—DeWitt Henry, editor of *Ploughshares*

"[An] anthology of brilliant miniatures. . . . You can space out your reading of these epiphanic delicacies over a week or even months. Dear Browser, I have to confess, I gobbled them up in a day!"

—Alan Cheuse, National Public Radio

FLASH FICTION AMERICA

JOHN DUFRESNE

FLASH FICTION AMERICA

73 VERY SHORT STORIES

Edited by

JAMES THOMAS, SHERRIE FLICK, AND JOHN DUFRESNE

W. W. NORTON & COMPANY
Celebrating a Century of Independent Publishing

Manufacturing by LSC Harrisonburg
Book design by Ellen Cipriano
Production manager: Louise Mattarelliano

ISBN 978-0-393-35805-6

W. W. Norton & Company, Inc., 500 Fifth Avenue,
New York, N.Y. 10110
www.wwnorton.com
W. W. Norton & Company Ltd., 15 Carlisle Street, London W1D 3BS

1 2 3 4 5 6 7 8 9 0

We wish to thank our Associate and Consulting Editors

Tara Campbell
Kim Chinquee
Hector Duarte, Jr.
Patricia Engel
Marcela Fuentes
Molly Gaudry
Yona Harvey
Brandon Hobson
Bryan Jansing
W. Todd Kaneko
Tara Laskowski
Christopher Merrill
Kona Morris
Sally Reno
Tom Williams

Thought is only a flash between two long nights,
but the flash is everything.

—HENRI POINCARÉ

CONTENTS

FOREWORD

When I read flash fiction I read with equal parts admiration and envy. I recognize the familiar compression of the short story in a piece of flash fiction, the way the shadow of the past and the urgency of the present and the weight of the future hover there all at once, bringing the reader into and then beyond the story. But there is something particular about the compact precision of flash, the way it balances movement and stillness, asking the reader to look closely at something that's just about to come undone. The best flash fiction can have it both ways, can make us believe that we can have everything at once too, or break our hearts by reminding us that we can't. It's a feeling that Amy Stuber's gorgeous "I'm On the Side of the Wildebeest" puts words to: *"Stay, just stay,"* the narrator says under her breath to every living thing, but of course the heart of the story is in knowing that everything can't stay put, and the heart of the story is also in seeing that it can, however briefly, be put before us and forever preserved.

I often start my writing classes by asking the whole class to bring in a piece of flash for the first week, in part because I get to hear the whole chorus of voices and in part because I find that when I ask them to compress, to give me the shortest version of what feels like a full story, I learn something about what a story means to them, I learn something about who they are, I learn something crucial about what they're trying to hold on to or escape from. I found the same satisfaction in the chorus of voices in this anthology: in doggie DNA tests that can't quite answer the real question, in lightning that strikes twice, in a calmly postapocalyptic landscape where transactional physical exchanges for the sake of survival can look like kindness, in a waitress who sees clearly how her table of wealthy customers see her, just a character in the story of how *the power of their money . . . could work other people like puppets*, in a sister whose quarantine connection to her lover through screens helps her find the words for her dying brother, in a pissed-off mistress who crashes a wedding and brings both personal and diasporic history with her, in a man who catalogs his lovers until one transcends the numbering system and emerges as wondrously specific. As a chorus of voices of some of the most compelling contemporary writers in the U.S, this anthology tells me that my country is pissed off and giddy and bold and grieving and dying and in love, that it is forever and already gone.

I read this anthology balancing my greed with my fear that it would be over too soon—one more story, I would think, and then another, because I could read quickly, after all, but the pace of my feeling couldn't keep up with the pace of my reading and sometimes I had to give myself the gift of sitting quietly in the aftermath of a story, of letting it linger. I hope that in whatever future this anthology finds you, you too have the space to sit with its many gifts.

—*Danielle Evans*

PREFACE

WHEN *FLASH FICTION AMERICA* WAS first conceived as an anthology it had a simple premise: to showcase some of the best contemporary flash fiction published in the early twenty-first century. It was to follow historically in the footsteps of *Flash Fiction International* (2015), *Flash Fiction Forward* (2006), and *Flash Fiction*, the seminal anthology that used the two-word term for the first time in 1992.

But in order to find these great stories and the authors writing them, we also had to face a more philosophical question: *What is America?* Social and political movements, plagues, floods, earthquakes, and hurricanes have come barreling down in recent years. The aftermath of which has become an opening up to how messed-up and monumentally, historically different we are from each other as we inhabit this country. In "Origin Lessons," Aimee Bender's new teacher insists, "We began all at once, everywhere." As editors we agreed to open up the book of American flash fiction, to lay it flat like the Great Plains, to manipulate it into the coasts and hollows, mountains, cities, and towns—to find the authors and characters living everywhere, harmoniously and not. In "Rhythm," Joshunda Saunders writes: "we get low low low so we can burst up & out like uncapped hydrants, flow out into these streets until the water seeps in, seeps out & we out."

There isn't an easy answer to what America is, but we were intent on digging into it. A Langston Hughes line came to mind: "America never was America to me," and in some ways that was our guiding principle in compiling this anthology. To find the stories that expand and pursue and challenge the definition of the United States. It's "the way you look for evidence of belonging . . ." Jasmine Sawers writes in "All Your Fragile History." We set out to find the evidence. And it was overwhelming. From online journals to print journals, magazines, and books we flipped and scrolled, read and reread, thousands of stories under a thousand words.

What we found was a wide array of flash fiction pushing at the form with nuance, grace, and grit. Stories that kicked aside an America portrayed with limited scope. Authors who unfolded, unpacked, and clicked a flashlight into the attic of this country. What we found is that flash fiction is alive and well in the twenty-first century, certainly ready, eyes wide open, for another thirty-year run.

In "Monsters," Sadis Quraeshi Shepard's narrator asks, "What would it be like, I wondered, to live without fear?" Emma Stough's Jenny notes, "Everyone has all the same diseases: insomnia, possession, indoctrination, childhood." Venita Blackburn writes, "They don't know anything about how we live, love, and die." These compressed stories take us into knowing as these tightly packed worlds open up. Some we already dwell in, others we try on, dip our toes into for a few pages. "Nobody thinks about the way sound carries across water. Even the water in a swimming pool," Amy Hempel writes in "Beach Town." As readers we're invited to eavesdrop. We like to be privy not only to the secrets but to how they're contrived, how they're floated across pools of water. Cassandra of Troy knows all the secrets in Gwen E. Kirby's "Shit Cassandra Saw . . . " and yet, "Cassandra is *done*, full the fuck up, soul-weary."

Flash Fiction America crisscrosses the country, like an epic road trip, east to west, north to south, on Route 9 and Highway 101, by plane, automobile, boat, and train. "Wichita was not what she thought," Serena laments in "I'm Exaggerating" by Kate Wisel. Chauna Craig's men drink bourbon on the rocks in Butte, Montana. Meg Pokrass gets to work in Midtown Manhattan. We touch down in New England and the Northeast, Midwest, West, Southwest, and South. Of course, many of the characters are completely lost geographically and otherwise. Like the narrator in "Something Falls in the Night" by Desiree Cooper: "You are fully dressed, but you have forgotten your shoes. You wait shivering at a bus stop. When it arrives in the darkness, it is nearly empty. You board, your feet numb and clumsy."

The idea of America wouldn't be complete if John Wayne didn't ride into the sunset in Matthew Salesses's "How to Be a Conqueror." If the sun didn't rise on some hungover souls. If birth, life, and death didn't cycle through with joy, pain, comfort, grief, confusion, and resolution. "The summer sun dissolved into golden, vaporish rays in the trees," writes Stuart Dybek in "Bruise." In the end, it's the beauty of language and story that unites this anthology. One glorious, shining sentence after another.

—Sherrie Flick

INTRODUCTION

TELL ME A STORY, our reader says. Make me laugh, make me cry, carry me away. Help me to imagine a more compelling world; help me to understand who I am and who these other people are and what we're all doing here and why we're doing it, and if you can do that with language that is fresh and provocative, with nouns that are precise and verbs that are muscular, and if your usage is prescriptively flawless or wonderfully flawed, and if you can make me sing to the music of your prose, if you can bring the news of your world to my world, if you can "tell it slant" and keep it short, so much the better. Telling stories and reading them are how we make sense of the world, how we amend our bewilderment. This narrative impulse is as necessary for our survival as breathing.

Flash fiction isn't new. We have had fables, of course, and folk and fairy tales, biblical parables, exempla, and Zen koans. We might also include anecdotes, jokes, and every bit of gossip we've ever shared over drinks or at the kitchen table, every mumbled disclosure in the confessional or secret whispered in bed, and every introductory exchange with strangers we've met at cocktail parties. All very short, all driven by narrative. In fact, flash might be the most prevalent form of storytelling there is. Anton Chekhov, who arguably invented the modern short story, wrote many very short stories of six or seven hundred words. Kafka gave us *Parables and Paradoxes* and Borges, his *Ficciones*. At the turn of the last century *McClure's* magazine published "Daily Shorts." In 1926, *Collier's Weekly* began printing one-page narratives. *Cosmopolitan* followed. For more than fifty years, beginning in 1920, Nobel Laureate Yasunari Kawabata wrote his spare and lyrical "palm-of-the-hand" stories. Hemingway wrote very short stories in his debut collection, *In Our Time*. Mildred I. Reid and Delmore E. Bordeaux published a craft book, *Writers: Try Short Shorts!* But then the form seemed to fall out of favor for a moment, only to be revived in 1969 when Robley Wilson took over the editorship of the venerable *North American Review* and treated us to "Four-Minute Fictions." Richard Brautigan gave the genre a boost with his compact and comic countercultural tales, as did Grace Paley and Luisa Valenzuela with their quick, emotionally charged stories and Sandra Cisneros with her luminous vignettes in *House on Mango Street* and Raymond Carver and Joyce Carol Oates and John Edgar Wideman and also Donald Barthelme with his enigmatic, postmodernist shorts. Then came the anthologies *Sudden Fiction* and *Flash Fiction*. The very short story was no longer an experiment, but a recognized genre. *The New Yorker* publishes flash these days, and *Duotrope* lists 483 markets welcoming flash fiction. Flash isn't new, and it isn't going away.

Flash fiction is a narrative (or it's not) that is distilled, cogent, concentrated, layered, allusive, textured, insightful, and unpredictable. It's short but not shallow; it is a reduced form used to represent a larger, more complex story. And like the gist of a recollected conversation, it offers the essential truth, if not all the inessential facts. Like poetry, flash benefits from arbitrary constraint. In the case for this collection, a thousand words, with one exception. Why a thousand? Because you have to draw the line somewhere. "Art lives from constraints and dies from freedom," Leonardo da Vinci wrote. Flash makes meaning through compression. And this word limit may be all we need to begin thinking in an unhabitual way. Less is more. Brevity is both the soul of lit and an invitation to undermine the narrative conventions of the traditional short story. But you need to write a lot to write a little. To be brief takes time.

Writing flash fiction is the art of omission. What you leave out is as important as what you leave in. "It's not the notes you play," Miles Davis said, "it's the notes you don't play." Flash esteems glance above gaze. This is fiction approaching haiku, the art of few words and many suggestions. And like haiku, flash fiction does not do our thinking for us but starts us thinking, does not explain, only indicates. Flash carries the collaboration between writer and reader to another level. The story is the call that awaits its response. The writer, we might say, evokes the images that the reader dreams with. In conventional stories, we expect that the central character will be changed as the result of their struggle. But plots in flash may be elliptical, off the page, implied rather than expressed, and so it might be the reader, not the character, who is changed. The reader may be left feeling radiant joy, profound sadness, or bewildering shock.

Flash fiction seems to operate like dreams, which have middles but not many beginnings or endings. You're already falling through the air, terrified and confused. How can this be happening? And you never reach the source of the gravity before you wake. A work of flash begins in the midst of things, advances quickly, and ends abruptly. The narrative is over, but the story goes on in the mind of the reader who has been surprised in the act of imagining, goes on in the direction suggested by the story. Flash fiction is not about a lifetime or a season; it's about a heartbeat, the vital center, the driving impulse of life.

Thirty years ago, in his introduction to the first *Flash Fiction* anthology, James Thomas expressed his pleasure at presenting stories of minimal and rapid trajectory and asked the question, "How short can a story be and truly be a story?" Here we are again trying to answer by way of example, in *Flash Fiction America*, exploring the varieties of cultural experience, telling our reader many very short stories, complete and resonant, which are all about all the ways all of us live in America today.

—*John Dufresne*

Flash Fiction America

Origin Lessons

Aimee Bender

WE MET THE NEW TEACHER for origin class. He was tall, with a mustache. He was our last resort. The family-genealogy class had failed. The trip to the zoo to look at monkeys had failed. The investigation of sperm and egg in a dish had failed. All were interesting, but they were not enough. Where did the sperm come from? Where did the monkey come from? Where did Romania come from?

He sat in a chair at the front of the rug.

We began all at once, everywhere, he said.

We sat quietly, waiting.

Has he started? someone whispered.

Yes, he said. I have started. We began all at once, everywhere.

We thought about that.

But before that?

He shrugged. Goes beyond what we know, he said. All we can know is the universe.

I thought we started in a dot, someone said.

He shook his head. He brought out his lunch in a brown bag from his briefcase.

No dot, he said. A dot is at a point, and if at a point, things are also not at that point.

We watched as he chewed a baby carrot.

A very well-packed dot, someone else offered. From which all things hurled free. Not unlike a suitcase.

Nope, he said. Everywhere, all at once.

Then what? someone asked.

After that? he said. Well, at first, it was fast. Everything accelerating fast. Everything wanting to get out.

Get out of what?

Poor wording, he said. Just rapid acceleration. Then it slowed down. Now expansion is accelerating steadily.

What expansion?

Oh, the universe is expanding, he said, wiping his mouth. We found that out in 1929. From Hubble.

We nodded. This made sense. It had been in a suitcase and then—

No suitcase! he said, stomping his foot. All at once, everywhere!

Someone stared to cry. Someone else pushed Martha into the rug.

How about this, he said. He put away his lunch bag and opened his briefcase again and brought out sock puppets to show us personified matter and radiation. So, he said, what happened was that, after around four hundred thousand years, everything slowed and cooled, and matter grew lumpy due to gravity, and radiation stayed smooth. Before that, the two lived evenly together.

He wound the two socks together and then moved them away from each other, and the lumpy sock got all lumpified, ready to form galaxies, and he stuffed a battery-operated light bulb inside the smooth sock so that the light beneath that fabric radiated.

Nice, we said.

The origin of galaxies, he said, with a flourish.

Are those your socks?

No, he said. I bought the socks at a store.

Won't the light bulb burn the sock?

No, he said, coughing. It is a specially insulated sock.

Are we accelerating right now?

Yes, he said.

Edgar grabbed on to his seat. I feel it! he shouted. He fell off his chair.

The teacher removed the socks from his hands. We can't feel it, he said. But everything is moving away from everything else, and it does mean that, in a few billion years, even our beautiful neighbors may be drifting out of reach.

He looked sad, saying that. We felt a sadness. In a billion years, our beautiful neighbors pulling away. Surely, we will not be here in a billion years. Surely we will be something new, something that might not conceive of distance in the same way. We told him this, and he nodded, but it was wistful.

He had set up a telescope on a corner of the roof, and we went up to take a look.

This is time travel, he said, narrowing an eye to set the lens. Because the light is old. We're seeing back in time.

No, we said, wrinkling our noses. We are seeing right now, today.

No, he said, the light has to travel to us and it takes millions of years. What you're seeing is time.

Excuse me, we said. We were embarrassed to correct him. He seemed so smart. What we're seeing is space.

It's space, yes, he said. It's also time. You're seeing what has already happened.

That's absurd, we said, though we did not move.

We make bigger telescopes, radio telescopes, he said, to see back all the way. We can go back thirteen billion years now! Almost to the Big Bang.

No, we said.

Yes!

You can see all that way back?

Yes!

And? we said, sitting up. The suitcase?

We pictured it at the end of a telescope. The longest, biggest telescope ever made. A tiny suitcase, of a pleasing brown leather.

Well, he said, leaning on the side wall. We can see very close to the beginning, but at around four hundred thousand years, the universe goes opaque.

We almost tossed him off the roof then. We were right there at the edge.

It's true, he said. We can see all the way to about year four hundred thousand! Can you believe that? But before that, it's veiled.

Like a bride? we said.

He smiled for the first time that day.

Sure, he said, relenting. Like a bride.

And she takes off her veil at four hundred thousand?

She does, he said. We see her quite well after that.

So who'd she marry? we ask, settling ourselves at his feet. When a bride removes her veil, it's the moment of marriage.

I don't know, he said, scratching his head. Everything? Us?

Boxing Day

Rion Amilcar Scott

DADDY'S PISSED. I CAN TELL 'cause I can hear his gloved fists slapping the punching bag downstairs. It's a flat *plapping* noise. The louder the sound, the more pissed he's become. He says every day he punches the bag is boxing day, but today actually is Boxing Day.

I would stay out of the basement, away from my punch-drunk father and every delusion he's used to sew himself together, but my mother's sent me to descend into his Hades to deliver a message.

He notices me and begins to speak as he punches the bag, breathing hard between phrases.

My father, he says, used to always tell me about the day after Christmas. How he and Grandma and Grandpappy and all the kids would head out to the beach. Can you believe that?

He stops to catch his heavy breath and then starts punching and talking again.

We suffering in arctic weather—the goddamn river's frozen and shit—and I bet your grandfather is swimming with tropical fish right now. When I was a kid all he did was tell me about it. *Look, kid, the days before you got here was the best, and now all we do is watch our breath steam.* Now he's back where he wants to be. Happy fucking Boxing Day!

Daddy is in one of his moods, that steady persistent low-level blue. Every word is a bomb filled with cynicism. I'm always surprised by the burn of his napalm.

That morning I woke early to catch some cartoons in the basement. My father says I'm too old for cartoons, so I didn't want him to see me slink downstairs. As I rounded the corner and approached the stairhead, I saw Daddy with his gloves hanging about his neck from a set of black strings.

Stay up here, kid, he said. I'm about to beat that thing till it cries. Yep, gonna be down there awhile.

He doesn't need to say, *I don't want you around.* His shrug, the curt dance of his eyes, they speak for him.

Daddy's blue moods never care about anyone. Every minute when he's like this I'm in a four-dimensional world made of endless time: hours laid next to hours, hours stacked atop hours into the sky. This broken man, reeling from daily compromise. Sarcasm and boxing the only things keeping him together. As for me, I'm one of many chains round his neck that hold him in a cold, tiny basement of mediocrity.

My father is shirtless and slick with sweat, swaying before the punching bag. He leans into his maroon opponent, clinging to the thing like he needs it in order to stand. Ref, he shouts. Ref! This motherfucker tried to bite my ear.

Dad.

Say hello to Tyson, kid.

Dad, Mom said there is not enough tofu for all of us, and it's your turn to cook and wash the dishes.

I'm the heavyweight champion of the goddamn world and that

woman wants me to eat bean sprouts? I need some red meat. A steak or something. *I'll eat your children.*

He bares his teeth and shakes his head and lays rapid-fire blows into the punching bag.

It's vegetarian day, Dad.

Seriously, kid, go tell your mother to jump in a lake.

I can't tell my mother to jump in a lake. When I'm back upstairs, I tell her he's on his way.

Later when my mother sends me back down into the dim, cold basement, Daddy is Muhammad Ali standing over Sonny Liston. He's Mike Tyson coming into the ring like a vicious animal. Then he's Tyson whimpering after losing to Buster Douglas.

His whimpering stops being a joke and crosses over into real tears, his face a rain-slicked street at midnight. He leans into the bag like Tyson leaned into Don King after his loss to Douglas. I rarely saw my dad embrace my mother the way he's hugging that bag. I don't know whether to turn and tiptoe back upstairs or to go to him, hug him in the way he says men are not to hug.

Dad, I say.

When our eyes meet, he squares his slumped shoulders and throws a weak set of punches at the bag.

Tyson in '90, he says. Good impression, huh? He wipes his tears with his forearm and punches the bag again and again and again.

Bruise

Stuart Dybek

S HE CAME OVER WEARING A man's white shirt, rolled up at the sleeves, and a faded blue denim jumper that made her eyes appear more blue.

"Look," she said, sitting down on the couch and slowly raising the jumper, revealing a bruise high on the outside of her thigh.

It was summer. Bearded painters in spattered coveralls were painting the outside of the house white. Through the open windows they could hear the painters scraping the old, flaking paint from the siding on one side of the house, and the slap of paint-soaked brushes on the other.

"These old boards really suck up the paint," one of the painters would remark from time to time.

"I've always bruised so easily," she said, lowering her voice as if the painters might hear.

The bruise looked blue underneath the tan mesh of nylon. It was just off the hip, and above it he could see the lacy band of her panties.

It was a hot day, climbing toward ninety, and as he studied the spot that she held her dress up for him to see, it occurred to him that even at this moment, it still might be possible for them to talk in a way that wasn't charged with secret meanings. Not every day needed to be imprinted on their memories. The direction their lives seemed, uncontrollably, to be taking might be changed, not by some revelation but in the course of an ordinary conversation, by the twist of a wisecrack or a joke, or perhaps by a simple question. He might ask why she was wearing pantyhose on such a hot day. Was it that her legs weren't tanned yet? He might rise from the couch and ask if she would like a lemonade, and when she said yes, he would go to the kitchen and make it—a real lemonade squeezed from the lemons in his refrigerator, their cold juice stirred with sugar and water, the granulated sugar whispering amid the ice, the ice cubes in a sweating glass pitcher clunking like a temple bell.

They could sit, sipping from cool glasses and talking about something as uncomplicated as weather, gabbing like painters, not because they lacked for more interesting things to talk about, but because it was summer and hot and she seemed not to have dressed for the heat.

Instead, when she crossed her legs in a way that hiked her dress higher and moved her body toward him, he touched the bruise with his fingertip, and pressed it more carefully and gently than one might jab at an elevator button.

Oh, her lips formed, though she didn't quite say it. She exhaled, closing her blue eyes, then opening them wider, almost in surprise, and stared at him. They were sitting very close together, their faces almost touching.

When he took his finger away she stretched the nylon over the bruise so he could better see its different gradations of blue. A pale green sheen surrounded it like an aura; purple capillaries ran off in all directions like tiny cracks, like a network of rivers on a map; there was violet at its center like a stain.

"It's ugly, isn't it?" she asked in a whisper.

He didn't answer, but pressed it again, slowly, deeply, and her head tilted back against a cushion. This time the *Oh* of her lips was audible. She closed her eyes and moaned, uncrossing her legs. They were sitting so close together that the sound of her nails scraping along nylon seemed to him almost a clatter the painters would hear. Her legs opened and he placed his palm against her and felt through the nylon heat, actual heat, like summer through a screen door.

He pressed the bruise again and again. Each time she reshaped her lips into a vowel that sounded increasingly surprised.

Outside, the house turned progressively whiter. The summer sun dissolved into golden, vaporish rays in the trees. The bruise—he never asked how she got it—spread across the sky.

Some Hard, Hot Places

Kathy Fish

MY BROTHER TALKS ABOUT THE time he was in survival training in the mountains and he had to eat a rabbit's eyeballs. He's on speakerphone in his hospital room, whispering.

Now that he's dying my brother has stories in his mouth.

I shouldn't be able to hear him but I do.

I met someone, I tell him. On a Zoom meeting.

My brother is much older. He's been dying for the entirety of the unprecedented times. The word *zoom* makes him laugh.

I laugh too, but suggest a video call for us. Maybe someone there could help him?

My brother has stories in his mouth but he doesn't want me to see him when he tells them. He's seventy-five percent morphine now and I am glad.

My lover and I write notes in the sidebar of the Zoom call.

The host doesn't know what she's doing. She mutes everyone, then asks a question.

We are all shrug emoji.

We are all rolling eyes emoji.

We are all rolling on the floor laughing our asses off emoji.

On the screen, my lover is just a rook's move away.

We flirt in the sidebar and grin mysteriously on-screen.

We agree to meet elsewhere.

We can't go anywhere, so we agree to meet elsewhere.

What do rabbit's eyes taste like? I ask my brother, because I'm beginning to doubt this story and I want to keep him talking.

My brother tells the story of taking psilocybin before a Moody Blues concert and seeing God.

He tells the story of a trip he took to Vegas with our dad. Hookers, he says.

He tells the story of putting a mouse out of its misery with a baseball bat.

My lover and I can't go anywhere, yet here we are.

I'm in his living room and he's in mine and I'm in his kitchen and he's in mine. We are in each other's living rooms and bedrooms and kitchens.

We, together, never look out a window.

We, together, never hear distant trains or smell snow.

We never breathe the same cold air.

Sometimes we watch shows together, from our own living rooms, and I watch him fall asleep.

We watched a whole season of *Star Trek: The Next Generation* and I watched him sleep.

During Zoom meetings, it's important to address each other directly to avoid confusion. So the others don't reply. We say each other's names as if to say, no, not you. *You.*

In his longest story yet, my brother tells of a sexual encounter in the woods with a priest.

It was pure, he says. It was connection, it was prayer, it was vigil. It was mushrooms and Chianti and the Holy Spirit. It was the glorious mystery of the Risen Lord. It was . . .

You wouldn't like how things are now, I tell him. Out in the world. You're better off.

My lover wants me to get closer to the screen.

We are in our own space, just us two. But I'm as close as I can get.

I cast flattering light on my body with the standing lamp, just out of sight.

My laptop sits on a stack of books so he sees me from above.

My neck looks better that way.

This is how it would be if we were in the same room. Taller him, gazing down at my upraised face.

My cat meows, jumps up on my lap.

I didn't know you had a cat, he says.

I lift her to the screen. Her tail tickles my breasts.

He wants to know her name.

Her name is Mavis.

I set her down, the only living thing I've touched besides myself in forever.

He puts on his shirt. He asks me what I miss.

Everything, I say. Annoyance, inconvenience, long lines, and lingering, grubby places, the hard, hot places.

I miss places.

I want to know what you smell like, I say.

I want to come out of a bathroom and see you French-kissing another woman on the dance floor.

I want to make a scene in the parking lot.

I could make a good goddamned scene if I wanted to.

The last time we talked, my brother called me by a different name. He asked me if I still loved him.

Do you still love me? he asked.

I do still love you.

I still love you, I said, because I knew whoever she was, it must be true.

Family

Jensen Beach

SOMEONE SUGGESTED SWIMMING AND SOMEONE else said that in this weather all we need is another incident. Someone recalled that there was an expression that perfectly explained this very moment. Someone said that yes they remembered it, lightning doesn't strike twice, and someone else said that as a matter of fact that's what happened to a friend. Someone said that no one believed this story the first time and so why should they believe it now. Someone said that they'd read an article on the internet about this topic and someone else said that, well then of course it's true. Someone suggested that everyone just calm down immediately. Someone began to walk away and someone reached out an arm to stop someone. Someone turned and said that they begged someone's pardon, but could they please release their grip. Someone struggled to hold on until someone else suggested that maybe lunch should be served, which turned the subject to food, which as usual had a calming effect. Someone prepared lunch and someone else set the table. Someone opened a bottle of wine and someone else accused someone of drinking too much. Someone lifted a phone to call someone about this and someone said, could you please put the phone down, lunch is served. Someone sat near the kitchen so as to fetch items from the stove and to refill serving dishes as necessary. Someone made a comment about someone's cooking and someone else found this indulgent, and someone else found it simply untrue. Someone said that it was raining now. Someone left the table and then the house until someone was in the yard and looking up at the rain, and the storm was large and billowing in the distance and the rain was still light above the house and in the yard as it rained on someone there. Someone pointed to the approaching storm and someone else remarked at how dark it had suddenly become. Someone said that someone had better be careful out there and someone else pointed to the clouds, now thick and black and seeming in some way to breathe as if such a thing were possible, and the rain fell in enormous drops and someone started to run for cover. Someone saw a flash of lightning and someone else said that, yes, we all saw it. Someone no longer appeared to be in the yard and someone remarked upon this change and someone else looked intently and rapidly at every part of the yard visible from behind the large kitchen window, which was now streaked with water. Someone else ran to the kitchen for a similar, but slightly enlarged, view of the yard. Someone sat still and hoped that someone was uninjured and someone else attempted to determine the likelihood of real life violating our most tested truths in this way, and as someone sat and considered this question someone seemed to recall that the expression someone had previously mentioned further qualified the circumstances of two lightning strikes with location. Someone said out loud that this was a variable someone had very foolishly forgotten and someone else said that that was no big surprise. Someone else said, what do you mean by that? Someone said that as a family we're always forgetting important details, and someone else said, do you mean forgetting or ignoring? Someone said to look out the window and someone else did, where they saw that someone was now lying on the grass near the house in a wet heap of someone. Someone said, did it happen? Someone said that it had and someone else said that it hadn't, and they all gathered there before the window in the kitchen through which they had all looked so many times but never together like this, and they looked for some evidence of the event they feared most, and they looked in every direction but could not see the past because time doesn't move in that direction, and so they looked for a long while and nobody saw anything at all.

A Notion I Took

Joy Castro

I JUMPED INTO THE SAN ANTONIO RIVER once, for a hundred dollars. After I got pregnant and had to quit dancing, I worked nights waiting tables at The Bayous down on the Riverwalk. The night I jumped, Marisa was still nursing, and my breasts were fat and swollen with it. The belly left was nothing, hidden under the black apron we all wore for pens and the money.

Eleven o'clock, we were still turning tables. *CATS* was at the Majestic, and we had a special menu to catch the people coming out late. They flooded the lobby, gabbing and impatient, all excited with their fancy clothes and the opinions they were saying. Maybe a hundred of them, and the manager freaking out, *we're out of this, we're out of that, you bus table seven right now or you're fired*, and the busboy getting stoned in the cooler when you go in to find more lemons. Fuck, what a night.

A four-top of men from Tennessee kept messing with me—business guys, not theater people. They were in their forties, fat, flush with ego and big gold watches in the candlelight, proud over some triumph they kept lifting their bottles to. Every time I crossed the patio with more salsa or another round, it would be something: "Baby, are all the girls here as fine—" and that kind of shit. Come to Texas, play cowboy for a week. But one thing led to another until I was saying the things I say when men flirt. Bold, dumb things. Then it was happening: a hundred lay flat on the table, the river stretched out like a grin, and I was giving my apron to another girl to hold. I smiled and waved from the edge of the safe cement while the whole restaurant looked on, holding its breath.

Standing there, I knew the plunge was only half of what they wanted: to see a woman do something crazy, maybe get fired, even— the power of their money that could work other people like puppets. That, I knew all about. And the other half I knew about, too: the girlie show when I'd get out, black hair streaming and sticking, wet brown flesh gleaming silver, mouth all vulnerable, opened for air, the white shirt transparent, clinging, showing the black bra, the full ripe slope of the breasts, nipples prodding, the nursing pads' little white circles the only surprise. The whole restaurant would gape.

Standing on the edge, I could hear already the sudden clapping when I climbed out, see the hot glazed rove of male eyes, the tight smiles of women applauding to show their dates they weren't bothered, of course not, why should they be? The laughter and looks that would follow me as I strode between the tables to the four Tennessee men and took my hundred. In my bra I would tuck it. And they'd roar.

The other waiters would look pissed, and the ratlike manager would write me up, furious, fidgeting with loose fabric at the knee of his khakis. But the owner wouldn't fire me. She'd shake her head, smiling, and wave him off, privately pleased that her restaurant might get known as a place where things happened, where things could get wild, where a waitress might jump in the river, who knew? Anything to stand out in a tourist zone as safe and planned as Disney.

The four Tennessee men would get a story to take back with them about those crazy big-titty Mexican girls down in San Antone: just like a border town, man, anything for a buck. You go there yourself. You try it. And me, I would get to take the money and the rest of the night off, listen to the manager bitch, go home to my apartment where my mom would freak out and switch back and forth between yelling at me, "My God, Iréne! What is this? What are you doing with yourself for God's sake?" and telling me all about her TV show. Finally she'd go.

It would be quiet, then, just me and Marisa. I'd shower and scrub off the scum and toxic waste, soaping and resoaping the nipples to make sure, and I'd put the hundred in the Catholic school jar under the bed and nurse Marisa, the whole time thinking, *Who the hell knows anything about me?* until we fell asleep in the big bed together. I could see it all happening like that as I stood on the edge in the dark.

I turned from them then, leaping and arching, flying for a second and then falling, falling through air and falling in water, the luke-warm rush of it filling my ears with silence, blotting out the clatter of dishes and quick kitchen disputes, the fake smiles at the table and the things you say to make people with money give some to you. All of it, gone. Just a rush of soft silence, the slippery liquid the same warmth as my skin holding me as I swept through in a shallow arch. It's a canal, after all, made for drainage and boatloads of white people. But deep enough. I felt my body slowing. *This water is filthy*, I thought as I kept going down, and I kept my eyes closed against it. *So filthy and polluted they dump dye in to make it blue for the tourists.* And I thought as I sank how soft the words sounded: *filthy, polluted.* I tried to think, *No real water is turquoise,* as its silk slid over me and my own weight pulled me down. *It's only filth, with color added,* I tried to think in the dark smooth quiet, but all I could feel was its pull like the pull of a soft door opening.

My X

Molly Giles

MY X NEVER FINISHES HIS SENTENCES. He'll start off with a "Did you see . . ." and then stop. When we first met, I thought it was charming. I'd prompt him. "Did I see what, darling?" Silence. After we were married, less charmed, I'd jump in with my own offerings: "Did I see the full moon last night, did I see the red dog, did I see the fat man in drag?" I was never right. My X would listen, correct me, and disappear. He could, literally, disappear, an act that should have made us money. "I think I'll go . . ." he'd say, and I'd chip in with a hopeful, ". . . to the store?" only to hear him say ". . . to India." One minute he'd be standing next to me and the next minute he'd be in a cab heading out to some seaport or in bed asleep or in the garden watering the roses he claimed I never took care of. At the end, in the lawyer's office, when I admitted that I never knew where he went, what he did, or whom he did it with, he shook his head sadly and said that was because I could not read his mind. "She's so . . ." he said to the lawyer.

". . . exhausted," the lawyer and I said together.

". . . impatient," he said.

It was true. And why not? Years had rushed by and I still didn't know him. In fact, that was what he often said to me: *You'll never know how much I love you*, he'd say, and then, not unkindly, he'd laugh.

After the divorce there were sightings. A friend saw him in an art museum trying on silk scarves. My sister saw him pass her on the bridge in a silver Jaguar. A neighbor heard him talking Farsi with an Iranian rug dealer. We decided he either worked for the CIA or the FBI or the DEA or all three of them. Just last week, five years after our divorce, I bumped into him in a bookstore; he was standing in a corner reading the obituaries in the *New York Times* out loud to himself. He was dressed in surfer shorts and a hoodie. He had grown a mustache and had a pair of mirrored sunglasses on.

"Hi," I said.

He looked up, unsurprised. "Oh hi," he answered. "How are . . ."

"I'm fine," I said.

". . . the roses?"

I took a deep breath. He looked thin and raggedy. It occurred to me he might be homeless.

"I'm having the Witherspoons over for lunch on Sunday," I said. "Our old neighbors. Would you like to come?"

"Do they still have their two . . ."

"Poodles? Yes."

". . . -timing son-in-law living with them?"

"Lunch is at noon," I said. "And I never slept with their son-in-law, if that's what you're thinking."

"How do you know . . ."

"What you're thinking?"

". . . whether he's still living with them or not."

"Noon," I repeated.

I was shaking when I left.

Sunday came and of course no X. The Witherspoons and I had barbecue and gin and tonics and had just settled into the living room to watch the U.S. Open when the poodles started barking and the son-in-law said, "There's a man in your backyard." I shrugged his hand off my thigh and stood up. My X was in the garden watering the roses. It was as if no time had passed. I went out to him.

"Did you see . . ." he said.

"No," I said. "I didn't. Hand me that hose, please."

He handed me the hose and I aimed the nozzle straight at him and the blast was so strong it knocked him butt-down and his fake mustache flew off. For a second I exulted. Then because I'm an idiot I dropped the hose and went to help him up but he tripped me and I fell down hard beside him as the water spiraled fast and cold over both of us. He wrapped his arms around me and rocked us back and forth on the grass, laughing, and I felt his old male strength and smelled his sour green-apple smell and for a second I was almost happy again. By the time I pushed him off and shook myself and stood, of course, nothing was left but a trail of damp footsteps in the grass, a thread from his hoodie snagged on the gate, tire marks on the curb. I ran out to the street as his bike rounded the corner, took my shoe off, threw it, missed. The last thing I heard was his voice, faint on the wind. "Don't worry, dear, it's not . . ."

"Funny," I shouted.

"Over," he said, and disappeared.

A Sailor

Randa Jarrar

S HE FUCKS A SAILOR, a Turkish sailor, the summer she spends in Istanbul. When she comes home it takes her three days to come clean about it to her husband.

He says this doesn't bother him, and she tells him that it bothers her that it doesn't bother him. He asks if she prefers him to be the kind of man who is bothered by fleeting moments, and she tells him that yes, she prefers that he be that kind of man. He tells her he thinks she married him precisely because he is the kind of man who doesn't dwell on fleeting moments, because he is the kind of man who does not hold a grudge. She tells him that holding a grudge and working up some anger about one's wife fucking a sailor are not the same thing. He agrees that holding a grudge isn't the same as working up some anger about one's wife fucking a sailor, but, he adds, one's wife, specifically his own, would never leave him for a sailor, and not a Turkish sailor. In fact, he says, she did not leave him for the Turkish sailor. She is here. So why should he be angry?

Now she becomes angry, and asks him why he assumes she did not consider leaving him for the sailor. Besides, she says, she and the sailor shared a Muslim cultural identity, something she does not share with her husband. She asks him if he thought of that.

He says he had not thought of it and that, even if she had considered it, she must have decided not to leave him for the Turkish sailor. He acquiesces that the Turkish sailor and she must have shared a strong bond over being culturally Muslim, because, he says, he cannot imagine what else she would have had in common with a Turkish sailor.

Plenty! she shouts. She had plenty in common with the Turkish sailor.

Her husband wants to know what she had in common with the Turkish sailor.

She had nothing in common with the Turkish sailor except that she was attracted to him and he was attracted to her and they spent a night in an un-air-conditioned room in Karaköy by Galata Tower. In the morning she woke up to the sound of seagulls circling the tower, zooming around it hungrily, loudly. The Turkish sailor had heard the seagulls too. Then she had left. That was really all they had in common: the cultural identity, the sex, and the seagulls.

She tells her husband this story. He asks her what she wants him to say. She tells him to say he is angry that she fucked a Turkish sailor, that he wishes he had fucked her in the un-air-conditioned room near Galata Tower. She tells him to shout it.

Her husband refuses to say any of it. His refusal is quiet, itself not angry.

When she sees him gazing placidly at her, and refusing to say any of these things, she understands that this is his way of getting back at her for fucking the Turkish sailor.

And she also understands that this, his lack of passion, his sense of logic, is the reason she fucked the Turkish sailor, and it is also the reason she came home.

Something Falls in the Night

Desiree Cooper

JUMP UP, RUN SWIFTLY OVER the hardwood floor. Don't worry about your thin gown or your ungirded body beneath. Creep into your son's room and pinch him from his dreams. Greet his frightened eyes with the fury of survival. Clamp your hand over his mouth to cork a scream.

Listen to sounds crashing downstairs. Lift the window sash to the sting of winter. Poise your child on the ledge, and push.

In the nursery, the baby cries. Dash to her side before she gives you away. Downstairs, the ransacking pauses; the living-room curio hangs mid tilt. They must have heard her little sobs.

A boot breaches the steps. Quickly, you lift the baby, crush her head to your breast to stifle her cries. Do you dive into the bathtub and flatten yourself against the porcelain, praying that the shower curtain is bulletproof? Do you roll with the child into the darkness beneath the bed? Cower behind the door armed with a golf club? Huddle in the bottom of the hall closet? Or do you stand in the middle of the room, await the shadows in the doorway, and fight?

Jump up, run swiftly over the creaky floors. You are fully dressed. You go first to the baby's room, where she is dreaming about the warm suckle of your breast. You lift her rudely, and her arms and legs startle. She opens her mouth to scream so deeply, no sound comes out. You swaddle her in the thick down of her cradle blanket, open the window, and throw her into the snow.

Downstairs, there is the creak of a stranger's foot on the bottom step. Blood pounds loudly in your ears. You can barely hear your son call, "Mommy?"

The footsteps come faster. You dart down the hall to your son's room, scoop him from the bed. His body is supple and ready for a hug, but you spit, "Shut up," through gritted teeth. He is shocked silent. You open the window just as the knob on his bedroom door turns. You dangle him into the night. You ignore the question in his eyes as you let go.

Jump up, swiftly over the creaky hardwood floors. You have been sitting up in the chair, waiting with a pistol in your lap. You slip by the bedroom door where your son sleeps in his footie pajamas. You glance at the room where your infant daughter shivers.

Downstairs, someone is talking loudly. Drawers slam and dishes shatter. You take one step on the stairs, which groan with the weight of fear. The house goes silent. Someone is listening. A shadow lengthens at the bottom of the stairs. The bedroom door opens and your son says, "Mommy?" just as you pull the trigger.

Jump up, run swiftly into the winter night. Look back at your sweet house, with its Williamsburg shutters and stained-glass door. Upstairs, your children sleep without dreaming.

You are fully dressed, but you have forgotten your shoes. You wait shivering at the bus stop. When it arrives in the darkness, it is nearly empty. You board, your feet numb and clumsy. There is a woman dozing against the window. The bus jostles her little boy awake. When he looks at you, he shrinks and whines, "Mommy?"

You point the gun and shoot.

Seconds

Terese Svoboda

SECONDS, OR CRANBERRY SURPRISE? SHE'S his sister-in-law, she can baby him.

Of course, Dad says. Both.

More gravy appears, potatoes, peas and carrots, the surprise.

She says she doesn't know what's keeping him, he hates cold food.

Dad moves the gravy around so it floods his plate. It's a warm Thanksgiving, he says, as if that has something to do with his brother being an hour late.

She fills his glass with red until he says he had white. Then she doles out so much whipped cream he actually spoons it back.

Her daughter-in-law leaves the table to tend the baby on the living room floor.

The second cousin, really just somebody they scrounged up to make light talk, says in all the eating of seconds and drinking of thirds and the spooning of dessert, How has his treatment been going?

He was happy enough checking out his new ranch yesterday, says his son. Won a bet from me on how long it would take me to learn the new irrigation system.

They drink, they eat.

Can't say we didn't wait, says the wife, showing them a blackened sweet potato.

They file from the table to the TV, the dishes stay on the table. Don't do them, says Dad. It'll make him feel bad.

I don't mind, she says, not sitting down on the couch, veering back to the sink. You can do them later.

Dad likes that, the joke of him washing up. He asks the baby if she wants her toes eaten, and pulls at each digit to make her laugh. Her mother gathers her back when she kicks but she writhes out of her arms for her daddy, who's searching the stations for football or a parade.

Dad slow-foots it to the lounger. There's gravy on his white shirt and darkness across his face. He scratches the side of his nose after he's settled and points at the cabinet on the wall. Wasn't there something in there?

The son sees the gap, the one empty rack. Sometimes he cleans it, he says.

His mother's in the kitchen, washing the pans, but listening. Water still running, she comes to the door.

Where? says her son, pointing at the rack.

She has no idea. The child cries and no one picks her up.

Dad says, Try the long barn.

The child hiccups her crying while the cousin says surely he's just driving around for air, a ride to calm him down for all the holiday celebrating or to see if a gate is shut—everything everyone's said twice already. Why that barn?

I don't know, says Dad. But don't you check, he says to the son when he goes for the coat closet. Call Pete to go with you.

The son is shaking now, a big-frame shake that usually with him is a sign of anger but not now. You call Pete, he says, I'm going. He puts the keys in his pocket, skips the closet for the door.

No, says his mother, into the room in two steps. No, you don't.

Shit, says the son. It's Thanksgiving. He's supposed to—

Wait, says Dad. I hear something.

They listen to what? The car door of a neighbor, a little too much booze in the slam? Nothing. But in the interim Dad whips out his phone, he 911s.

As if such a call could solve something, the others listen. Of course 911 isn't local, no Pete they can get reassurance from, just a recital of regulations: Missing persons aren't missing for at least a day. No help at all.

She punches in the numbers on her own phone. Her daughter-in-law passes her with the baby on the way to the kitchen, the baby tapping her arm, a comfort motion.

Pete says he'll come over, she says, he says he hasn't had enough turkey.

We won't see Pete for another hour, says the son still at the front door. Pete has money on the game.

I said it's important, says the wife.

You don't want to go, says Dad in a voice that says he doesn't either.

You stay here, says his mother. His wife agrees, the baby sucking at her bottle, she forbids him.

Did he take his pills today? the son asks. Now plaid-coated, he's the image of his father, just about as wrinkled, and just as stubborn.

Of course, says his mother.

But did he swallow them?

How can I tell? She turns to face the kitchen door, she just turns.

Dad closes his eyes. Wait, he says.

It's about two minutes later that Pete's car pulls up and Dad pumps the lounger upright. Of course they all hope it's not Pete. That would mean what they sense could be true. The son runs to the door and out to where the two of them, Pete and the son, talk and then leave without a hello or anything to anybody else.

Dad plays with the baby, a peekaboo that she likes, then cries about, Dad's peek is too shrill and her mother too desperate for calm. She should take the baby home but she can't.

The dishes are done.

A car parks in the drive just ten minutes later, and all of them inside are out on the carport coatless. The son says Pete's called the coroner, the son says he didn't go in but when he enters the living room, dropping the keys while trying to repocket them, his face isn't his father's anymore, it's bent, it's creased and drained. He's seen what he's seen.

Mom, says the son. Mom.

She has backed up back into the house and is crossing one arm over her chest, then the next, and the sound she makes wakes up the baby. If you'd only—sooner.

He shakes his head. After holding his mother and then holding his wife, he says to Dad, How did you know?

Dad says he guessed. He liked that long barn. Sooner or later, he says. He had it in him.

The baby reaches for her father and he takes her just as his wife moves away. Together they almost drop her.

Exotics

Dantiel W. Moniz

A MONG THEMSELVES, THE MEMBERS CALLED it the Supper Club; to us it was only our J-O-B, and no one, not them or us, spoke of it outside of the building's walls. Concealed in the center of the city in a plain, tan-brick building that could have been the dentist's or the tax attorney's office, the club was exclusive in the way that too much money made things. We couldn't have joined—not that we wanted to, we often said. Even if *our* fathers had handed us riches from their fathers and their grandfathers before them, made off of the lives and deaths of black and brown bodies, none of us would want to be complicit in such terrible opulence; we only swept up the place.

We took the jobs. Of course we took the jobs. We were citizens with citizens' needs: food and housing and medical care. Our children wanted and we desired they be allowed their want, that they sometimes have it satisfied. We didn't ask for much, much less than the members themselves, only that we might afford to be human, and in this way, the pay, cash in hand, was hard to beat.

Once a month, the members gathered in the night, wearing elaborate half-face masks in the likenesses of pigs and dogs and cats that hid their eyes but left their mouths free. While we poured tart cherry mead, fetched fresh cloth napkins, procured new spoons for ones that had fallen, we observed them: a walrus tipping back raw oysters; a big-eyed cow knifing marmalade onto toast; a peacock shimmering in a gold dress, sloshing pink champagne onto the floor. We cleaned it up. We swept crumbs from the linen. We cleared plates between courses and some of us might have drawn our fingers through ribbons of decorative sauce or nudged unbitten nibbles into the palms of our hands. If we caught one another doing so, we pretended that we hadn't. At every dinner, our faces were bare; the members wanted to know us, though they pretended we had no power. We didn't know that we did. They conversed around us as if speaking through air, and we came to know most intimately what they thought about the world. One night, over fugu ceviche, a jackal said: The Revolution was never about freedom. We just wanted more kings.

They were the kings, so they laughed.

The Supper Club specialized in exotic meats—the dining table raised on a platform, the eating itself the art. The members devoured main courses of stuffed gator over dirty rice, emu in raspberry sauce, anaconda slivered into hearty stew, and slabs of roasted lion they joked came direct from Pride Rock. They declared ortolan passé, though once we witnessed the tiny bodies disappear beneath the further shroud of napkins, and through their wet smacking, heard the crunch of delicate skulls. They were jeweled animals eating lesser animals, and to each other, with our eyes, we communicated our disgust. We did not prepare the food or choose it. Of course, we served them; we did only our jobs. We fed our children and kept the roofs above their heads. We watched the members gorge themselves in January, February, March and April and May. We collected our unmarked envelopes as they licked extravagant gravy from their fingers.

In November, the members cried, Next month must be the rarest! Bigger, better! We deserve! Their mouths always watering for the next meal before they'd finished the last. A panda draped her arm across the gilded chair of a buffalo, her husband, and said, For Christmas let's have something truly special. Maybe the last of something, and us the only ones to taste.

On the night of the last supper, while we set the table with crystal stemware and festooned mistletoe above the archways, we heard the sleepy cries from the kitchen, the shh-shhshing of the chefs. We heard the lullabies, ones that had been sung to us and that we now sang, the melodies cleaving down to our bones. We were angry! Of course we were. We didn't want this. We didn't condone it—but what could we do? We brought the dishes to the table to gasps of nearly erotic antic-ipation and stepped back and dropped our eyes. If we didn't look, we could still pretend. Their silverware filled the room with music.

My God, we heard a canary say quietly to a sheep, her hands at her mouth. We knew, if they could, they'd eat Him, too.

And afterward, once the floors were clean, the table stripped, the dishes washed, and the cutlery polished, once it seemed that the club had never been, we stood in line for our money. As a bonus, a nod to the year of our dedicated service, each of us was given a white bag as we left by the back door. Merry Christmas, the chefs said. Bon appétit. We took the bags; we tucked them under our coats. None of us spoke. What could we say? In the parking lot, stepping into our used cars, avoiding each other's eyes, we shrugged. We excused ourselves. Any-way, we might have thought, haven't we always eaten the young?

How Many

Bryan Washington

THE FIRST ONE TAKES YOU back to his place, on Mandell. He asks you to top him and you do and that's it.

The second one chats you up. You don't even make it out of Ripcord. There's that room by the emergency exit, and you grope each other against the wall until it's obvious that nothing's happening. But of course you keep trying anyway, and then one of you stumbles, and then you laugh, and he laughs, and someone bangs on the door.

The third one takes you back to his place, and you're nearly undressed when he changes his mind. He looks at your dick, and then he looks at your belly, and then he shakes his head, and that stuns you into silence. You don't even slam the door. There's an 85°C Bakery by his apartment, and you buy something so sweet that you can't help but blush.

The fourth one's exactly your type, but he's married. Oops. He pays for a drink, and then another, and that's when he tells you. He offers you a third. You politely decline, but you think about it for days afterward, grimacing, shaking your head.

The fifth one takes you home from Blur. You decide to let him fuck you. It works without a hitch, and afterward, in bed, with your head against his chest, he smiles and says he has a boyfriend. After you've left, you pull your car into a Whataburger, where you scream, and you scream, and you scream.

The sixth one is actually a fluke, because you meant to talk to his friend, who was taking too fucking long in the bathroom. But the sixth one is funny. He wiggles his nose. His hoodie's too tight. You talk in the bar, and then against the trunk of his car, smoking up all of his menthols. He says that you don't need to fuck each other senseless just yet, but you take him to your place anyway, and you have clumsy sex. You finish. He doesn't. You don't mean to let him spend the night, but that happens. He leaves in the morning, and he doesn't text or anything.

The seventh one is really the seventh and the eighth because they are a package deal. You suspect that this will be unnecessarily complicated—but it isn't. They've got it down to a science. When you leave their townhouse, in East End, you feel like a ball of light.

One day, the sixth one spots you out in the world, at your gig bagging groceries. You debate acknowledging him, and then he asks where you keep the bottled water.

The sixth one takes you to a bar in a part of the Heights you hadn't known about. You don't touch each other, and later you'll think about that not touching, and how it was more arresting than any way you could have possibly touched.

The sixth one texts you a few days later. You grab dinner at this place by his apartment in Alief. He orders for you—some impossibly spicy noodle dish. You stand in front of the restaurant afterward, two chubby people plugging the doorway, and you're the one who says, O.K., can we? Is this all right? Do you want to?

And the sixth one says, O.K. Yes. We can.

So you do.

The sixth one's gone when you wake up in his bed—but, this time, there is a text. You debate waiting an hour or five, stalling him. Instead, you immediately message him back.

The sixth one makes a point of being surprised when you ambush him at work, which is a thing that you'd warned him you'd do. He is a nurse, and he is in scrubs, and he asks if you want to eat in the cafeteria, but the hospital reminds you of your mom. You can't finish your food. The sixth one takes you out for ice cream instead, and it drips all over your shoes.

The sixth one doesn't fuck you exactly the way that you want, but he's willing to learn. You, too, are willing to learn. You find that there are many things to explore, new and exciting frontiers of skin and tissue. You exhaust the joke about going back to school, and how whatever it is that you're doing feels like the opposite of dropping out.

The sixth one tells you all of the nicknames he's had, and then you throw in yours, until they become something like a poem: bear, black bear, brown bear, panda bear, red panda, doughboy, butterball, cookie, doughnut, sweetcake, bumper, baby-talk variations of your first names, baby-talk variations of your last names. You promise to call each other by your given names only, a promise you are doomed to break—instantly, simultaneously.

One day, the sixth one wakes up beside you, tracing your groin with his tongue. He says, Six months! Can you imagine?

You can't.

The sixth one doesn't have anything discernibly wrong with him, and you feel generally O.K. when you're around him. But this is a foreign feeling. Reality television and telenovelas and K-dramas have made you wary. What's a relationship without conflict?

The sixth one starts leaving his shit at your place. You start leaving your shit at his. In this way, you cancel each other out. Neither of you remembers if there's a scientific term for this.

The sixth one goes to work and comes back to your place. You go to work and come back to his place. You look up, one day, and a year has passed. A year! Nothing has gone wrong. There is no conflict.

The sixth one is always leaving his phone around, all of the time. You think of that thing your mom used to say, about how there will always be trouble if you look for it.

One day, the sixth one says he wants you to penetrate each other simultaneously. You didn't know that this is a thing two men could do, until you do it, straining your wrists, and you know that you'll never do it with anyone else.

The sixth one asks you to move in with him, on the day you've decided to ask him to move in with you. Finally, a dilemma!

The sixth one organizes his things around your apartment, room by room, before he leaves town for a nursing conference. You gawk at him from your complex's parking lot, frowning exaggeratedly, waving both hands.

The sixth one is still out of town when you're sipping a Diet Coke at JR's. You don't know that the ninth one is the ninth one until you say, O.K., and then you fuck him in your car. It isn't even that great. The ninth one tells you he likes you, and you say that he should probably go. You settle your head on the steering wheel, and the horn sounds until someone knocks on your window.

You remember: Newton's Third Law! A problem inside of a problem!

The sixth one is back in Houston, and you wait until he's settled and he's come a few times to tell him. You say it offhandedly, as if it were burnt toast or a lost pair of shades.

The sixth one packs his things so quickly! He finds socks that he'd lost for weeks! Lost books! Lost boxers! His wallet and his keys and his shoes.

The sixth one blocks you. Doesn't call. Doesn't text. No D.M.s.

The tenth one is the eleventh one is the twelfth is the thirteenth is the fourteenth is the fifteenth is the sixteenth is the seventeenth is the eighteenth is the nineteenth is the twentieth is the twenty-first. The twenty-first!

The twenty-second one leaves your apartment, and after you lock the door you lie on the floor. You don't cry. You just lie there, breathing, and then the sun rises, and you go to work.

One day, the sixth one comes into the grocery store, even though there are many in his neighborhood. But he doesn't come for you. In fact, he walks a perfect circle around you.

But everyone else is so busy that, eventually, he asks for your help finding the things on his list.

You both walk from item to item, checking them off. Then you ask to ring him up, too, and there is a look on the sixth one's face, as if this were the biggest decision of his life.

The sixth one says, No, that's O.K. Someone else can do that.

But he hasn't walked away, either. He stands there.

So you ask another question.

You ask the sixth one if it'd be O.K. to grab lunch one day? To sit down? Just as friends?

You watch the sixth one weigh the decision. You taste it before it leaves his throat. It's a familiar palate. Delicious, frankly. You swallow it whole.

Not Daniel

Deesha Philyaw

I PARKED IN THE SHADOWS BEHIND the hospice center, and waited. I held a box of condoms on my lap, Magnum XLs. It was like being sixteen again, except this time I bought the condoms instead of relying on the boy. This time the boy was a man I had mistaken for someone I'd gone to junior high with when our paths first crossed two weeks before at the main entrance of the hospice center. I was coming, he was going. I thought he was Daniel McMurray so I stared longer than I should have, and he stared back. Later that evening, I'd run into him again coming out of the room across from my mother's. His mother had breast cancer, mine ovarian.

I checked my phone: *10:27.* I'd timed the Walmart run for the condoms pretty well. Not-Daniel would be down in three minutes. To throw Nurse Irie, the night nurse, off the trail, we never left or returned to the floor at the same time. Her name wasn't really Irie, but I called her that behind her back because she was Jamaican. She was also mean as a snake. I had complained to the head of the center about her, suggesting that her brusque manner was better suited for the morgue. But Nurse Irie liked Not-Daniel. She didn't cop an attitude when he asked questions about his mother's care. He told me she even joked with him late one night as he walked around the floor in his skimpy running shorts: "Boi, you keep walking around here in those itty-bitty tings, someone might mess around and give you a sponge bath."

Nurse Irie was not a stupid woman. Perhaps she would put two and two together and figure out that Not-Daniel and I were . . . what were we? What do you call it when your mothers are hospice neighbors and the nights are endless and sleepless and here's someone else who spent the day talking to insurance companies and creditors and banks and pastors and relatives and friends, some more well-intentioned than others? Someone else who is the dutiful son to your dutiful daughter, another family's chief shit handler, bail bondsman, maid, chauffeur, therapist, career advisor, ATM. Here's someone else who both welcomes and dreads death as it loiters in the wings, an unpredictable actor.

What do you call it when that someone else wears a wedding band but never mentions his wife by name? A wife and two kids back home in the next state over. Don't ask, don't tell.

At exactly ten-thirty, Not-Daniel tapped the passenger-side window. For a few moments, we sat in silence the way we always did at first. Sometimes I would cry, sometimes he would too, because we could out here, beyond the reach of our mothers' Jesus, nurses on autopilot, empty platitudes, and garbage theology about God's will disguised as comfort. And then, eventually, one of us would speak.

But this night . . . how to begin? Pick up where we'd left off the night before? When yet another rambling conversation about funerals and selfish siblings suddenly became kissing, became my T-shirt off, became my nipples in Not-Daniel's mouth.

This is how we began: Not-Daniel took the box of condoms from me, removed one, and then set the box on the dashboard next to my phone. Then he set his phone on the dashboard. I knew his ringer volume, like mine, was on the highest setting, because the call, that call, could come at any moment. Then he took my face in his hands and looked at me. I dropped my eyes.

"No," he said. "I need you to be . . . here. All of you. Here."

Lifting my eyes to meet his, I felt like Sisyphus pushing that rock. In his eyes, I saw *wifekidsdyingmother*. I blinked, and blinked again, until my vision cleared.

In the backseat, Not-Daniel undressed me, undressed himself, and then buried his face between my legs. I reached over my head, clutched the door behind me, and cried as I came over and over again.

By the time Not-Daniel put on the condom and pulled me to my knees, my legs were limp and useless. He turned me away from him, pressed his palm against the center of my back, and pushed me forward. He draped his body over mine and entered me. He was rough, but not unkind.

I wondered whether he was thinking what I was thinking: What if one of our mothers dies while we're down here rutting around, as my grandmother would say?

But in the cramped space of the backseat and of our grief and our need, there was no room for guilt or fear. Only relief.

And that's what I told Not-Daniel when we were both spent, our damp backs sticking to the leather seat.

"*Relieved?*" He frowned and then smiled. "Relieved? Then I failed to deliver the goods."

"No, no," I said. "You . . . delivered the goods. The goods were delivered. And received. But I do have a question . . ."

"Shoot."

"Were you worried that one of them would die while we were down here?"

"Thought never crossed my mind."

"Really?"

"Really. Listen, I can either deliver the goods, or I can think about my mama, dying or not. I can't do both."

And then I laughed, even though I felt like I shouldn't have. Even though nothing was as it should be.

Beach Town

Amy Hempel

THE HOUSE NEXT DOOR WAS rented for the summer to a couple who swore at missed croquet shots. Their music at night was loud, and I liked it; it was not music I knew. Mornings, I picked up the empties they had lobbed across the hedge, Coronas with the limes wedged inside, and pitched them back over. We had not introduced ourselves these three months.

Between our houses a tall privet hedge is backed by white pine for privacy in winter. The day I heard the voice of a woman not the wife, I went out back to a spot more heavily planted but with a break I could just see through. Now it was the man who was talking, or trying to—he started to say things he could not seem to finish. I watched the woman do something memorable to him with her mouth. Then the man pulled her up from where she had been kneeling. He said, "Maybe you're just hungry. Maybe we should get you something to eat."

The woman had a nimble laugh.

The man said, "Paris is where you and I should go."

The woman asked what was wrong with here. She said, "I like a beach town."

I wanted to phone the wife's office in the city and hear what she would sound like if she answered. I had no fellow feeling; all she had ever said to me was couldn't I mow my lawn later in the day. It was noon when she asked. I told her the village bylaws disallow mowing before seven-thirty, and that I had waited until nine. A gardener, hired by my neighbor, cared for their yard. But still I was sure they were neglecting my neighbor's orchids. All summer long I had watched for the renters to leave the house together so that I could let myself in with the key from the shelf in the shed and test the soil and water the orchids.

The woman who did not want to go to Paris said that she had to leave. "But I don't want you to leave," the man said, and she said, "Think of the kiss at the door."

Nobody thinks about the way sound carries across water. Even the water in a swimming pool. A week later, when her husband was away, the wife had friends to lunch by the pool. I didn't have to hide to listen; I was in view if they had cared to look, pulling weeds in the raspberry canes.

The women told the wife it was an opportunity for her. They said, "Fair is fair," and to do those things she might not otherwise have done. "No regrets," they said, "if you are even the type of person who is given to regret, if you even have that type of wistful temperament to begin with."

The women said, "We are not unintelligent; we just let passion prevail." They said, "Who would deny that we have all had these feelings?"

The women told the wife she would not feel this way forever. "You will feel worse, however, before you feel better, and that is just the way it always is."

The women advised long walks. They told the wife to watch the sun rise and set, to look for solace in the natural world, though they admitted there was no comfort to be found in the world and they would all be fools to expect it.

The weekend the couple next door had moved in—their rental began on Memorial Day—I heard them place a bet on the moon. She said waxing, he said waning. Days later, the moon nearly full in the night sky, I listened for the woman to tell her husband she had won, knowing they had not named the terms of the bet, and that the woman next door would collect nothing.

When Chase Prays Chocolate

Christopher Allen

CHASE IS THIRTY-SIX. His hands are rubbing his wife's shoulders, but his thoughts are readying themselves for escape. "Chase, please. It's too hard." She turns her head to look at him, but now Chase is five and leaping onto a granite kitchen countertop. He swivels in midair and lands. Sitting. His wife says again, "Chase, please. It's too hard." The landing's never smooth. And then there's always the awkwardness of turning to kneel, to reach the third shelf and the dwindling bar of chocolate his mother (never) uses to bake. He pulls back the label that reads "Pure Baker's Chocolate" and sinks his teeth deep, hard into a corner.

Chase is forty-nine. Dribbling sounds are coming from the bath and his wife. His heart races at the thought of being caught clicking through porn sites. He swallows hard, a dark memory of chocolate coating the back of his throat. He's five again and kneeling on the cold, hard countertop. Mommy's asleep on the couch. He nibbles on the chocolate and tries to make his knees—first the left, then right—feel

old and innocent at the same time. That would be perfect. Chase lusts
for the dusty, drab quality of pure chocolate without all the sugar, butter, and sprinkles. In the bathroom a plug glugs from the drain. A hair
dryer roars. He clicks back to CNN.com, deletes his cache, swallows
his memory, and smiles. Chocolate in its purest form, he thinks, is like
a life uncorrupted. In the thunder of his wife's preening, he shouts,
"Chocolate liquor, soy lecithin."

People aren't pure. They have a troubling number of ingredients.
They have retinas and freckles, fists and curly hairs. And thoughts:
weeping thoughts, raging and perverse thoughts. They have nipples
and knuckles and dilemmas. They have lips and hopes and vertebrae,
which some animals don't even have—but thoughts most of all. Chase
keeps a list of people ingredients in a canister on a high kitchen shelf to
remind himself that innocence needs a ladder. And that's why he prays.
He's five and forty-nine, sixty-two and twelve and twenty-three. But
most of all five. His latest people ingredient—number 3042—is a little
demon called corticotropin-releasing hormone, which Chase doesn't
understand completely, but he knows it makes him mad.

Chase is nineteen. And five. He's taking his new girlfriend to see
Jaws. She smells like jasmine; he hopes he smells like a Hershey's bar.
He swallows and scoots the chocolate back behind a can of baking soda
and shimmies off the counter. But his mother is standing there when
he turns around. "Little man, what have I told you about climbing—"
A palm stings his face as the movie starts and his girlfriend reaches for
his trembling hand. She tickles his palm as Mommy holds a cold cloth
to a rising bruise on Chase's cheek. "Chase," she says, "I was angry.
That's all." But the tiny bits contaminate us, he thinks, gripping his
girlfriend's hand, white and skeletal in the cinema's pall. "Anger," he
whispers, "is like salmonella." "Chase, you're hurting me." His girlfriend is trying to pull her hand away. "Anger's like a demon," he says

to his mother/girlfriend. "No," his mother says—steely now. "Not like that at all. It's nine o'clock. Time to say your prayer."

Chase—always and ever five—falls to his knees. He raises pinched-shut eyes to the shelf he's too small, too old to reach, and prays: "Chocolate liquor. Soy lecithin. Chocolate liquor. Soy lecithin."

The Gospel of Guy No-Horse

Natalie Diaz

A T THE INJUN THAT COULD, a jalopy bar drooping and lopsided on the bank of the Colorado River—a once mighty red body now dammed and tamed blue—Guy No-Horse was glistening drunk and dancing fancy with two white gals—both yellow-haired tourists still in bikini tops, freckled skins blistered pink by the savage Mohave Desert sun.

Though The Injun, as it was known by locals, had no true dance floor—truths meant little on such a night—card tables covered in drink, ash, and melting ice had been pushed aside, shoved together to make a place for the rhythms that came easy to people in the coyote hours beyond midnight.

In the midst of Camel smoke hanging lower and thicker than a September monsoon, No-Horse rode high, his PIMC-issued wheelchair transfigured—a magical chariot drawn by two blond, beer-clumsy

palominos perfumed with coconut sunscreen and dollar-fifty Bud-
weisers. He was as careful as any man could be at almost two a.m. to
avoid their sunburned toes—in the brown light of The Injun, chips in
their toenail polish glinted like diamonds.

Other Indians noticed the awkward trinity and gathered round in
a dented circle, clapping, whooping, slinging obscenities from their
tongues of fire: Ya-ha! Ya-ha! Jeering their dark horse, No-Horse,
toward the finish line of an obviously rigged race.

No-Horse didn't hear their rabble, which was soon overpowered as
the two-man band behind the bar really got after it—a jam probably
about love, but maybe about freedom, and definitely about him, as his
fair-haired tandem, his denim-skirted pendulums kept time. The time
being now—

No-Horse sucked his lips, imagined the taste of the white girls'
thrusting hips. *Hey!* He sang. *Hey!* He smiled. *Hey!* He spun around
in the middle of a crowd of his fellow tribesmen, a sparkling centu-
rion moving as fluid as an Indian could be at almost two in the morning, rolling back, forth, popping wheelies that tipped his big head and
swung his braids like shiny lassos of lust. The two white gals looked
down at him, looked back up at each other, raised their plastic Solo
cups-runneth-over, laughing loudly, hysterical at the very thought of
dancing with a broken-down Indian.

But about that laughter, No-Horse didn't give a damn. This was an
edge of rez where warriors were made on nights like these, with music
like this, and tonight he was out, dancing at The Injun That Could. If
you'd seen the lightning of his smile, not the empty space leaking from
his thighs, you might have believed that man was walking on water, or
at least that he had legs again.

And as for the white girls slurring around him like two bedraggled angels, one holding on to the handle of his wheelchair, the other spilling her drink all down the front of her shirt, well, for them he was sorry. Because this was not a John Wayne movie, this was The Injun That Could, and the only cavalry riding this night was in No-Horse's veins. *Hey! Hey! Hey!* he hollered.

I'm on the Side of the Wildebeest

Amy Stuber

I'M WITH MY FAMILY WATCHING bats circle through the dusk around the upper rim of the Grand Canyon when the bank calls to ask if I've purchased $1,279 of perfume, liquor, and cigarettes in Montreal in the last hour. It seems unexpected, the phone agent says, and I imagine the list of my actual purchases from the last two days: gas, pretzels, candy in cellophane bags, one night at a Best Western in Santa Rosa, New Mexico, where the hot tub was questionable, but we all sat in it anyway because after ten hours of driving, much of it on two-lane highways in western Kansas where the whole world was feed lots and semis driven by addicts, we were willing to take one more risk.

It's the summer my daughter turns thirteen and eclipses any human-woman loveliness I might have had. She's cut her waist-length hair, and that seems to have focused something in her. I imagine her in five years buying perfume and liquor and cigarettes in Montreal, and strangely I want that for her. I do. At eighteen, I rode my bike in the dark drunk, darting between cars. I slid down the brick side of a two-story building on a dare. I did not count the number of strangers I fucked in unfamiliar bedrooms. Now the lines at both corners of my mouth make me look like I'm in a Dust Bowl photo. It's hard to look forward because forward is just this but more so. I try to swear off vanity. What are my options? I'll age in that Eileen Fisher way: thin, drapey, neutral sweaters but kind of elder ballerina on her day off. Or maybe I'll age in that Iris Apfel way, all big glasses and ten necklaces and fuck you for trying to tell me to shrink and fade.

My daughter sits on a rock so perfectly bouldery it seems like one of those fakes people use for landscaping or in theme parks, but it's the Grand Canyon, so I assume it's real. She rubs at the mascara she only weeks ago started wearing, and a bat hovers in front of her face for just a second. She doesn't flinch. She just stares at it, and I realize she's the badass I always thought I was.

My son runs back and forth repeatedly, covering the same ten-foot path over and over. It is a thing he does that other people think is weird but that I think is endearing. Everything is orange and red and dry, and it all seems like a clear window into a very-near-future America: waterless beyond resurrection. There's definitely a cruelty to the fact that my children's childhood is this doomsday prophecy of climate change, micro-greens, ugly hybrids, and Trump, while mine was bell-bottoms, Twinkies, skateboarding, *Soul Train*, and only a shadowy sideline concern about possible nuclear war.

My son stops running for a minute and stands near the rock where I sit with my husband. "Wildebeest seems like it should be spelled *b-e-a-s-t*, but it's not. It's *b-e-e-s-t*, which makes no sense," he says. He's spent the whole day in the car watching *Planet Earth* DVDs with their grand aerial shots of migrating African herds. My husband, who is practically Google, likely has an explanation for the odd spelling. He knows everything, and it's equal parts useful and annoying. "Well, actually," he starts, so I tune him out and watch a family speaking Japanese go right up to the edge of the rim with their phones. They all take the same picture and then back away from the edge, and I let out my breath.

Apparently, wildebeests migrate in larger groups than any other mammal, except—soon, I think—humans. Gas stations will dry up. Burned-out cars will rest between charred trees. My daughter will be an adult woman, and maybe she and some person with whom she has regular sex and meals will take off in looted REI gear, along with all of us, pack animals, heading north to some place that isn't burned or underwater.

The sun has set, and the sky is pastel and dusty and thick with bats, but there's nothing orchestrated about their weird bat movement. They fly more like balloons whose knots have been loosened, so I can't view them as any kind of planned, murmured warning.

We all climb into the car, which is trashed with Cheez-Its and gummy worms and empty cups with plastic lids askance, everything crisscrossed with cords and chargers. My daughter's face glows its odd alien moon in the backseat, and my son puts his feet through the space between the door and my shoulder, so I can reach back and hold them in my hand.

Someone in Canada is drinking our liquor and smoking our cigarettes and spraying our perfume into showy clouds on every person in arm's reach. A few days ago, herds of animals went racing away from the geysers at Yellowstone, and my daughter became convinced it meant a world-ending super-volcano was coming, and the sooner we could get to California the better.

At a hotel near the Grand Canyon, we find ourselves in another hot tub. This one is cleaner, and there are fewer drunk people in American flag swimming suits in the pool next to it. There is a wrought-iron fence around all of it, but the gaps between the iron staffs are wide enough to let just about anything in or out. My daughter steps out of the hot tub and jumps into the pool. She and my son float on their backs, while the sky turns a solid purple and the orange mountains are like actual arms around them. "Stay. Just stay," I say, under my breath and to every single thing.

Jenny Watches *The Exorcist*

Emma Stough

IN HER SLEEPLESS ROOM WITH the shades drawn and a bowlful of neon peach rings. Blue TV light is radioactive, but after years of exposure, Jenny's skin has grown a thick, radio-proof layer. It is gummy to the touch.

Jenny remembers sleep like a matchstick remembers flame: quick and devastating.

The archaeological dig at the beginning of *The Exorcist* is the scariest part of the movie because every single cast member was buried alive. Well—wrong film.

The archaeological dig at the beginning of *The Exorcist* is the scariest part of the movie because of that stone creature and how it seems, at first glance, to be more or less the height of a real man. It even has the eyes of a real man. And the priest—future exorcist—sweaty, covered in sand and dirt, squares up to face the stone devil, foolishly, briefly, looking right into the dead stone eyes.

And in the background: big red ball sun. Is this about to be an all-American baseball movie?

Jenny likes creature features. As a kid she made a miniature cardboard town and collected ants from the sidewalk for population; they stomped through cardboard streets, monsters of her own making.

Jenny puts the peach rings on like real rings and she is engaged ten times over. The TV light bleeds out from its square confines in squiggly blue waves. Pulsing against her gummy skin.

Conceivably, every actor in *The Exorcist* is a real actor, and so the mom, playing an actress within the film, is doing a double-excellent acting job. That's twice the acting.

Jenny tried to make movies with her ants, but their unions were resistant, their demands too many. She spent hours—unending, dreamless—planted on her stomach, watching their brazen descent from cardboard to carpet to wall to the tips of her fingers, up her arm. *Who is your God?* she asked as they disappeared beneath her shirtsleeve. *Have you no devil to fear?*

Jenny's observations:

1. Little girls born in America are well-mannered (prior to possession).
2. The American medical system is full of guys who are totally willing to do a bunch of complicated procedures on a child who says "cunt" to them repeatedly.
3. Is this film about parenting, the devil, or both?
4. Everyone has all the same diseases: insomnia, possession, indoctrination, childhood.
5. Possession is a bureaucratic process in the Catholic Church.
6. Exorcism, like sleep, is scary, cold, and unfamiliar.

Jenny is out of peach rings and there lies the priest at the bottom of the stairs, concrete blooded beneath him.

A picture of Jenny's childhood home: two-story, blue-sided. Three steps leading to front porch, three flowerpots on the right, three flowerpots on the left. Easy and familiar shapes. Inside, the shadows of things, the quick black dart of whatever unfelt memory, the slow march of ants from her bedroom out into the house.

Jenny thinks the picture of the house is a prison in which her good sleep is jailed. She thinks if she walked up the steps, crossed the threshold, creeped up the stairs, pried open the bedroom door: she would find herself asleep, unbothered, blue with rest.

At the end of the film, Regan, good as new, waltzes out of the house in matching hat and coat, and her mother is telling the only not-dead priest that her daughter doesn't remember anything, anything at all.

Jenny thinks forgetting is more complicated than that. What out-of-body experience—especially one so biblical—doesn't leave a stain?

Jenny is also run-out-of-her-body: Where there might be rest, a chasm (where there might be a soul, the devil). Some girls are happiest in shade-drawn bedrooms, made up of their own undoing.

What Jenny thinks the epilogue looks like:

Regan returns to California and gets a horse just like her mom promised and the sun yo-yos up and down in its regular yellow and orange and pink and it seems like things are going just like they should, just like childhood, but somewhere between the school dances and family vacations and quiet moments reading next to a window, Regan feels something inexplicable rapping down deep inside, pinching at the shape of her inner self, the cluster of organs keeping her alive; and though she doesn't remember peeing unselfconsciously on the floor in front of party guests, doesn't remember scurrying down the stairs backward, spider-like, doesn't remember her head rotating impossibly in full 360s, she still feels sometimes, if only briefly, a sluice of the old voiceless pain, something like being rinsed over—silently, brutally, constantly—in a thin coat of blue paint.

Sink Monkey

Alyssa Proujansky

IN THE VIDEO, THE MONKEY sits in a woman's bathroom, legs dangling. I don't actually know that the monkey is a boy, but still I think *he*. I watch the video on my phone, sound off, curled on my side in my bed. I watch it over and over. Sink Monkey is what I call him—though he is actually sitting on the edge of a bathtub. Sink Monkey has a large head, long, tufty fur. Heavy eyelids. Expressive eyebrows in constant motion. They go up, up when the woman's hands move into the frame, down as she washes his spindly toes. She cleans the bottom of his feet with a cloth. Pats them dry, places them gently on top of each other. I press my palms to my abdomen. I've been bleeding all day, though nothing like before.

Sink Monkey is the only way I've been able to imagine going through with the pregnancy. Whenever I pictured a human child, I felt nothing. I've been ambivalent for weeks, going on long walks with Ethan, talking in circles. Neither of us wants a child—in fact, it was one of the first things we agreed on. But as we talked, the question evolved: Was it an accident or an "accident"? On a scale of one to ten, how badly *don't* we want one?

Mandy texts and I press pause on the video. I've been swiping away texts all day—she's the only one I'll answer. *I feel like I caused it*, I write, by not wanting it enough. *Every time I go to say miscarriage, I screw up and say abortion.* Then I hate myself for using those words. I have no claim on either. I deserve nothing, I think—not grief, not sympathy.

I text Mandy a long paragraph about ambivalence. About two robust cells floating in fluid. How I'm stuck, as always, in the space between them. How this stuckness encroaches on all aspects of my life. But as I type, I buzz with a secret: I can still feel Sink Monkey curled inside me, warm and protected.

While I wait for her reply, I replay the video. I think *dear* about each of Sink Monkey's features. Dear tummy, rounding out over his legs. Dear face, turned up toward the woman as she cleans his ears with a Q-tip. Dear legs, hanging gently over the lip of the bathtub. Dear eyes, fluttering closed as she combs the fur on his chest with a wide-toothed comb.

Mandy texts back a flurry of *sorrys*. She ignores the ambivalence paragraph, which feels like a kindness. She wants to know whether it hurt, and I sit up. I pause the video at my favorite part. The woman is preparing Sink Monkey's toothbrush. He's touching his mouth, craning toward her.

The internet, I write, *says it's like bad period cramps. It's nothing like that. Like, not even remotely.* I tell her that now I know what contractions are like. That I can only describe the smell as *kind of like honeysuckle.* Then I can't breathe. *Gonna try to sleep now*, I type.

I go back to Sink Monkey, try to focus. I list words about his eyes: *Trusting. Eternal.* I write down whatever I want, no matter how stupid. But as the woman moves behind him, I notice her arm. Pale and puffy, like she never goes outside. A scaled rash creeping from wrist to elbow. Who am I to think that Sink Monkey is happy? It's not like I'm a *primatologist*, I think, in the hacked-up voice Ethan and I use to mimic our neighbor. I turn off the video and then I turn off my phone. I lie on my back and stare at the ceiling.

I think: *Drink water, eat toast. Take iron, take B vitamins.* I can see myself leaving the bed, walking to the kitchen. I can see myself *having, getting.* I imagine these good things raining down into the glowing chamber of my body. Repairing Sink Monkey, making him thrive.

The Touch

Kimberly King Parsons

Born landlocked, the animal trainer had been plagued all his life by whale thoughts. It made no sense. He had never seen one, would never, still his dreams brimmed with the giants. He couldn't swim, wouldn't even tolerate a washrag on his face, but in dreams he glided alongside great pods of these beasts in silent slow motion. Or his nightmares—the crisp terror of coming across a dry one, dying or dead somewhere in his city. A heaving rib cage on the boulevard, a loose, meaty heart unearthed by a garbage plow.

The thing that bothered him most about whales: They are out there somewhere whether you see them or not, bobbing in the black depths. This knowledge wrecked him, somehow. If the animal trainer couldn't conquer whales, elephants would have to do. Land leviathans, they had that same throb of gravity. Their big wet eyes, the dumb lumbering that hid their great minds.

Riding was his goal at first, then standing one-footed, supremely confident with his boot in a pool of loose skin.

"Nothing but a big, baggy horse," he liked to say.

The thrill of looking down from their backs, the surprising speed he could muster in them. He taught his elephants to turn in all directions, to bow down and rear up. At first his commands came through a series of whistles and clicks, but soon his herd performed whole shows by rote.

Of course, what looked like effortless collaboration came at the cost of brutality. It was about breaking them down, dismantling the thing that made them bigger than you. His father taught him that. An elephant can stop a show just by sitting. She can rear up and rip clean through a tent, trample children if she wants to. But a good trainer, if he has patience, will always, always prevail.

~

The papers nicknamed him the Mastodon Masochist. His first break was a five-thousand-pound Indian called Romeo. The name was ironic—Romeo was known as an "ugly" in circus parlance, and thought to be untrainable. Called a waste of money by the Barnum expedition after he demonstrated his temperament early on, Romeo went rogue on a dock in Ceylon, crushed a captor's skull underfoot.

The animal trainer spent his days correcting, forcing, anticipating every gesture of the huge beings he knew not to trust. Then at night, the show. The ticket count, the boss happy drunk or sad drunk, depending on the numbers. Tent energy. The ringmaster warning about pickpockets, the pickpockets then noting which specific pockets, which trouser legs the audience members touched. That world of knives and fire. The concentration of the crowd, keeping acrobats aloft with their thoughts, or else wishing, waiting for sudden death. Nauseating band music. Clown after clown. The rest of the show such a bore for the animal trainer, hacks the lot of them. His mantra said aloud each night before taking his mark: "Get ready, motherfuckers." He needed the attention, hated himself for needing it. A joke he told to hide the hurt: for a big topper, applause is like making love to a widow woman—you really can't overdo it.

After the show he got his cut of the take. Sleep was impossible, the high from his act stronger than any speedy drug, so he made his way to Lulu's. He got a deep discount on the girls there, though it didn't matter much. That place was like playing the ponies—you always came out broke. It was worth it to him: that thought-stopping supernova of bought sex. The animal trainer had some celebrity because of his work in the circus, but the truth is, the elephants were a bonus—he would have made a name for himself at Lulu's without them. His father taught him to do one thing well. Do it and keep doing it until you're dead. Turns out the trainer could do two things. The girls called him Touch, and they were always happy when he turned up.

Then he was back on the streets of his neighborhood, a bad place to be at night, even for a man like him. Yawning to look casually brave, or else muttering and shaking change in his pockets to look crazy. Avoiding shadowy passersby, walking a wide berth around trouble that was not his, staggering home to wash whatever girl off his belly, hanging his animal clothes on the line outside his window so the stink wouldn't keep him awake.

He loved women, but he couldn't wait to get back to his elephants. After Romeo there was Jumbo and Cleopatra and Frankie and Jumbo II, Indians and Africans and swollen Indians with mutilated ears passed off as Africans: boatloads of the sickest, saddest lot of half-dead jungle uglies ever to heave onto American soil. The shape of them in the dark, unstabled, unchained but never leaving, waiting for him. Their bulk before the sun came up.

The trainer's ear against their sides, the wet heartbeats. The purl of slow blood in them. It was the same indifferent roar he heard when he listened at the inside of any seashell. The cupped promise of a distant ocean—the sound of its deep wonders massive, utterly unknowable. An impossible transmission he held in his hands.

At the Taxidermy Museum
of Military Heroes

Steven Dunn

I VOLUNTEERED. IT GETS ME OUT of work three days a week, plus it looks good as extra duty on my brag sheet.

Towering over the expansive asphalt parking lot is the mirrored atrium, tapering to an apex, giving way to sleek white facades of its four wings, a cross. On each side is a circle of flagpoles with drooping flags. In front a plaque reads: *These flags will forever be flown at half-mast in honor of the heroes who gave their lives for freedom.* Inside each circle is a bronze statue lying with arms out, palms to heaven, helmet cocked. Adjacent bronze rifle. Scattered bronze bullet casings.

I walk inside the atrium. Conditioned air envelopes me as the stained glass casts rainbow patterns on the marble floor at my feet. On a platform in the middle is a soldier, crouched in a shooting position, stuffed white fingers curled around rifle trigger, one eye squinting, the other staring straight ahead.

I meet the lead taxidermist for orientation after she descends on the escalator behind the soldier. I see you're admiring our work, she says, looking over her glasses and placing a loose gray dreadlock behind her ear. Yes, I say, it looks really lifelike. She says, Honey, we all look *life-like*. Huh? I say.

We're all just an approximation of life, she says. Even death is just another approach. Taxidermy is a faithful representation of life in that liminal space in between.

She unlocks a Staff Only door and tells me there are four levels going down, each for a different part of the process. We descend concrete stairs, illuminated with emergency-exit green light, to level three, where we walk into a fluorescent white room with glossy white floors, gun-gray cabinets, and a grid of steel tables with evenly spaced holes on the surfaces, and a sink nearby. I circle my fingers along one of the holes. To collect the drippings, she says.

Taxi means to arrange, she says, and of course *derm* means skin. She walks over to a large steel and glass door, above which a red digital display indicates five degrees Celsius. They are ready to be mounted, she says, pointing inside, where flesh hangs loose on the men like shirttails. There are droopy black holes where there were once eyes.

This is only a processing center, she says. We will ship bodies to five other museums being built, once they are up and running. Lord knows when, but hopefully soon, we're so backlogged here.

This way, she says. Ahead is another large door, where digital red announces it is zero degrees Celsius. A clipboard hangs next to it, white pages with columns of black text. This is our storage room for bodies in transition, she says.

The room is vacuum-sealed and illuminated with motion-activated fluorescent light. Stainless steel trays are stacked four high, four wide, separated by an aisle. I can't tell how far back they go. Each tray holds a stiff body, faceup, covered by a white sheet.

We have to be careful not to let the temperature of this room fall below zero, she says, because ice will form in the body tissue and the skin will lose its wonderful elasticity. The bodies we can't use go down to the fourth level, that's the crematorium. Families can choose an official urn for the hero's ashes.

The second level is where the skins are mounted. Rows of off-white muscled mannequins with hollow eye sockets pose: saluting, lying in sniper position, standing in shooter position, throwing grenades, crouching, running.

Next to each mannequin is a short gray cabinet with shallow drawers. She slides out the top drawer. Glass eyes with brown, blue, and green irises nest in egg-crate foam. Next drawer: eyebrows and eyelashes, many shades of brown, black, and blond. The third drawer displays silicone hands with manicured fingernails.

We use these, she said, because it's too difficult to remove the real hand skin, and this way we can position the fingers to pull a trigger, throw a grenade, or salute. The fatty parts of the face, like the lips and cheeks, are also filled with silicone, she says.

We walk to a mounting station, where she introduces me to Camilla, who is hard at work. Camilla looks up, but goes right back to stitching skin around the back of a head and down its neck. Brown-iris eyes peer out the front. The lips are full and skin is stretched tight across the shoulders.

Back up on the first level the mounted bodies are fitted with uniforms. Boots are polished, placed, and laced up on the soldiers, sailors, marines, and airmen. Their hands are fitted with rifles and handguns. A Navy SEAL has his face painted black and green. A Marine wears his dress uniform: blue pants, black gold-buttoned coat, left breast draped with medals, white-gloved hand saluting from the black brim of his white cap.

Now the lead taxidermist tells me it's time for me to do my part.

Follow me, she says, and we go back down the concrete stairwell to the fourth level, the long rows of refrigerated bodies, again. But this time a cadaver is laid out on a steel table with a man standing beside it, tapping a clipboard.

This is Patrick, she announces. Our volunteer is here to help. Just in time, Patrick says, and glances down at the body. This one wasn't good for much; we need to get him onto this stretcher and over to the crematory. Could you grab the other end of the sheet?

The cold yellow toenails scrape my wrist. Patrick grins unhappily. The skin has been removed from the cadaver's head and upper body, revealing gray muscle. But the skin is still attached from forearm to fingertips. From hips to toes. And his penis is still intact, but with a smooth line cut around the pubic hair. I wonder if there is a family to claim his ashes.

The White Girl

Luis Alberto Urrea

2 SHORT WAS A TAGGER FROM down around 24th St. He hung with the Locos de Veinte set, though he freelanced as much as he banged. His tag was a cloudy blue-silver goth *II-SHT*, and it went out on freight trains and trucks all over the fucking place. His tag was, like, sailing through Nebraska and some shit like that. Out there, famous, large.

2 Short lived with his pops in that rundown house on W. 20th. That one with the black iron spears for a fence. The old-timer feeds shorties sometimes when they don't have anywhere to go—kids like Li'l Wino and Jetson. 2 Short's pops is a veterano. Been in jail a few times, been on the street, knows what it's like. He wants 2 Short to stay in school, but hey, what you gonna do? The vatos do what they got to do.

2 Short sometimes hangs in the backyard. He's not some nature pussy or nothing, but he likes the yard. Likes the old orange tree. The

nopal cactus his pops cuts up and fries with eggs. 2 Short studies shit like birds and butterflies, tries to get their shapes and their colors in his tag book. Hummingbirds.

Out behind their yard is that little scrapyard on 23rd. That one that takes up a block one way and about two blocks the other. Old, too. Cars in there been rusting out since '68. Gutiérrez, the old dude runs the place, he's been scrapping the same hulks forever. Chasing kids out of there with a BB gun. *Ping*! Right in the ass!

2 Short always had too much imagination. He was scared to death of Gutiérrez's little kingdom behind the fence. All's you could see was the big tractor G used to drag wrecks around. The black oily crane stuck up like the stinger of the monsters in the sci-fi movies on channel 10. *The Black Scorpion* and shit.

The fence was ten feet tall, slats. Had some discolored rubber stuff woven in, like pieces of lawn furniture or something. 2 Short could only see little bits of the scary wrecks in there if he pressed his eye to the fence and squinted.

One day he just ran into the fence with his bike and one of those rotten old slats fell out and there it was—a passageway into the yard. He looked around, made sure Pops wasn't watching, listened to make sure G wasn't over there, and he slipped through.

Damn. There were wrecked cars piled on top of each other. It was eerie. Crumpled metal. Torn-off doors. Busted glass. He could see stars in the windshields where the heads had hit. Oh man—peeps died in here, homes.

2 Short crept into musty dead cars and twisted the steering wheels.

He came to a crunched '71 Charger. The seats were twisted and the dash was ripped out. Was that blood? On the old seat? Oh man. He ran his hand over the faded stain. *Blood*.

He found her bracelet under the seat. Her wrist must have been slender. It was a little gold chain with a little blue stone heart. He held it in his palm. Chick must have croaked right here.

He stared at the starred windshield. The way it was pushed out around the terrible cracks. Still brown. More blood. And then the hair.

Oh shit—there was hair in strands still stuck to the brown stains and the glass. Long blond strands of hair. They moved in the breeze. He touched them. He pulled them free. He wrapped them around his finger.

That night, he rubbed the hairs over his lips. He couldn't sleep. He kept thinking of the white girl. She was dead. How was that possible? How could she be dead?

He held the bracelet against his face. He lay with the hair against his cheek.

When he went out to tag two nights later, 2 Short aborted his own name. Die Hard and Arab said, "Yo, what's wrong with you?"

But he only said, "The white girl."

"What white girl, yo?"

But he stayed silent. He uncapped the blue. He stood in front of the train car. *THE WHITE GIRL*. He wrote it. It went out to New York. He sent it out to Mexico, to Japan on a container ship. *THE WHITE GIRL*.

He wrote it and wrote it. He sent it out to the world. He prayed with his can. He could not stop.

THE WHITE GIRL.

THE WHITE GIRL.

THE WHITE GIRL.

Skin

Sejal Shah

THIS IS WHAT THE WHITE BOYS SAY: your hair. Your skin. This is what the black boys say: we together, together. This is what the Asians say: you date out too, I can tell. This is what the Jamaican boys say: I never liked you Indians. This is what the desis say: Get out of Massachusetts. Move to New York.

This is what the white boys say: but we would have brown children. And: Color doesn't matter. And: Why are you so obsessed with it. We're all Americans, right. How are we that different? My parents would love you. My older brother would want to go out with you. Your skin is your best feature.

This is what the black boys say: you got such nice eyes, girl. Your people have such big eyes. If you dressed hip-hop, you'd be my wife. We're almost the same. What is that dot, I like that dot. Never pay for a guy. What are you doing after. You saving it for your husband? Don't give it away to the white boys. Why not come home with me?

The brown boys are silent. I can't find them, can't see them at all.

Sometimes there is a table of them, sitting on the far side of the blue wall. They are talking in Hindi. They are laughing in Hindi. We pass each other on the street, slightly embarrassed. If we looked, we'd have to say hello. Countries and questions suggest themselves between us. If we stopped to talk, if we went out for coffee, friends would ask when's the wedding, and oh, we love Indian food.

The brown boys, desis: They are too short after the white boys. You are too brown after their white girls. You look at each other helplessly. You are instant family, and then the instant passes.

Some of them remind you of your father when he was a student. He was thin then, wore the Third World mustache above his grin. How he looked in pictures: young.

This is what the brown girls say—where are the good ones? There's no one here at all. We say: let's go salsa dancing! Hit garba-dandiya raas. Let's go bhangra-hip-hop-reggae dancing: Springfield, Hartford, Manhattan, Queens. We are driving up and down Route 9, up and down 91, up and down Main Street. We pass Emily Dickinson's house, yeah, there was a woman who understood: why even bother? Just stay in your house and write. We'll go to Net-IP next year. We'll think about going to India next year. We'll think about finding someone later. In the meantime, New York.

The problem with white boys is not just that they're white. That they would even think such things. The problem with black boys is not only that they're black. That they would constantly be trying to cop a feel. The problem with desis is not only that they remind you of your father, your five crazy uncles. The problem with Western Mass is not just that you like this place. That you stand out in the snowy whiteness, that their mountains are really moderately-sized hills, that this is where you live. That you are a brown girl here, never just a girl.

This is what they all say: You'll publish first. Hey Arundhati Roy, hey Jhumpa Lahiri, where's your best seller?

Here is a story about where you live.

Here is your best seller.

This is yet another story not about India.

Bigsby

Maurice Carlos Ruffin

THAT'S THE WAY IT WAS when I was younger. I never had a hard time getting a date—I'm not bragging. I'm not, I swear. Probably because I grew up with three sisters, y'know? The chicks always liked me. Black chicks, too. Man, if I went out, they'd give me the eye. You know women don't just look a guy they don't know in the face. Amirite? Yeah. I dated some. There was this one in college. I haven't thought about her in some time. Aisha. She got closer to me than most. By junior year, I was staying at her apartment more than in my own dorm. We got along well. Did everything together for a while. Picnics in City Park. Day trips to the beach in Biloxi. People would stare. At first, I thought it was because she was so good-looking. She had this shape. I mean not just her hips and stuff. Her face was heart-shaped. And those eyes. We fizzled out.

That's right, then I met Samantha. Those redheads, bro! Dammit. Why you always got to drag that ghost out the closet? You want to know what happened with us, Kyle? I'll tell you what happened. Then don't ever bring her up again. This shit whiskey is giving me a headache. Order something better. Don't be so damned cheap. Samantha was perfect, and we fell in love quick. It wasn't just the usual things like compatibility and looks. She was ambitious. She wanted to make an empire with me. Her father was older and had this company that put video poker machines in all the bars. I know it don't sound like much, but do you know how many bars there are in New Orleans? That family was loaded, and she wanted to take over one day and keep expanding it.

One day, I came home to our condo downtown. She was my fiancée by then. We were considering a June wedding. We were talking about buying a house in Old Metairie, starting a family. Her parents would cover the cost of everything. They would have to. My family had nothing to contribute. I had less than nothing. That day, the condo was so quiet. I thought Samantha was out for a jog or maybe down at the coffee shop. But she was sitting on the bed holding some paper. Her face was blotchy. She looked terrible. She asked how I could lie to her the way I did. She threw the papers at me, but they fell on the floor. I'm thinking she's accusing me of running around on her, like she'd hired a PI or something. But I wasn't like that anymore. I picked up the papers.

It was one of those breakdowns from a company that checks your DNA. It wasn't her idea. She said her mother must have swabbed a cup I drank out of or something. I was furious. I mean, who does that, bro! I could've punched a hole in the wall. The percentages were highlighted. I had plenty of points on the European side of things like Irish and Italian, but it also said twenty-four percent sub-Saharan Africa. This was news to me, and that's what I told Samantha. She said she wasn't a bigot. But she had to think of her parents. What would she tell her friends? Her Nana? I moved out about a week later.

Yeah this better, Kyle. This real whiskey. No, I don't think that sheet was right. I think all that computerized mumbo jumbo is bull-shit. I know my family tree. My great-grandparents were still alive when I was little. They had roots in Sicily. I know my heritage. Fuck! Get me another shot of this. Don't be cheap. Make it a double. Funny thing is, years later, I ran into Aisha at that festival they throw out in Ponchatoula. Yeah. The one with strawberries. And we kind of picked up where we left off. Eventually, one night I told her about those papers and she was all like, "I sho reckoned. You ain't got no pink in yo' skin. That's why you so fine." She didn't really talk like that. She was snooty—had gone and got herself an English Ph.D. Taught at a college. Spoke better than I do. A couple of times, I told her that sheet was wrong, but she just nodded. We didn't end up lasting that long the second time around. I couldn't have her loving me for something I'm not.

Over There

Patricia Q. Bidar

CHARLES IS MY BLOOD AND what he feels, I feel. From the overhead vent, a soft breeze cools the sweat of his neck. I experience the small blessing of it, seeing him lean soft arms onto the checkout counter. My brother is dressed in the same black suit he wears to all our dinners. Charles is bald-headed like me, although my bony pate is covered—in the way of middle-aged men and ballplayers like the young Turk I saw near the refrigerator section of this CVS—in a ball cap.

The cashier assumes my brother and I are strangers. It is true we haven't greeted each other. Before him on the counter is a cheap, lime-green phone charger. It's clear he's been here awhile. The cashier beckons me to the second register. Charles regards the charger.

"What happened?" I call over. The cashier is ringing up my eggs, bacon, bottle of wine. I am using CVS as my market. Also, my bank. I press the buttons that add $20 "cash back" to my tab.

"My charger! I just bought it this morning," my brother says, looking past my face. "It was stolen. From the coffee shop!"

"Your phone charger was stolen?" Now it comes to me: My brother's smell. The greasy suit, the unwashed hair.

A small line is forming. The cashier gives a little huff. "I told you, sir, it's about $11.95 with tax," she tells Charles. I am alert to the small note of irritation. It isn't often I am witness to my brother's lived and public days.

"Are you at the shelter over near the church?" I continue, sliding my card back into my wallet. The cashier shakes her head slightly. She wears those gigantic, bamboo-style gold hoops that were popular twenty years ago. The kind that have to be hollow since they aren't elongating her lobes.

I know our conversation can wait. Charles and I are meeting for an early dinner. It's just happenstance we're both here at CVS across the parking lot from the coffee shop where apparently Charles spent at least part of the afternoon.

I've bought the wine, the breakfast supplies as a kind of reward for myself, I guess. A way to recognize my immense humanitarianism, meeting my brother at a neutral location to buy him a patty melt and some coffee, which he'll ask to have refilled at least five times before we shake hands goodbye.

"Could you . . ." the cashier gestures to the line.

"I think he's next," I say, leaning over to palm Charles the twenty. My brother gives a brusque nod. Passes wind. Isn't it the strangest thing, how a person's farts can smell the same after years and miles and the horribly timed breakdowns?

"Yeah, no. The Berkeley Shelter. Took the bus." He flashes the flip phone as if to show the cashier, me, and the line of tired workers who are waiting that he does have a machine to be enlivened by the charger. I start for the door.

"Gotta have a phone," says the young Turk in the baseball uniform. Kindly, I want to believe. I startle when the glass door emits its electronic chime. My brother is the first to guffaw.

"Yo, Charles," I call back to my brother. He gives me a little half salute that was a thing of his in high school. Our yearbook mentions it under his photo. "I'll see you over there, man."

I have a couple of minutes to pop my trunk and deposit my bounty. Wine to soothe me after our visit. I'll empty the bottle, imagining my brother telling the bus driver, then his dorm-mates at the shelter about his brother hooking him up with a brand-new charger and a princely meal. All the coffee he wanted.

I'll still be thinking of him when I awaken in the morning, temples thumping, and gauze-mouthed. I'll think of my brother's half salute as I fry up my bacon and eggs, grease seeping into my clothes.

The Pregnancy Game

Michelle Ross

Gwen points to Minh and me and says, "You're both pregnant." To Tahlia, she says, "You're not pregnant."

"Yes!" Tahlia says.

"And you?" she says to Gwen, who stands apart from us, the cue stick to us racked balls. Gwen cracks her neck. "I'm a Right to Life Activist. Kind of like the robber in *Settlers of Catan*."

"You steal our babies?" Minh says, picking dirt from underneath her nails.

"Fetuses, technically," Gwen says. "They're not born yet. But no. What I steal is everything but the fetus."

I feel myself shiver even though it's August. We're in the woods behind Gwen's house. Pine trees like thick arrows point toward the bleached sky. Ozone depletion, particulate matter.

Gwen has created a game board on the forest floor by making a trail of the pink paper plates purchased for her older sister Patrice's baby shower, a baby shower that never took place. All Minh and Tahlia know is that Patrice "lost the baby," a phrase that makes me think of my dad's frequently misplaced car keys.

Minh, Tahlia, and I are the pawns. Gwen has brought along the fuzzy white dice she won in a claw machine at the arcade. A game turn consists of a player rolling the dice, then walking the designated number of plates from start, picking up the plate where she lands, and turning it over to read what it says. There are two messages beneath each plate: one for pregnant pawns, one for unpregnant pawns.

Gwen must have spent hours writing on these plates, planning out the rules. That's typical Gwen. The first time she spent the night at my house, my mom went on about how precise Gwen is. "Whoever heard of a little girl measuring out the amount of toothpaste on her brush like that? And did you see how long she chewed between each bite of spaghetti?" she said to my dad. "She counts to forty," I said. "Good lord," my mom said.

Gwen says that because Tahlia isn't pregnant, she gets to go first.

"Why?" Minh asks.

"Because it's the rule. Pregnant pawns always go last," Gwen says.

"Not in the real world. What about those expectant mothers parking spots?" Minh says.

Gwen rolls her eyes. "Seriously? You think that's a perk worth getting excited about?" She looks to Tahlia and tells her to roll the fuzzy dice.

The dice rolls over brown pine needles and stops when it bumps against a cone. Five. Tahlia reads her pink paper plate aloud. "You're a slut who had casual sex and then took a morning-after pill. Go back to start."

Tahlia laughs, flips her hair. "Hey, I'll take slut over having babies any day." She walks back to the start plate, rejoining the rest of us.

Minh says, "Is she back at start because she had casual sex? Or because she took a morning-after pill?"

Gwen says, "Morning-after pill mostly."

Minh is next. She rolls a six. The paper plate reads, "You ended up pregnant as a result of being raped. You got an abortion. But in your state, it's illegal to get abortions in rape cases. In fact, your rapist can sue you for doing so, and that's just what he's done. Go back to start."

Minh says, "How is that even a thing? A rapist suing his victim?"

"It's a thing all right," Gwen says.

"Well, what if I lived in a state where it's legal to have an abortion in the case of rape? Would I get to go forward then?"

Gwen looks to me. "Frances?"

Though I can't see the horizon beyond all these trees, I know the sun is starting to set because I spot a mosquito on my thigh, its long legs reminding me of the stitches in Gwen's forehead when she fell off her bike a few years ago. I flick the mosquito away, worry about blood diseases. I say, "I don't think moving forward is the objective of this game."

Gwen nods her head in approval.

"What is the objective, then?" Minh says. "To further overpopulate the planet? To turn women into baby-incubator automatons?"

A mosquito lands on Gwen's arm and she smacks it dead. Rubs the residue onto her denim shorts. She ignores Minh, says, "Frances, it's your turn."

I reluctantly retrieve the fuzzy dice, which is slightly damp and more brown than white now. When I release it, the dice rolls into Gwen's pristine white sneaker and stops. Three. I walk slowly to the third paper plate and pick it up. I stare at it.

"Read what it says." Gwen smacks another mosquito, this time on her neck. Again, she wipes the residue onto her shorts.

I read, "Your fetus is not viable, but it's post–twenty weeks." I stop.

"Read," Gwen says again.

I suck in my breath. "So you must continue to carry the pregnancy even though there's no chance the baby will survive after birth. Move forward six spaces and read the next plate."

I look to Gwen, my best friend since we were five. Her face is stone, but I can see through to the jagged mineral deposits, the hollow cavity inside.

I don't move.

"Forward six," Gwen says.

"Gwen," I say.

"You can't quit," Gwen says. "No quitters."

Still, I stand there. Minh and Tahlia look back and forth between Gwen and me. Somewhere a police siren sharpens, then dulls. Dogs bark.

Gwen walks over to me. Says, "I'll go for you, then."

Before I can say anything, Gwen raises her hand. Smacks my cheek. Minh says, "What the fuck?"

I grit my teeth so as not to cry.

Gwen holds open her hand to show me the mosquito bits and the blood. My blood. I wait for her to wipe it onto my shorts, since it's my blood, my dead mosquito, but she doesn't. She wipes the mess onto her own shorts. She moves forward.

Monsters

Sadia Quraeshi Shepard

T HAT SPRING MY WIFE COVERED the walls of our living room in newsprint. She would draw one monster per day, she announced, and once they were on the walls, they would no longer wake her up at night.

For three months she dragged sticks of charcoal across the large sheets. Long, wide slashes that inked her fingertips perpetually black. After the first hour, the body was always in place. Their slack jaws resting on thick, bubbling necks. Their shining eyes and knife-like fangs.

In early March we went to the doctor for my wife's biannual checkup. Because you're immunocompromised, the doctor told her, you'll have to be doubly careful. I nodded, writing the information down in my notebook in a pantomime of calm, trying to appear in control while a low, throbbing panic began to radiate from the base of my skull.

On the way home we found an old armchair on the street and hauled it up the two flights to our apartment, then felt silly for doing it. Were we crazy to have touched the chair? We let it sit for three days on the landing before dragging it into our living room and swabbing it down. Newly sanitized, it joined my office.

While my wife drew I sat crunched over my laptop, telecommuting. I can make enough for the both of us, I told her. I wanted her to keep drawing. Images of the ceilings and spare rooms of my colleagues grew familiar to me, as did the interruptions of their children. I grew fond of the hum of their televisions off-screen, the patches of yard I sometimes glimpsed outside of their windows. Most were too polite to ask about the monsters that hovered at the edges of my screen. I never offered explanations.

What would it be like, I wondered, to live without fear? In the apartments around us we heard our neighbors moving around their spaces. Working, talking, fighting sometimes. Their music became our music. Their restlessness seeped into the walls and mingled with ours. The ash from my wife's charcoal settled into the corners of the room. Her drawings expanded from the walls to a pile on the floor, growing like a bulwark against the enemy. We spoke to our faraway mothers and begged them to stay inside.

I called the market on the corner and asked the owner if he could send one of his nephews with bags of onions, rice, and lentils. In the four years we'd lived here the grocer and I had never communicated in our common language. Brother, he said, his voice thick with regret, I have only Uncle Ben's.

At the end of each day my wife stepped back from the walls and stood with her arms at her sides, looking at what she had made. Then she walked to the bathroom and I knew not to disturb her. There she shed her clothes in a pile on the floor and ran a bath as hot as she could stand. She soaked her tiny frame until the heat had penetrated the cords in her neck and the claw of her fists had broken open. She used an old sponge to scrub the pads of her fingertips until they were pink and new, and emerged steaming from the bath, her eyes bright, wearing one of the large men's kurtas she wore at home.

This was a kind of nightly triumph. Some nights we exchanged a bottle of hand sanitizer for wine and climbed out on the fire escape to drink it. A toast to our health, we said, as we joined in with the cheers that erupted on our street every evening at seven. On nights that we had no wine we drank milky chai.

Now that her drawings covered our apartment my wife was able to sleep or wake at will, seemingly immune to caffeine. I was not so lucky. On those nights that I couldn't stay asleep I crept back into the living room, listening to the sound of sirens.

I stood in the middle of the room and dared myself to look at the monsters lit by the dim glow of the streetlight. I stared at the scales of their skin, their wet mouths hanging open to reveal the forks of their tongues. I closed my eyes and listened to their sharp keening, trying to drown out the wheezing and clicking of the ventilators, the flat lines of the monitors. Then I toasted them, taunted them, told them that they didn't scare me anymore, even though they did.

The Weatherman's Heart

Tessa Yang

RUMORS ROLLED THROUGH TOWN THAT the weatherman was dying. We gathered around the television to see if we could tell.

What were we expecting? Parched, yellow skin, and brittle hair, and lips drawn back in a skull's livid smile? The weatherman appeared unchanged. He was tall and tan with his dark hair parted on the right side, and he spoke of rain. That summer, the talk was always of rain: when it would come, how long it would last, whether it would be one of those fine passing mists or a real storm, good and strong, soaking the dry lawns and filling the birdbaths until they overflowed.

"He's not dying," said one of us with disgust as the news went to commercial.

"Is *too*," insisted another. "My mom says he's got sickness inside him. In his heart. He'll be dead soon. Just wait and see."

So we waited.

Under the blazing June sun, we ran wild through the long, empty days. We pried dried-out frogs from the creek bed with our mothers' garden spades. We prepared toxic salads of crushed beetles and fungus scoured from rotting logs. We cupped our hands around moths, clapping away the white dust of their panic that stained our fingers and palms. Sometimes we imagined our parents in their offices, vents breathing a stale chill into their vacant faces, but we felt no pity for their plight. In their absence we could write our own laws: Tattletales faced abandonment; crybabies, thirty seconds beneath the hornets' nest to prove their valor. We laughed, fought, swore, and formed hostilities and alliances that evaporated faster than gobs of spit on the sidewalk. And in the evenings, confined to our separate houses, the day's filth reduced to grimy circles around bathtub drains, we looked on as our parents watched the forecast, dismayed to see the drought enduring and the weatherman still alive.

So we made a bargain: his heart for our rain.

The origins of this sacrificial arrangement remained elusive. It seemed to rise from the cracked earth and linger like a vapor in the air, and once we inhaled it we could think of nothing else. In the beginning our daydreams were modest. A swift, efficient heart attack. A night's sleep that darkened to forever. As the earth hardened like concrete and the wildflowers bowed their wilted heads, our visions grew crueler. Lightning strikes, car crashes, nosedives from the tops of buildings, drowning, burning, a ninja star to the back of the head. We shrieked these fates at one another like insults, digging fingers into sunburned arms. We could not believe the weatherman's selfishness. We could not accept that he would dare to go on living and deny us the rain that was rightfully ours.

Romping through our adjoining backyards no longer satisfied us. We entered the sweltering shade of the woods where twigs snapped like matchsticks underfoot. We ventured into the pasture where cows nosed the yellow grass, a gleaming heat rising from their spotted backs.

Inevitably, the tunnel drew us. Once its yawning mouth had been a stand-in for every fear of every dark thing that slouched from basements and cracked closet doors, but our rage had filled us with a reckless bravery. We struck out. Our voices resounded grandly off the concrete walls: *Death by fire! Death by decapitation!* The creek had long since vanished. The tunnel was dry as a boneyard and deliciously cool. Nearest the entrance, we could make out the chalked slogans and initials of those who had come before. We may have spent a whole day down there, immune to hunger and thirst, squabbling over the laws of our new kingdom.

When we climbed back to the street, we encountered a world engulfed in darkness. The sky hung close as a ceiling. There was no breeze, yet every leaf seemed to quiver with some private anticipation. Raindrops began to fall on our stunned, upturned faces. Within moments it was a downpour. We ran through the pasture and the woods, slipping in our flooded sneakers. We had to use our hands as visors to keep the water from running into our eyes. Our backyards were seas of frothing mud and soaked, flattened grass. We sought shelter under the overhang of the nearest porch, watching as our bare vicious summer-world collapsed under the rain's driving force. There was no thunder. Lightning did not flare and blister above the trees. There was only the rain, the long-sought rain, which now that it had arrived felt only like punishment—and that was when we remembered our bargain.

We fumbled for the door, patting down pockets for keys, forgetting in our horror which of us this home belonged to. We stumbled into the living room, trailing mud and water, and someone dove for the TV remote and there were several seconds of near-hysteria as we searched for the right channel. A commercial was playing. A jingle for a grocery store. We managed to collect ourselves. We sat down and waited. Outside, water surged from the overwhelmed gutters and made long curtains through which nothing could be seen. The air conditioner clicked on. We sat there, shivering in our wet clothes, waiting for the weatherman to appear.

Shit Cassandra Saw That She Didn't Tell the Trojans Because at That Point Fuck Them Anyway

Gwen E. Kirby

LIGHT BULBS.

Penguins.

Bud Light.

Velcro.

Claymation. The moon made out of cheese.

Tap dancing.

Yoga.

Twizzlers. Mountain Dew. Jell-O. Colors she can eat with her eyes.

Methamphetamine.

T-shirts. Thin and soft, they pass from person to person, men to women, each owner slipping into different teams—Yankees, Warriors—and out again with no bloodshed, no thought to allegiance or tribe. And the words! Profusions of nonsense. The Weather Is Here, Wish You Were Fine. Chemists Do It on the Table Periodically. Cut Class Not Frogs. Words everywhere and for everyone, for nothing but a joke, for the pleasure of them, a world so careless with its words. And not just on T-shirts. Posters. Water bottles. Newspapers. Junk mail. Bumper stickers. Lists. Top ten Halloween costumes for your dog as modeled by this corgi. Top ten times a monkey's facial expression perfectly summed up your thoughts on NAFTA. Top ten things your boyfriend *wishes* you would do in bed but is too afraid to say. Cassandra has not noticed a lack of men telling women what to do. Perhaps this will be a pleasure of the future, a male desire that goes *un*spoken. A desire that is only a desire, and not a command.

Then there are the small words, the private words, hidden within romance novels, mysteries, thrillers, science fiction, fantasy. Heaving bosoms, astronauts, and ape men. Pulp paperbacks that live brief but fiery lives, the next torrent of words so swift behind they must sell or be destroyed, only enough space on the shelf for the new.

And lives, of course. Cassandra would rather see only the fictions, the objects, the colored plastic oddities of the future, but she must see lives as well. Here are two little girls. They sit in the dirt and dig at a boulder. When it is finally unearthed, the possibilities! A passage to the underworld, a buried treasure, a colony of fairies—anything but dirt. It is essential that they never succeed, never dig up the boulder, and of course they don't. Their plastic shovels move the dirt aside; new dirt, dusty and thin, blows across their eyes. One of the girls becomes an engineer. One is raped by her college boyfriend. This second girl will run a bakery on an island where she loves to hike. She will have three children, all boys, and she will die when she is quite old and quite unwilling to go. Her boys will have lives too. Everyone does. Lives on fast forward, on silent, even the best life, even her own, swiftly boring.

Cassandra is tired of running at wooden horses with nothing but the flame of the smallest match.

She is tired of speaking to listening ears. The listening ears of the men who think her mad drive her to madness. She wishes she could move far away to an island and own a bird. She never will do this because she knows she never does. It is said that Apollo gave Cassandra the gift of prophecy—this is true. It is said that, when she refused his advances, he spit in her mouth so that she would never again be believed. A virgin the same as a seduced woman the same as a violated woman the same as a willing woman, all women opening their mouths to watch snakes slither out and away.

Cassandra is *done*, full the fuck up, soul-weary.

Still, as Troy is sacked, as she clings to the cold marble legs of the statue of Athena in the sacred temple, she cannot accept what she knows to be true. That soon Ajax will arrive and rape her. He will smash the statue of the goddess she worships and curse his own life; and worse, her goddess will not help her, will turn her shattered face away. Cassandra will be carried across the sea, made another man's concubine, bear twin boys, and be killed by Clytemnestra. But before this comes to pass, there are visions Cassandra burns to share with the women of Troy.

The women of Troy might listen. They know that Cassandra's curse is their curse as well. That Apollo spit in her mouth, but it was only spit.

Here is what she might show them.

Tampons.

Jeans.

Washing machines.

The cordless Hitachi Magic Wand.

Elastic hair ties.

Mace.

Epidurals.

And here is the best thing of all, the thing that makes Cassandra smile as the men storm her temple, exactly as she has always known they would: someday, Trojan will not be synonymous with bravery or failure, betrayal or endurance, or the most beautiful woman or the most foolish of men. A Trojan will be carried in every hopeful wallet, extracted with abashed confidence, slipped over the shaft, rolled to the base. Perhaps the Trojan men would laugh if they knew, or be humiliated, or pause to think about the indifference of history and the hubris of the man who hopes to be remembered. But the women, once they saw that blue streamer unfurl, the women would rejoice, would wave it over their heads like a new flag, like a promise of better things to come.

Customer Service at the Karaoke Don Quixote

Juan Martinez

CUSTOMER SERVICE AT THE Karaoke Don Quixote is main thing we worry about. Because if customer doesn't go here, will go elsewhere, and soon no customers go here period. We treat them special. We feign bad foreign accent to make feel better. We not decide on particular region—because if customer is from said particular region, or customer's family is, is no good, no? No. Is no good. Is little Italian, little Polack, little bit here and there. Is good.

Because it gets customer singing. Customer service is number one priority for us. We say, You sing, you sing! Is person drinking? Yes! Is good, for beer and spirits make person sing, and people singing is good. They buy more beer and spirits. And intoxication is good because is no cover charge. Is good, because people like singing great works of literature, and is good because they drink more, so more profits.

First we start with *Don Quixote*. But soon we branch to postmodernist stuff, because customers want, and customers is always accurate: They say, Barth! Barthelme! Pynchon! Coover! We say, OK.

We say, is good. Also postmodernists drink. Minimalists, they don't drink so much. Is poetry good? No, is no good. Poetry karaoke, is like haiku, sonatinas—no good, no one sings. Classic is good: Melville and Tolstoy and some other peoples—big hits, big big hits.

Is reason for accent? Is annoying you? Logic? Logic is, these are shy peoples—literature peoples is shy. Is sitting around reading, no much dancing, maybe some drinking and then dancing, but stiff, you know? Is people reading travel, you know? The *New York Times* travel section? Also travelogues and such. Is dreaming of going elsewhere, maybe finding charming out-of-the-way spots with kindly innkeepers, lovely foreign women, also big motherly types that feed them exotic soups and ales and such. And maybe, in this fantasy of going places, they're thinking they might let go a little because no one knows them, right? So we feed that fantasy a little. Is good, is people happy. Is good business. People sing: They sing *Quixote*:

<<En un lugar de la Mancha, de cuyo nombre no quiero acordarme, no ha mucho tiempo que vivía un hidalgo de los de lanza en astillero, adarga antigua, rocín flaco y galgo corridor.>>

Or sing dubbed international public domain version.

"In a village of La Mancha, the name of which I have no desire to call to mind, there lived not long since one of those gentlemen that keep a lance in the lance-rack, an old buckler, a lean hack, and a greyhound for coursing."

Is good! Business is good. We have many franchises. As for matter of customer service—customers happy, is always happy here—service-wise we are number one. Soon we open in La Mancha—is ironic, no? Waiters feign heavy American accent. Talk loud. Slow. Is good. People feel OK singing. Is happy.

Soon: IPO. T-shirts. Website. CDs. Is good!

Bone Wars

Laura Citino

THIS KID IS TRYING TO tell me that Brontosaurus didn't really exist. He wears a black T-shirt halfway to his knees, skinny like they all are. These kids get bused in from tri-county or the group homes because a day at Suffolk City Dino Park is a cheap way to occupy restless eyes and destructive little hands. Most of them get right to vandalizing. Some of the park people hate these kids, but I like them. They're easy, really, so easy to help.

"I don't know, buddy," I say. "We got one right here." I gesture like I've been taught to the animatronic sauropod creaking its head back and forth above us. From where I stand, I can see the bolts in its neck, green and yellow paint rusting. I'm supposed to be doing rounds to make sure the tri-county kids aren't clogging toilets or scrawling DICK on the flat boulders along the walking path. This job is low stakes. No flashing lights or emergency tracheotomies, no rollovers in cornfields. *A positive step forward*, was what I wrote on my application.

"Brontosaurus was a mistake," the kid says. His nose runs and he keeps slinging the back of his hand across his face. Snot doesn't freak me out. In EMT school I always had the strongest stomach. Blood, vomit, the strange clarity of viscera, no problem. "They thought they discovered another species but they didn't," he says. "It's just an Apatosaurus with a funny head."

My first day, José quizzed me on dinosaur knowledge in the break room while he sorted through OSHA videos. Velociraptor means *Swift Seizer*. Dimetrodon means *Two-Sized Tooth*. José can't wait for me to see the Dino Park in the fall, how the flaming leaves enliven the machinery. I like his faith in my future here.

I say, "Did you know that Brontosaurus means *Thunder Lizard*?"

He looks at me with suspicion, caught off guard by how much of a dweeb I am. These kids are hard to impress. Even the dumbest ones just know things, but I'm trying to get into the habit of automatic goodwill toward others, the belief that someone, somewhere, is having a worse day than I am. The potted ferns rustle and I pull José from his hiding place, pluck the joint from his lips. José loves kids. He places his long fingers on the back of my neck. "Oh, Carlotta," he says. "These are the most majestic creatures to ever walk the planet. We have to help him. This could save his life."

I flinch. "He's right here."

The kid says hi. He says his name is Carter.

José pinches his eyebrows together, rearranges his face into one of deep concern. "Carter, are you telling my beautiful friend here that Mr. Brontosaurus isn't actually real?" He winks at me. The kids always ask if the adults here are dating or married, as if that'd be the most natural thing.

Carter stomps his foot. "Brontosaurus just isn't the right name of that thing. Somebody switched the skulls." He has the face of someone who has never been told, I believe you.

José says that the admittance of failure is not my strong suit.

Carter says, "Well, she stinks."

Kid, I can admit failure anytime. The ease with which I admit failure would blow your fucking mind. The history of prehistoric discovery in America is fraught with lies and deception, one-of-a-kind fossils destroyed out of hand simply for the pleasure of undercutting another man's work. How's that? And I knew the guy was dead. The car was crushed in like a pop can, this guy hung by his seat belt, bleeding out at a speed that seemed impossible to me. His femur was white and clean. But I thought maybe he needed to breathe. That's why I jammed my little knife into his throat. That's why I did it, even though I didn't need to, because I was surprised by all that white.

José grabs my hand and holds it tight.

Here's another. When I was a kid, I visited a park just like this one. I screamed the whole drive home because I thought the dinosaurs were alive. Carter says that we create and destroy in equal measure and José says, Babe, he's got a point, but I knew all their names. I knew they would follow me home. We found the bones. Even when we are wrong, the bones will still be real.

The Logic of the Loaded Heart

Amber Sparks

I f John is three, and John's mother is six times his age, how old was John's mother when John was conceived in the back of Al Neill's pickup truck after a Styx concert in Milwaukee? If John's parents spend 100 times zero days being actual parents to John, how many days' total is that? Does your answer change if John's mother sometimes bought him Mr. Pibb and lottery tickets when she stopped at the gas station on her way home from work?

Extra credit: Please calculate the probability that at his mother's current age, John will drop out of school and work in a burger joint while playing lead guitar in a heavy metal band called The Slaughterhouse Four.

When John is six, his father goes to prison for attempted robbery of the Rocky Rococo Pizza in Delavan, Wisconsin. Please calculate the probability that The Slaughterhouse Four will open for Def Leppard at the Minnesota State Fair in what will be the brightest shining moment and impossible dream of John's life.

At thirty-six, John has three ex-wives, one current wife, and nine children. (Holy shit, John.) If John still works in fast food, and his youthful good looks have sunken like a shipwreck with the passage of time, how many women in this bar will go home with him tonight?

How many women will go home with John tonight if John's band, now called Shards of Death, is playing tonight at this bar? Does that number increase or decrease if John is wearing a T-shirt that says "Swallow or It's Going in Your Eye"?

Amy has had five Amstel Lights, and her blood alcohol level is .08. If John is fifteen years older than Amy, how many hours will it be until she wakes up in his apartment, hungover and horrified by her poor decision-making?

If John's wife comes home from her night shift at Perkins at that precise moment, and her anger level is rising at a rate of three millimeters per second, what is the volume of John's wife's anger after the approximately fifteen seconds it takes John to put on his pants?

Extra credit: How many minutes until John's wife threatens to take the kids and the money and leave? How many days until John's wife sneaks into the basement at three in the morning and puts holes through his favorite electric guitar with a long series drill bit?

John hires a man to kill his wife, and agrees to pay him thirty percent up front, and the rest when the job is completed. If the total amount is $100,000, how much will the hired man get up front? And how many years will the judge subtract from or add to John's sentence if he was high on crack cocaine when he ordered the killing? Bonus question: If John is $1.1K in debt and agrees to pay a contract killer $100K, how long does John have to live?

John's band has had four names—but not at the same time. The first year, John changes his band's name and he changes it again at evenly spaced intervals over the course of twelve years. How many years separate each name change, and how many years will the names "Viking Fists" and "Ogres' Blood" cause the judge to add to John's attempted murder sentence? Does it even matter? Will John have a new life in prison? Will it be better, or maybe at least cleaner, tidier, than the one outside?

Bonus extra credit: If John's mother at fifteen and his father at twenty were given extraordinary foresight, would they have fallen in love? Would they have stood in line, in the raw cold rain, for those Styx tickets? Would they have listened to the nostalgic-yet-aspirational lyrics of "Come Sail Away" and thought, We *could* set an open course for the virgin sea? Would they have climbed into the back of that pickup truck in the afterglow, nails and bolts under bare skin and school and plant shift not withstanding? Would they have purchased extra condoms at the five-and-dime? Would they have wanted to preserve all they had—or would they have taken a chance, anyway, because when love sings down the microphone and strikes you, who can say what would happen if you failed to swoon and fall at its feet? Who can say whether A leads to B leads to C or how many apples John ended up with in the end? Who can say why the loaded heart defies all logic, like an unfinished word problem, like a riddle written in the human dust of a crowded barroom?

The Art of Losing

Julie Cadman-Kim

I SUSPECT, AS I HUG HIM on the train platform, that he has oranges in his pockets—despite what they must have cost him. He'll want to pretend like everything is normal, of course, and I'll let him like I always do.

"Hi, Dad," I say.

"Hey, Boots." He's aged significantly since the last time I saw him, but I say nothing, just lean over and kiss his face, weathered and speckled with sunspots like an old saddle. If he notices anything changed about me or the city drowning in the rising tides behind me, he doesn't mention it.

"Good trip?"

"Long as it ends with me by your side, it's a good trip in my book."

This was the last time he'd be making the journey by train because it was the last trip this train was ever going to make. While the passengers are still disembarking, the repo-scavengers waiting on either side lower their green caps and set to work sawing through the steel tracks before they have a chance to cool. I'd expected it, of course, the end of train travel—the expense was too great, the risk too large; diseases traveled by train, experts said, and terrorists. All planes were grounded just a year earlier, and though I've had plenty of time to get used to it, there's still something inexplicably devastating about the death of modern transportation.

A single pitted orange finds its way from Dad's fingers into my palm. It's probably riddled with worms or so sour it's inedible, but in my hand right now, it feels like the most solid, wonderful thing in the world, like snowfall and fresh air and waiting in line at the grocery store with a wallet full of cash.

"Well, let's get you home," I say, avoiding stepping around the damp clumps of tan and white feathers peppering the platform.

"Western wood peewees," Dad says, looking down and sucking on his teeth like he's got something stuck in them. "Migratory birds. Should've been in Mexico by now. Probably all mixed up like the rest of us."

I fight the urge to help him down the platform steps, to take hold of his bicep, still skinny despite his weatherproof anorak. I hope he'll make the best of it with me instead of just giving up like so many have, letting the warm, acidic water carry their bodies away, a strange new kind of fish that float facedown instead of belly-up in the now-dead oceans. On the radio this morning they announced our weekly rations will be reduced again, and, like the earlier announcements about planes and trains, I said another silent goodbye to the way things used to be, the way they'll never be again.

I had traded a promise of sex with my neighbor so he'd ferry me and my dad back home in his old fiberglass skiff. He's nice enough, Craig, but niceness means different things these days. I'm glad he agreed in the first place, even though he made me take my shirt off and give him a hand job as means of a deposit. After I finished, I surprised myself by kissing him on the cheek. Sure I was blushing, I turned away.

"What was that for?" he asked.

Because fifteen years ago I would have thought you were cute, I wanted to say. *For agreeing to let us use your boat even though there's no point in anything anymore. For letting me give you the one thing I have left to offer.* Instead, I just tucked my hair behind my ears and pulled on my shirt. "For old times' sake," I told him.

Now, in the boat, Craig's eyes are heavy in his face. He seems collapsed somehow, like the thing holding him up inside has snapped. Next to him, Dad looks almost strong, capable like he used to be when I was little and he'd take me camping for weeks at a time. "Joanie," he'd said when I was eight and crying about some minor injury, "listen close and you'll hear the love song of the varied thrush." I had stopped crying, and there, clear as anything, was the trilling single-tone whistle of a tiny orange-breasted bird who knew exactly what he wanted in the world.

Now, Dad turns to Craig and smiles. "I appreciate you giving us a ride, Craig; good to see people still looking out for one another."

I roll the orange in my fingers and try to catch Craig's glance, but he doesn't look at me, just keeps his hand firm on the rudder, his eyes watching the new horizon.

Dimetrodon

Justin Herrmann

Each time a car door shuts outside the tiny rental, the muscles in Lydia's chest tighten. Each footstep on the pavement, a possibility he's found them. Back in southern Illinois, birds don't even rise at this hour. But this is Alaskan summer and every neighbor might be up at this awful hour loading fishing gear into their boats and truck beds. Each sound nudges her awake. Sunlight spills through cracks in the blinds enough for Lydia to see her daughter Emily on the mattress next to her in a sweaty tangle, an unnatural-looking position that alarms her until she catches the faint sound of Emily's snoring.

~

Gary's been on the road in a rented Subaru four nights, the most sleep he's had a few hours in a church parking lot in Minot, North Dakota, before crossing the border. He descends the steep hill that leads into town. A spit curves into the bay, a skeletal finger pointing toward mountain ranges with valleys shrouded in glaciers. He drives to the spit, parks. HANDMADE SOAP, FISHING CHARTER, BEAR VIEWING. The air is thick with odors of ocean brine and fryer grease. The loudness of the wind on this exposed strip of land surprises him, as does the chill on his bare neck and cheeks. Clean-shaven, short hair, Dockers shorts, a disguise of sorts, so maybe even a wife who ran away with her husband's child might not recognize him at first. Tourists pose with massive freshly killed fish. A teenage girl in rubber overalls guts and fillets the fish on a large metal table, says, "Looks prehistoric, but nothing tastes better."

Clearly distance brought Lydia here.

The night before she left, he sautéed vegetables in a wok while she paced, texting. Already in a mood, she stepped on Emily's favorite toy, a hard-plastic dimetrodon. "Pick up your fucking dinosaur," she said.

He knew how things could go. Even so, he said, "It's not a dinosaur."

It built from there. She struck first.

Emily was two when she was in his life. By the morning of her third birthday, she was gone.

~

Lydia cleans rooms at the lodge at the end of the spit. Her coworker Meg helps run sheets through the mangle. The warmth of the sheets reminds her of folding clean shirts, then about peeling those same shirts from a firm body, the way he'd touch her. Then she thought about the last time Gary touched her, his body weight pressing her against the kitchen floor, the crook of her own arm constricting her throat.

"Saturday, honey," Meg says, "Derek's taking you out on the bay." Several men have asked Lydia out in the months she's been here. She's declined all previous offers. It seems Meg has made it her mission to introduce Lydia to every bachelor in town. Commercial fisherman, fishing guides, fish processors. All men here seem skilled with knives. This comforts and terrifies her.

~

In town a few days, Gary's seen the sun at midnight, and again at four a.m. He's seen Salmon bacon, salmon sausage, even salmon-flavored vodka. Today he saw his wife get on a boat with another man. Now, through the windshield of his rental, he sees Emily scaling the side of a wooden playground ship. Her hair is short like his. She pays little attention to the barfly-looking woman that brought her. Barfly pays attention to her phone.

~

Talking doesn't come easy, so Lydia and Derek talk about their kids. He has children from a previous marriage. He asks about her ex. Lies about Gary come easy.

Derek's family owns oyster farms. He steers the skiff toward a meadow of blue buoys. He hoists a basket from the ocean that looks like a laundry hamper, opens the lid, removes a couple oysters the size of chicken eggs, takes a knife from a pocket of his frayed jeans, unfolds it. His fingers look small and dirty near the gleaming blade. A quick twist of the blade forces open the shell. He digs the point underneath the flesh. She's never eaten anything still alive before. She hesitates, then uses her finger to push the flesh into her mouth. It feels like the inside of someone else's cheek.

~

A kid runs up the slide, slips, falls hard. Barfly glances. When she sees it's not Emily, goes back to her phone. Other kids have stopped playing, watch the mother console the screaming child, as do parents. Not Emily, she climbs.

Gary opens the Subaru door, the plastic dimetrodon in his grip.

~

Lydia is barefoot, knee-deep in the bay's cold water. She helps pull the skiff onto shore. She can't help but think of that dimetrodon Gary went on about, waiting motionless in the shallows for prehistoric sharks to wander close. She pictures Precambrian teeth, or Permian teeth, or whatever-fucking-era-before-the-existence-of-dinosaurs teeth, full of bacteria-harboring serration, piercing her calf, dragging her through the shallows to the shore.

"Goddamn dimetrodons," she says aloud.

She hadn't thought Derek heard, but later, on the hard mattress in his cabin, he says, "There's plenty that'll kill you in Alaska. Dinosaurs aren't one."

Not a dinosaur at all, Gary said the night she left. Stories are written in our bones. Dimetrodon skulls reveal they're distant relatives of ours, mammals.

That, she could believe.

~

A brontosaurus grazes on gigantic flowers. Purple, yellow, orange. It inspects cigarette burns near a purple one. The dimetrodon creeps from under the dense motel pillow, slowly at first, and just like that the long neck squeezed by Emily's fingers is also gripped by solid plastic jaws, shaken, dropped on the comforter. Gary slides the dead bolt into the lock. Draws the blinds shut.

"Daddy," Emily says. "When's Mama coming?"

He smiles at her, strokes her hair. "Sweetie," he says. He takes the tiny, wounded brontosaurus from the comforter, sets it upright on the nightstand next to a bag of salmon jerky. Outside, car doors close. "Shh," he says.

Gray

Bergita Bugarija

I RESERVED MY LAST DAY IN town for the museum of contemporary art, the famous one. A must-see, Madge said when I told her about the trip. The fourth floor would change everything, she gushed, her voice breathy. Hardly, I thought, but didn't have the heart to crush her zeal.

I entered the concrete and glass box. I don't mind minimalism. Although the vast, sprawling lobby was scary. A block of white granite in the middle, the reception desk, seemed like a life raft in a sea of spooky echoes. Murmuring multitudes studied colorful floor plans that, if followed as recommended by their own Madges, would change their lives.

First floor, Lichtenstein. Okay. Second, Mondrian. Fine. Third, Warhol. I get it. Kind of. And then the fourth, the inevitable: a square of gray. A mockery posing as art, and all of us, certainly the Madges of the world, in on the prank.

Well, not me.

No one can tell me that a piece of gray-painted canvas stretched on a frame is art. And the worst kind of gray, at that: nihilism gray. Not charcoal, not pebble, not mouse, not elephant, not concrete, not rainy day. Not smoke gray. Not ash gray. Not stone gray. Not gray hair gray.

Just gray. The synthetic kind, artificial like its callous attempt to make us second-guess our sanity, forgo our common sense, our instincts, our sensory grounded reality.

It's not even that, like so much of contemporary "art," the gray square made me feel I could have done it. Of course I could have. In five seconds. Madge's hologram appeared before me emitting the art community's worn-out comeback: *You could have. But you didn't.* You know what? I wouldn't have made this even if I could, or, for that matter, because I could! This shameless practical joke that went too far. Seriously, is this what I traveled miles for and paid money to see? This pretentious nonsense posing as a provocation, I suppose. Of what?

Oh, Madge . . .

Gray square like a gray cat; neither bad luck nor good fortune, just whatever. Not a majestic humpback whale gray, not a dewdrop-translucent playful gray, none of the mystery of the fog gray. Even smog gray is more enigmatic than this dull one venerated at the world's esteemed museum. Not moon, not London, none of the fifty shades from that bestselling erotic saga I never read but a friend told me all about. Even gray aluminum wall installations at any of the countless nondescript corporate headquarters have more depth and texture, more soul.

I don't think this gray was even painted on the canvas, the charlatan artist didn't even bother that much. What most likely happened is this poser bought a gray tarp from a knockoff Gucci handbag trafficker who used the cloth to bundle and transport the illicit cargo. So fascinating. Right, Madge?

My skin started to itch at the edge of my sweater sleeves.

The color of elegance, they say, of fine Italian suits. I say a war-zone tent has more charm, more layers, more emotion. But no, let's attribute to this gray square some deeper message, elevate it to a pedestal of a cliché metaphor like "the gray zone" symbolizing the absence of clarity and straightforwardness, the visual representation of the relativity zeitgeist. Or maybe it's a social commentary on the gray economy, or a racial paradigm shift—the whirlpool of humanity in which all mingle victoriously color-blind.

But wait. Maybe gray is a trickster. Officially achromatic, inoffensive, unassuming. Hmm. Who are you kidding? What are you hiding, gray? Are you afraid that the nuance would overwhelm our fragile brains, so we'd better not take a closer look?

I crossed the masking tape on the floor delineating the art's personal space bubble.

Now up close, I inspected the travesty, and guess what? It's pixelated. And the pixels are not even gray but purple, peach, black, brown, indigo. Each pixel aware of its pigment, each more colorful than the next, playing their part, each anything but boring and meaningless, anything but meek, anything but safe. But all decidedly lying low, partaking in a camouflage orgy to create a deceivingly idle, harmless gray puddle, shun the attention, perpetuate an illusion of sameness, equality. All under the pretense of offering a generous respite for our overstimulated irises prancing along, uninterested in truth, preoccupied with distraction, counting on all to pass by unaroused, mindless, lifeless.

Neutral? Nice try, gray. All those pixels. What for? To glorify opacity and indecision? How brazen. How weak.

Just as the sweaty half ovals radiating from my pits reached my bottom ribs, the guard hushed that the museum was closing in a

few minutes. I walked out the exit and breathed in the fresh darkness, the streetlight-polka-dotted night, the ease, the order, the calm
black-and-white.

Still, I was angry as anyone denied closure would be, fuming at
Madge and the stupid gray square for wasting my life, for weaseling
its way to that prestigious piece of wall real estate, blasé and arrogant,
while so many worthy of the spotlight whimpered in bleak anonymity.
How did the "artist" con the curator? How could the curator suspend
all reason and allow that garbage to pass for art? What did they see?
What could the "piece" possibly mean, what could it evoke, stir up?
That drab, mute piece of nothing.

Good Boys

Honor Levy

WE'RE ON THE ROOFTOP WITH the boys. The boys are calling girls dogs, like, "She's a dog, a total dog." They don't mean bitches. They just mean dogs. If they wanted to tell us that a girl was a bitch they would say, "She's a bitch, a total bitch." When the boys say something, they mean it. That's why we like them. We're not dogs. That's why they like us. That's why we're on the rooftop.

The house has three floors. The ceilings are high. I know that if one of the boys fell off the rooftop he'd die. I know that none of the boys will fall off—not tonight, at least. Tonight, they're not roughhousing or drinking tequila or annoying me. They've left the tennis rackets on the second floor, and they want to tell us about their trip to Greece. In Greece, the cigarettes are cheap. They filled an entire suitcase with little yellow boxes of George Karelias and Sons. They say we can smoke as many as we want. They're proud. The cigarettes are so cheap. The boys are so proud. We laugh. Zoe laughs like Tinkerbell, the air whistling between the gaps in her teeth. She's definitely not a dog.

I know we're high up. I know our lives would be ruined if one of the boys fell, but tall plants are growing on the edge of the rooftop and I can't see the cobblestones. If I could see that little cobblestoned street and the boys' little Smart car, it would be easier to imagine them falling. It would be easier to remember that I'm in Paris. It would be easier to laugh like Zoe, like Tinkerbell, like a real girl, a girl who is not a dog.

I can't see the Panthéon or the observatory or the park. I can see only the boys and their tanned stomachs and the scrapes they got from falling off the moped. We could be anywhere. We could be back in New York or near my house in L.A. or at some Airbnb in Berlin. I'd like to go to Berlin, to dance with the boys at Bergheim, to eat *knafeh* with Zoe, to see the Reichstag or whatever, but the boys don't want to go. Athens is the new Berlin. In Athens, the cigarettes are cheap. I thought Kraków was the new Berlin. The boys laugh and shake their heads. I can smell their wet-puppy-dog hair.

The sun is setting and the sky is so pink. Pink like the canopy bed I never got, like Kirby, like peonies, like the cheeks of a girl who the boys have just called a dog. I stand at the edge of the rooftop holding my phone just above the plants, trying to take a photo, trying not to drop it. The boys tell me that if I want something to post on Instagram they'll text me a Greek sunset. I'm not going to post anything. It's just for my grandma. They want me to show her a Greek sunset. All their grandmas are dead. In Greece, the sky gets even pinker, like, way pinker. The Greeks have four words for sunset. One for each of the boys. Tomorrow, they leave to work on their barbed-wire sculptures at some studio space in Normandy. Tonight, we're in Paris, but all they want to talk about is Greece. They wish they could have stayed, stayed away from Paris, from Normandy, from Bennington and Bard, from the rooftop, from all this. Their moms have ovarian cancer. Their girlfriends are pregnant again. They're sure to fail a class next semester. In Greece, none of that matters. In Greece, they sail on boats and make sketches of naked marble women and all sleep in one king-size bed. In Greece, they touch sculptures of gods. In Greece, they put their art history education to good use. In Greece, they were happy. We want them to be happy. We let them tell us about the olives and the stray cats and the monks and the night they crashed the moped and the windmills and the dead dolphin and the economy. I want to ask them how many dogs they saw, but then again I don't really care.

Dogs are girls who care. Girls who ask too many questions are dogs. Dogs comment on how high the ceilings are. Dogs want to know who this rooftop really belongs to. Dogs ask what your dads do for work. Dogs post sunsets on Instagram. Dogs throw up when they drink tequila. Dogs beg for games of rooftop tennis. Dogs ask where the Eiffel Tower is. Dogs wear too much perfume. Dogs stink. Dogs get mad when the boys kiss me or Zoe. Dogs don't know how to keep it casual. Dogs whine. Dogs don't want the boys to be happy. Dogs want to be held after sex, to be petted, to be taken care of. Dogs make a big deal when you get them pregnant. Dogs don't know how to just take care of it while you're with your boys in Greece. Dogs are too loud. Dogs get excited too fast. Dogs need you. Dogs just don't get it. Dogs don't get to hang out on the roof. It's too high, they're too wild, they might fall, and then we'd have to catch them or something.

I'm Exaggerating

Kate Wisel

SERENA WORE A NAVY TWO-PIECE SUIT, sensible flats, twisted-up hair, a buttoned collar over the wrist—read the faded *blah blah blah* script. Her first flight was to Wichita, and she had asked Niko if he knew what Wichita looked like from the sky. She wanted to hurt him. For him to picture her cloud-height, off the ground, sixteen hundred miles to the middle, untouchable.

She scooped ice and twisted bottle caps. Balanced her palms on headrests during dips. The aisle a tightrope. It rattled: the overheads, the ice, her fingers. Sometimes the pilot and the copilot looked like the cops who rapped on her door the month before. In the cockpit, their hands on the gears against the bright, complicated look of the control panel. The backs of their heads against the bright, complicated look of the sky. She cracked the front door, chain off the bolt, swollen eye. Her smile a cross, index finger against her lip. Niko was passed out in boxers, in the bedroom, in a deep sleep. The cops pushed through, ignored her.

"I made a mistake," she said. She paced, the blood in her hair graffiti orange and stiff. Blood on the white table, sprays of droplets from huffs where her mucus went loose under the break, her wrists twisted back.

"I'm exaggerating!" she told the cops, then recognized it as something he would tell her. Right in her ear like a basketball coach fighting the sideline.

"Get up," Niko would say. "You're faking all of this."

Wichita was not what she thought. Little Rock, Providence. Nowhere she'd been, or belonged, but all familiar. She had a day off in Spokane. Bumpy wheels of luggage by her heel, she roamed down Division Street, smokestacks spilling filth up toward an ocean-colored mountain. Janis Joplin on a brick wall, fingers outstretched. Toward the river, the smell of spoiled milk and a sign: Near Nature, Near Perfect. Pine trees that could see inside homes and for miles.

Back on the plane she found passengers to their rows. Locked in the Clorox blue of the bathroom, she fingered her new insignia, a wing pin she wore like a crucifix and to sleep. And on the dark seat, facing backward, going forward, she thought of what to do. This she thought of terminally. What was down there. What wasn't. There was no losing of a baby or liters of liquor in desk drawers.

Maybe there was a lost baby; to be exact is to lie.

She had enough money to run up a credit card. There was a lease, the stain of their signatures, one under the other. Hers under his, as if he could hold her down with ink.

Somewhere above Lake Superior she heard an infant's cry. It was a saltwater gargle, as disturbing and rangy as a vocal warm-up. She walked down the aisle, nearing the sound, and found a mother dozing on the seat. She lifted the infant from the mother's sleeping arms. Her T-shirt was splotched with milk at the nipples, her slump vaguely sexual, like she'd been slipped a mickey.

Serena strode the aisle with the infant in her arms, its wail an emergency. It filled the cabin with an engine-like force, though those fat-ringed thighs kicking against her stomach went nowhere. She watched as a businessman's eyes popped open. She gazed at them, felt his shock upon waking. Midair. Midshriek. She palmed the little one's wet head, the mask of a soft wet scalp under her eyes. The seam of her lips by an ear the size of a bottle cap.

She whispered, "Hey there."

She whispered, "Don't be quiet."

She whispered, "Keep screaming."

The Beauty and the Bat

Diane Williams

"PLEASE DON'T SAY THAT about me, Diane," Rae said.

"Well then," I said, "you have always worked like a dog."

"Babka," said a lady who joined us. We were at Rae's.

And the lady had a piece of cake on a plate and she sat down behind a slant-top desk that appeared to cut off her head at the neck.

But her face was a vivid face I would have been proud of, had it belonged to me, and it was fully in sight until she ducked down to fork up the cake.

Who was she? Should I have known?

As I mulled this, Rae's daughter—came in to ask—"How do you murder (she meant, how do you *pound thin*) chicken breasts?"

The lady chased her back out—as the pricking of my wig clips against my scalp grew worse.

So, then I was left alone and irritable with Rae, who was saying, "A rolling pin."

And who is *Rae*?

She is my cousin who lives with her paradisiac vistas of Central Park, delphinium with peonies in a vase, and there's the herringbone floor.

In her kitchen, I saw the pink lobes of the chicken breasts beneath plastic wrap.

"Did you wash it first?"—the lady, who was waving a heavy discolored utensil—was asking Maud—that is, Rae's daughter.

And then the lady turned to ask me, "*What are you doing here?*"

"Tea would be nice," I said.

I saw nearly an entire babka tucked beneath a glass dome.

"And, may I have some cake, please?"

Maud had left the room and the lady did not turn back to answer me and with her tool she began again slapping at the meat.

Then the door opened and a young man—my son—stood there and was not invited in.

"What are *you* doing here?" the lady asked.

"Be nice to me!" he said.

"Close the door! Go away!"

With both her arms briefly stretched above her head, she looked like a woman whose identity I knew I should have known.

Surrounding her, on the surfaces, were peas in their pods in a vine leaf, green bowl, and some drops of blood.

I stepped farther forward over the checkered black and white linoleum to where there is a charming view of a sphered copper church roof that draws to a point, with a golden cross atop it.

A pair of pigeons were busy mating on a parapet, and this looked so hazardous. I could feel talons—Do pigeons even have them?—digging painfully into my back. And then I was distracted by a large, proud aqua mix-master.

Not immediately, but I turned just in time to see the beauty put down her bat.

Speaking of beauty, she was standing in the awful fluorescent light—her heaving and her lifting well over by then.

Would now be the time to take the cake?—I thought.

I admired the color of her shoes, how her hair was coiled and braided. I knew who she was well enough, by then—a competent woman in earnest who didn't like me.

So, she did get excited when I just shoved the bowl of peas aside to make more room for the cake's cover.

While I ate my first mouthful, I saw her mouth open and close as I opened and closed mine.

What she did do—she posed quietly.

All that she said was, "You are Diane Williams? Do you even know what most of your friends say about you?"

James Brown Is Alive and Doing Laundry in South Lake Tahoe

Stefanie Freele

STU IS DRIVING TO South Lake Tahoe to take his postpartum-strained woman to the snow, to take his nine-week-old infant through a storm, to take his neglected dog on a five-hour car ride, and to take himself into his woman's good graces. And, he's hungry. Stu has considered more than once stopping the car on the whitened highway and plunging himself over a cliff, so he could plop into a cozy pile of snow and hide until his wife is logical again or the baby is able to tend to itself, but he's not dressed warmly enough for months or years in a snow bank, has no snacks in his jacket, and he must focus on The Family. The Family of four: the woman, Stu, their baby, the dog. It is almost blizzarding, the windshield wiper fluid is frozen, the window is frosted, the dog is antsy, the baby whimpering, the woman—who should be happy, she nagged for days to go to the snow—is intermittently admiring the snow and whining about cramped legs. Stu is trapped, by the car, The Family, his own legs, and the snow, which is falling, falling, falling.

~

Megan's legs are killing her, mostly because her shoes don't fit. Her man thinks that her feet will go back to a previous size after she loses the last eleven pounds. No shoes fit and she just knows her three-hundred-dollar ski boots will be terrible. She removes her shoes—she should have done this miles ago—and feels instant relief. She is also relieved that the baby is calm. The baby coos and says "eh" and "oooh" and wiggles his little fists. The dog lies with her head on the baby's car seat. Megan remarks that this is adorable. Her man grunts.

~

Phillip, who is nine weeks old and does not have control of his muscles just yet, sees the dog's head and would like to touch her, especially the black circle around the dog's eye. However, Phillip's little fists go every which way, but not that way. He grunts little noises when his fists don't do what he wants them to do.

~

Beebop, the dog, wishes she had a yellow squeaker toy. Like the one at home. The yellow one sitting on her round bed. If she had the yellow squeaker toy, she would squeak it and thrust it into the fist of the baby. Perhaps the baby would throw it for her, because her man and woman never throw anything anymore.

~

Stu is afraid to talk because his woman might cry again. She cries a lot lately, even though he is working harder than he ever has before, is bringing in a good paycheck, and is taking The Family on their first vacation. Instead, he is silent. The snow is falling, falling, falling, and he thinks he might just have to pull over, run out into the snow, and scream into the darkening forest. But, then he might get lost, and have to eat his horse, like the Donner party. But he doesn't have a horse, and the Donner party ate themselves and their horses in North Lake Tahoe, not South. They didn't have cell phones.

~

Megan is trying not to cry. She is sick of being fat, sick of being a milk machine, sick of not having her own income, sick of being dependent on her man, and sick of not knowing what to do when the baby cries. It is her first baby and sometimes she doesn't think she has any idea of what she is doing. She feels like an imposter and is terrified someone will catch on very soon and point at her, yell at her, and take her child away from her, because she is a crybaby. She knows this is stupid and feels even more like crying when she realizes the stupidity of her stupidity.

~

Phillip watches the dog blink and this is interesting. But, a flailing fist pops up and punches Phillip in the eye and he lets out a cry.

~

Beebop curls into a ball away from the crying baby who has just punched himself in the eye. The cries are a lot like the sound of her squeaker toy and Beebop lets out a world-weary sigh.

~

Stu hears the dog sigh, the baby cry, and notices his woman's discomfort. He is helpless and wants to say something, but knows if he says anything, anything at all, even something he thinks is nice, or helpful, or pleasant, or cheerful, his woman might weep. And then he'd have two criers and one sigher.

~

Megan squirms and through the snow reads the signs on the hotels and restaurants. The car stops at a red. In front of a laundromat, on the sidewalk, stands a dark man with black hair in a leather jacket. He wiggles thick eyebrows up and down and squints in the snow as he smokes a cigarette. Megan speaks. "Hey, look, James Brown."

~

Phillip hears his mother's voice—her happy voice—and pauses.

~

Beebop lets her tail wag once and sits up. Mom's happy. Mom's happy.

~

Stu catches sight of the man. His woman is correct: There stands a guy who looks just like a happy James Brown. "He's alive and doing laundry," Stu says.

The man's eyebrows wiggle. He looks over toward The Family and opens up his jacket revealing a shirt that reads glittery, GIVING UP FOOD FOR FUNK.

Stu's woman grins. "It *is* James Brown, downtown."

The dog studies James Brown while whapping her tail on the baby's car seat.

The baby says, "Oooo oooo."

"Right on, right on." Stu presses the button, lowering the windows. Cold pine air drifts in.

His woman lets her arm out and brings back snowflakes on her sweater to show everyone.

Nothing Is Ever One Thing

Robert Scotellaro

THE PLANE CRASHED INTO the mountain. It had lost altitude suddenly, irredeemably. There was chaos in the cockpit. Seat belts clicked shut, oxygen masks dropped. Then a monstrous fiery blast . . .

Roger, speaking in gasps after running through the airport, deposited that red face of his over the boarding counter and complained fecklessly. How the hell did he know it would take so long . . . Those ridiculously long lines . . .

"I'm sorry," the boarding agent said, peering into all that fury. "That flight has taken off some time ago. You'll need to rebook."

"*Fuck!*" he said, slapping his hand down hard on the counter, and a security guard rushed forward.

Roger rocketed through traffic. Till he couldn't. There was a foundation makeup convention he desperately needed to be at. There was a promotion waiting to fatten his wallet if he got it right. This new project he'd pitch. This new old product with a fresh new name and ad campaign he'd pitch. The clients he needed to get onboard would be there, and he knew the script by heart. But there was a plane to catch between him and success, and now he was the one, *goddammit*, who needed to get onboard. Just his luck that there was more traffic than he expected, and that friggin' goldfish. *What was he thinking?*

He was scrambling out of the bedroom with his suitcase when he saw his young daughter in the hall crying. *Now what?* he thought, looking at his watch. She had a small fishbowl in her hands with a goldfish floating on the top of the water, her tears dripping into it.

"14 Karat," she said, then sobbed. His wife was already downstairs, naked under her robe, fixing lunch for their eldest to take to school.

"I'm so sorry, hon," he said, patting her head. "Let's flush 14 Karat down the toilet together, so it can go in the ocean. Be in the big water where it belongs."

She hugged the bowl against herself tightly. "No!" she screeched. "He'll go to hell then!"

"Hell?"

She released one hand and pointed down at the carpet. "I want him to go to heaven," she said. "We have to bury him like Grandpa, for him to go to heaven."

For God's sake, he thought, but went with her out back and buried it under the honeysuckle. There was a little girl ritual and a little girl prayer in whispers as he bowed his head and glanced furtively at his watch.

While slipping on his trousers he looked out the window. After three days of incessant downpours, it had finally let up. He stood there sunlit. The storm had moved on. Perhaps that meant something, the storm moving on. Clear skies. That maybe he'd get some kind of break. He went over some pitch lines in front of the mirror. Maybe longer than he had time for. But so much was riding on it. When he felt he was ready, he grabbed his suitcase/the doorknob. Then he heard it from the other side of the door. Thought, *What the hell . . . ?*

The alarm clock startled him awake. His wife stirred. He pulled back the comforter and gazed at the teepee his erection made of his boxers. He didn't want to cut it close. But there was still time. A quickie wouldn't change much. And besides, he needed to rid himself of some of that tension that was building. He strapped on his watch without looking at it, reached over, with a pestering hand, into all that warmth . . .

The Combat Photographer

Dave Housley

THE COMBAT PHOTOGRAPHER NEEDED health care. Not for a piece of shrapnel in the knee or a stray bullet to the shoulder, not for injuries sustained while running to the site of a car bomb, or thrombosis or malaria or even food poisoning. There was a baby on the way, and his wife was drawing the line.

I'm sick and tired of it, the combat photographer's wife said. Sudan. Afghanistan. Iraq. It's one thing to leave me for months at a time. It's another to leave your child.

It's what I do, the combat photographer said. I'm a combat photographer.

The combat photographer's wife tapped her foot and folded her arms across her belly. You have three months, she said.

~

At the interview, the museum people were awed. This is amazing, they said, flipping through the images of severed body parts, burning twisted metal, mass burial sites. This is, the head interviewer gulped and brushed his hand over a picture of a Sudanese ten-year-old with a machine gun and a Chicago Bulls T-shirt, this is courageous work.

The combat photographer nodded, made the face he made when people looked at his work—something between humility and gritty determination and recognition that yes, this was courageous work but somebody had to do it.

The salary was slightly less than he had made as a freelancer, but of course there was a 401K, paid vacation, flex time, optional life insurance, and disability and tuition reimbursement. There was health insurance.

~

The combat photographer marveled at how easy it could be to live as a normal person. He rode the subway, read the sports section, lingered over morning coffee in the photography studio while the museum filled with school groups, tourists, and families. In the studio, he had absolute control. No wind, sun, monsoon rain. No bullets biting through the air. He photographed the museum's natural wonders, exhibits that were being archived—the skulls of beaked whales, ghost orchids, stegosaurus bones.

He ate lunch at noon, took coffee at three, and left promptly at five-thirty. He often lingered in the front of the museum on his way out, watching the children gape wide-mouthed at the museum's dinosaur displays.

He thought of the unborn child in his wife's expanding belly.

You were so right, he said.

She smiled and put her hand over his, then placed it on her stomach.

Two months, she said.

~

The combat photographer was not used to being supervised.

Could you maybe move a little faster in the studio? his boss said. Things are starting to back up a bit.

The combat photographer gave her the look he gave people when they were looking at his work.

Thanks so much, she said. We're just super-glad to have you on board.

~

The combat photographer found himself at the Vietnam Veterans Memorial. He took pictures of things left at the wall, homeless veterans in tattered wheelchairs, older men saluting the names of fallen comrades, their hands feeling the marble as if searching for a pulse.

For a few minutes his hands worked on their own, adjusting, focusing, loading another roll of film. And then he looked around. Teachers led school trips. Tourists ate ice-cream sandwiches. Joggers lumbered past.

Six weeks, he thought. The combat photographer went back to work.

~

The combat photographer found himself bypassing the subway for the four-mile walk home. Occasionally he would find his heart quickening, the old adrenaline kick in his blood. He would pick up his pace, walking and then jogging down streets he had never seen before.

After a few minutes he would hear the sirens or would arrive at the accident scene to find motorists arguing over a fender-bender, police filling out forms.

He would put away his camera and trudge homeward.

He tried not to think about what was happening to his body and mind, to his combat photographer's soul, but it was a long walk and unlike similar walks he might have taken in Mogadishu or Kashmir, there was nothing to do but think.

~

The combat photographer started drifting into the front of the museum. Things were happening there, he knew, if you had the patience and the right kind of eye. He found unusual scenes—a young husband and wife arguing in a darkened corner, two school groups staring one another down, security bullying street people out the museum's giant doors.

~

The combat photographer had his three-month review. I think you need to spend just a little more time in the studio, his boss said, tapping the back of his hand with a manicured nail. Less time at the front.

The combat photographer thought about giving her the look he gave when people looked at his work. But then he looked at the work laid out in front of him—dinosaur bones and flowers and fossils and bugs.

More time in the studio, he said, no problem.

~

The combat photographer waited for his phone to ring. The baby was two days overdue. He hunkered down in the studio, took what seemed like the same pictures he had been taking for three months.

He fought the urge to go to the front of the museum.

The phone rang. It's time, she said. The combat photographer hurried into his office, gathered his things.

The fire alarm rang. He ran into the hall. People were frantic, crying, scurrying toward the back exits. He could hear pandemonium in the museum, sirens getting closer.

It's real, a security guard shouted. Fire in the archives.

The combat photographer walked back into his office. A calm settled over him. He looked at the cell phone, his packed bag. The sirens were just outside. The smoke was getting heavier.

The combat photographer grabbed his cameras and his camera bag. He opened the door and ran toward the fire.

Solo

Rita Zoey Chin

WE WERE MARRIED THREE DAYS when we lugged our new telescope out into the snow. Vastness, mystery, turbulence of light—I wanted them all with you. But when we looked through the lens and found only a small ghostly Saturn, we left that leggy instrument like a bent scarecrow in the yard and walked up a long hill to what felt like the edge of the earth. Your hands swiped gently up at the sky as you named the constellations, each syllable a puff of white smoke into the cold. I could already see the faces our children would have.

We could have jumped. We could have fucked in that darkness. But we descended the hill quietly, and ten years went by. We didn't have children. We had five suitcases. One day, I packed two of them, and I drove away.

We were married six years when I met a man. We spent an evening together, and those hours were a bridge from which I never returned. I didn't know how to tell you about him. It seemed that to tell you about my grief would have only made it ours. Nothing is simple, and everything is simple. Maybe if I'd conjured the words, they would have formed a different kind of bridge, between us.

He was upside down. I'd arrived at the concert late, and that was the first I saw of him. Immediately, I shifted in my seat and pointed my knees at him—an exact movement, the line from my knees to the line of his body straight as a horizon. And then in some yogic flash, he was upright, strumming his guitar, slithering lithely around the stage, into and into the music he was making. He was alone up there, bare-chested and barefoot and moving like surf.

When the concert was over, I stood on the autograph line. I'd never asked anyone for an autograph before, but on that night, I was an animal following musk. I couldn't say what one person looked like in that crowd. There was just the landscape of it—this rocky bunch of slightly moving heads all focused on one man who could and could not be seen, depending on your vantage point. I was in the back, so all I had were the heads. But the line was moving slowly, and after what seemed like a second concert of chatter, I was nearing the edge of the terrain.

A space opened, into which I gazed, and saw him. He looked small somehow, just standing there off-stage in his leather jacket, with his sheared-bare head and a vulnerability that was raw and surprisingly tangible. His eyes were nearly transparent, an echo of blue, and I saw there was something guttural in his throat, something not yet heard.

The next night, I found myself blazing through the highway miles like some crazed stalker to see him do it all again. And then I was pivoting myself so that my knees formed the end of the arrow between us. And then I was on the autograph line again, with a different CD.

And then I was in his hotel room.

We closed the door and faced each other, and we traveled through the million mirrors of each other's eyes, and no one flinched, and no one spoke, and standing there we crossed a threshold, we looked into the eye's black hole and were fearless with our exploration. I don't know how long we stood there. But I know that I was bared back to dust.

In his bathroom, I splashed water on my face and fingered the bristles of his toothbrush while he cooked vegetables and garlic in a hot pot on the hotel room desk. We sat on the edge of the bed and ate.

He moved like a snake. He lunged at me, this wide rush of him, and if I hadn't been shivering from a combination of desire and fear, I might have chuckled. But when he leaned in, when he got almost to kissing but not kissing, the walls fell away and the bed dropped away and my skin held nothing in anymore, nothing that really mattered anyway, and I could feel and hear and already taste his breath, and when his lips took my lips, I knew then that what I was experiencing was drawing a line—even with the world temporarily erased, it was drawing a line between me and the rest of it: I would always be alone.

He didn't sing to me, but he pulled out a flute, and he played it softly against my neck. Again, I said, and he played it against my sternum, which pounded back against the vibration. Again. He played it along my waist, against my hip, and down the dip of my belly. And the sound, mellifluous and persistent, did not stop until I devoured it, until I took it into me wholly, while outside there were stars I couldn't name.

Dear Nnamdi

Tyrese L. Coleman

SAT 8/15 6:03 AM

I shouldn't show up today, but I'm coming to your wedding. The *American* wedding. I will stand when the minister asks if anyone objects because I do, and I've always wanted to attend a wedding where that happens. I'm a law student, I know how to object. I've got evidence to sustain. Your poems. Dick-pics. Clothes in my dresser. Toothbrush in my bathroom. Morning calls. Morning wood. You. Here. Sleeping. Now.

Maybe I am a whore like your mother thinks.

But my bed is warm, my body still slick and tender.

Maybe we made a baby.

SAT 8/15 11:28 AM

Just so you know I don't care about *Miss Nigeria*. The opposite of me with her bright cocoa skin, flawless weave, makeup expertly applied. Yes, I know what she looks like—saved your picture from the Metro section. *Two doctors, first generation, prominent families, two weddings—here and in Nigeria—homes in D.C., London, Lagos.* Tell your Igbo-bougie mother you taught me how to make fufu. My southern accent doesn't mean I'm stupid, just as much as her being asked to repeat herself because her words start with O's wide like butts in kente cloth doesn't mean shit either.

1. I will be an attorney. A judge! 2. You were my first, my only. 3. My father is a professor, my mother a chef, my sister a nurse. 4. I am a good woman.

But—Miss Nigeria is Igbo.

Congratulations. You found a suitable wife.

Your precious mother hates the sight of me. I'm impure, I know, I know. My best friend says light-skin women have nothing to complain about. She pulls my hair like I'm a doll, tells me I need a tan: my legs are Perdue chicken thighs. That shit ain't funny. My yellow-brown thighs signal wantonness, physical proof of brown legs split for a white dick—you know—we talked about that. Late night, ganja filled our chests, and we pontificated: Ann Petry's *The Street*, the sex-crazed mulatta tragedy of Sarah Jane in *Imitation of Life*. Literature doesn't provide happy endings for women who look like me. Real life doesn't either. The night you told me about her. Said she didn't matter. Appease your mother, you said. Does Miss Nigeria know your poetry? The idleness of writing doesn't seem to fit your mother's ideal of a good Igbo boy. She hates the influence of my pale otherness on you, yet I know nothing but black.

Black, not African.

"Never African. Never Nigerian. Never Igbo. Never for you." Your mother chastened when we met as if you were bringing home a stray dog.

But on some western shore, my ancestor was sister to her ancestor, and they *stole* mine. I'm no longer littered with sand, not enough grit to grip when the boat leaves, and we are tied feet to wrist. This will get me in trouble, but I speak what's in my bones. It's our bones from another lifetime, Nnamdi, lying at the sea bottom. If you marry her, they will never make it home.

SUN 8/16 4:32 AM

This is not an apology.

I handled myself well. Had your mother not put her finger in my face—her sculpted head wrap quivering with each chicken-like neck jerk—if she had just sat down like the lady she claims to be, if she had not called me *akata* with her nose wrinkled like she smelled shit, or like I was shit, and what was I doing there, who the hell did I think I was, then I might not have had to raise my voice and tell the church where you were at 6:03 a.m. I know you said that word doesn't mean *nigger*, but that's how she said it. I know! If anyone out of us is a nigger, it's me.

I am not begging you to take me back.

But, when she slapped me, was there any part of you that wanted to act? My face cracked, red, glowed with tears and blood vessels. You watched while every woman there spat in my face, your male cousins laughing, high-fiving behind your back. Did your heart stir? Eight years, and you can't protect me?

Friends warned me about Nigerian men. We've all dated at least one, a black woman's rite of passage. It's ignorant to generalize. Not *all* Nigerian men are like you. But, you don't make it easy. Or is it just men? That's what Amy Winehouse is singing to me. We staring down this dark liquid tunnel numbing my face, my body, what's left of my mind. What is it about men? *What iis it ab-boouut men?* Amy and I, we commiserating.

I saw the real you at the altar. Beautiful—no doubt, that's why

I love you. The ceremony in a golden dusky light, you were an eclipse. In you seeing her, I didn't perceive romantic love. Nah. Greater. Greater than what I thought we had. I see it now. Saw it when you cried at the sight of her—pride instead of love. Your heart sang some language I don't understand. Pride greater than any love you could ever have for me. I have no culture. I come from plain old slavery and miscegenation. She's your lifelong dream. Of dances and song and food and family and hope and everything else. She's your mother, and her mother, and her mother. She's the reason why you're here. The reason I fell for you. And for you . . . I could never be for you.

I'll take a wash for the past eight years, and just say I'll see you next lifetime. Maybe then we will both make it through the middle passage. Or not. I've got work tomorrow. Come get your shit.

Scrape

Utahna Faith

TAMENY LEANED INTO LEXINGTON AVENUE and waved. The taxi driver sped past. "Rude fuck," she said. She backed into the sidewalk swarm of bodies and was turnstiled between a tall woman in a suit and an Asian man wearing a baseball uniform. She felt weak and pressed her way across the sidewalk and into the first food shop in front of her. The signs looped elegant and swirly. The usual yards and yards of buffet under hot lights, spices in the air, voices she couldn't understand. Eyes on her. DESERT SHRIMPS written in block letters next to Arabic printing on the card above one metal bin. She tonged out a morsel and held it in her palm, considering it.

"Eat it or I'll shoot."

She turned her eyes but not so much her head. He was thin and beautiful. Frightening.

"Is that a gun in your pocket or are you glad . . ."

She couldn't finish.

"I'm glad," he said. He took the food from her hand and put it to her lips. She bit. Crunchy. Salty. Spicy. A little juice, a little oil, something that felt like a fish scale, something that felt like a twig.

"From the sea?"

"From the air. Locust."

Peripheral vision, a box of plastic forks, a framed poster of a stallion, a man in a flowing robe gesturing with one arm, impassioned, like a preacher. Wings and legs in her mouth, crawling, flying.

She wanted to spit but swallowed instead.

~

Tameny's hotel room on Fifty-First Street was smaller than her closet on Mulholland. The bed, narrow and covered with a worn velvet quilt, pitched and wiggled when she sat. The stranger didn't mind it. He pulled her down onto creaking springs, a hand-sewn flower garden beneath her. Early skyscraper twilight and city buzz pushed in through the wavy glass, the tall and narrow window. His eyes were more lapis than purple. Spite, the word in her head for a moment then gone, her incisor pulling a drop of blood from his plush lower lip.

What if she were to rip down the polyester curtains, tear them into strips, bind his legs and wrists with them? Would he let her? Would the air fill with dust, skin flecks, microscopic bits of toxic industrial fiber? Would he know everything she knew?

His mouth moved down her throat, to her chest, and she was drifting. The pull at her nipple shattered. He sucked at the milk that still came, taking it. She pushed him away and he raised his head, smiling at her for the first time, moving his tongue like a cat licking cream.

She wanted to feel a battery of fists over her head, her back, she wanted to feel her own blood dripping like the milk that was dripping out of her. She would do it herself if she could, bludgeon that woman who had decorated a nursery in constant sunlight, who had framed in linen a distant view of the Pacific, whose husband would be staring at containers of frozen milk lined up like soldiers in the deep freeze, whose dimpled cherub would be swatting away a bottle in the arms of a Guatemalan nanny.

She tilted her face back, away from the man's eyes. She pushed his head down. Tears he didn't see, milk that belonged now to no one. She heard soul music through the pasteboard walls that made claustrophobic spaces out of once-grand rooms. The occasional beep from a smoke detector. She wanted a razor or a scalpel, a mace or a hammer. She wanted to let out her own blood.

~

A noise rose above the constant city roar, quick and harsh, followed by an extra cacophony of car horns, shouting. She unwound the sleeping man's arm from her curves, sat, moved to the window. She could raise the pane a couple of feet, press her face against iron bars. Tonight the air was heavy and carried a slight tinge of factory-made skunk. It was a long way down. Red lights. Sirens. Fuzz behind her eyeballs, the clock flickering midnight. She was hungry. What was that she'd eaten? A plague.

He lifted his head, eyes opening like a baby doll's. His pupils were huge and glinting in the dark room and the sky-high city light. She crumbled onto him. Down. She knew she could wreck him. Wreck herself. If only.

There was a phone on the wall and another in her backpack.

She wanted to swallow but spit instead.

Why I Could Never Be Boogie

Lisa Teasley

BOOGIE AND I MEET AFTER SCHOOL 'round four to race the turtles, or ride our bikes to the liquor store and back. Boogie's a bit slower than me, which bothers him 'cause I'm a girl. And Boogie is so fat—I think he's no more than ten and only a head above five feet, weighing up there in the two hundreds of pounds. Boogie is *huge*. But he's cool, shows me the hangs around Washington Boulevard and the Avenues—I just got to my Grandma's in L.A., and there's nobody but her, and Boogie next door, to show me what to do.

'Round seven Boogie has to go inside to scratch his father's dandruff and oil his scalp. Boogie's old man has long, good, wavy white hair—I think Boogie and his folks have a lot of white in 'em. Boogie is creamy-colored with fleshy fat, which is fine, 'cause Boogie's still pretty. His father too, who sometimes lets me come in and watch as he sits on the floor under Boogie. He has long black eyelashes that he looks at you from behind in his sneaky sort of way. He pats my butt whenever I leave, and I turn around and smile because I know he means good.

Other times I'm not allowed inside because Boogie's mother works. She's a nurse over at one of those fancy hospitals somewhere—I know it's fancy 'cause Boogie said the patients arrive in limousines! Imagine that. I even seen a fancy car pull up in front of Boogie's old rinky-dink yellow house. I couldn't see who got out 'cause Grandma pushed me from the window. Don't know why she did that.

But Boogie and I, we're going through some lows, 'cause Boogie's getting shit 'bout his fat and his smell, and I'm getting the big-titty, big-booty shit at school. But Boogie and me, we've got the turtles, we got our bikes, the liquor store, and we've got each other. So today we ride our bikes to the store for some Now and Laters, but I have to go to the bathroom *bad*. Grandma's not home yet from cleaning the Birds' house in Bel Air (The Bel Air Birds, I call 'em) and I left my key at home before school this morning, and we can't go to Boogie's 'cause his mother's working. So we beg the liquor store owner if I can use the bathroom, and we try and explain the situation, me close to tears, and the man just keep shaking his head no. I can't see Boogie 'cause my eyes are burning and I'm starting to cry, now the hot pee is stinging as it streams down my legs into a dusty, yellow puddle on that asshole's cracked floor. I feel sick, and Boogie's pulling me by the arm out of the place, and he's getting me on my bike. I ride home behind Boogie, sniffling, feeling hot and red as a beet, the piss drying to a thick stickiness between my thighs and legs, and on the inside of my sock.

Boogie's father answers the door with a "no-you-can't-come-in," because Boogie's mother's working. Now Boogie's throwing a tantrum, and yelling, "Who gives a shit if she sees that old white bitch anyway!" I don't have a clue what Boogie's talking 'bout, but Boogie's father grabs him by the ear, clamps his mouth, and slaps him hard on his fat cheek. But the odd thing is that he pulls us in the house anyway, and I'm allowed to go to the bathroom to clean up.

The house feels dank and clammy inside, and I hear this muffled, retard-like voice coming from across the hall, so I peek, and there in the bedroom with the door half open is Boogie's mother in her nurse uniform, and a white woman with black eyes, blue cheeks, and bandages covering everything else on her face. The smell of medicine and the look on that battered woman's face sends me to terror, I can't help it, I scream. And now Boogie's shoving me into the bathroom, and he closes the door, hugs me up, me, smelling high with pee like that, and we stay there, me, still terrified, until Grandma comes to fetch me.

Grandma puts me in the bathtub at home, the soap smelling like lemons, and Grandma's hands, huge and soft with rough lines, splashing the bubbles over my body, 'til it soothes me to sleep. I wake to the smell of fried bananas, black-eyed peas, and coconut rice. I hug Grandma from behind and ask her what's wrong with that white woman at Boogie's.

"She had a face-lift," Grandma says, and so I ask her what that is, and she says, "It's when doctors cut your face and then sew it up to look younger."

I say I thought the woman was hiding from thugs who beat her up. Grandma says, "You could say that too."

I'm completely confused, and Grandma's laughing and says, "She's just hiding while she heals up, and she wanted a place where nobody would see her. Boogie's mother's been keeping white women like her for years now. Extra money, you know."

I say to Grandma, "Wha' da' ya mean where *nobody* can see 'em? *I've* seen 'em, *Boogie's* seen 'em. Boogie's mother *and* father's seen 'em." Grandma just laughs.

I'm mad. That beat-up white woman gives me nightmares. And now Boogie and me stopped talking. I play by myself with the turtles, and ride my bike to the liquor store alone, where every time I look to see if my pee has left its mark anywhere on that asshole's dusty, cracked floor.

Rhythm

Joshunda Sanders

SUNUP TO SUNDOWN, A HUNDRED shades of Black girl beauty. Caramel & pecan-colored, rays springing from our lips, mouths full as golden balloons, sweet as Jolly Ranchers. Sugar bubble gum breath, tongues grape purple, hair deep brown or bright pink or braided royal blue, slicked with shea butter & coconut oil, edges smooth & dry elbows oiled like our thirsty shins.

We stay ready—we don't need to get ready. We spring after winter, a breeze of competition. Eyes prying youth open to look inside at our becoming, hips spreading womanhood wide east & west.

Bass flying through rattling windows, energy lodged in earth thrumming, shoulders curved in, protecting our hearts & the fly chains at our necks from the chill as our bodies learn to be the sounds of the city.

Our souls sway to drums that never stop pulsing. Our feet never stop moving. If we can't move, we don't exist. We are some bodies, so: we rock, we roll, we slay with Janet Jackson levels of control.

Spring, a short bridge to summer, means time to show these people we mean business.

We pound out hood Morse code on cafeteria tables, rocking steady, swaying up against the wall with our loves, legs scissored, hair turning back from the humidity we make as we become songs.

We grown with every moment we steal, singing to our own soundtrack. Tamika & Amecca & Ayana & Monique make another party with us, names like songs, like prayers rising from the Atlantic floor so we would always be music.

A drumbeat, a declaration, a love song. A step, a cheer, a chant with our mouths, the beat vibrating from hands on flesh. We make celebration between the long hours of what else is there? Passing notes or sending texts or watching the timelines & scrolling & scrolling. Sweat reminds us we are alive & we are here & we are planted.

We want to move our body south & north & rise up in freedom. We are Six of Wands tarot cards blooming victory. We are radiant Empresses of earth, stepping & dancing, winding hips all in the street.

These Air Maxes were made to stomp to the rhythm. It is ours & it is from Africa, to Brazil, to DR, to Trinidad, to Grenada, to Harlem & The Bronx & Queens & Brooklyn.

When it's time to step & clap, step step clap, we get it popping. A force all its own: launching.

We own these streets when the rhythm come down. We came to rock. Rhythm is our national anthem, our prayer; is our religion, is the hope & the dream of the rebel. We not just dancing to the music you hear, but the music you can't, the lyrics in our blood, the thrum of the soil, our ancestors dancing, singing, swaying with us, quaking the earth.

We predators, bitch, not prey. Give us back our smiles from your staring, your leering. Snatch back our proud chests, titties aloft, from your grubby-ass hands. We say our rhymes together & cast a circle big as the city, wide as the river we shake down to our core, we lift up like we are praising Oya & Eggun & Oshun.

Our rhythm is praise for the sky. Teeth shining white in the sun. We give you our bodies, our daily bread, just to dance. When we step & snap & slap our skin to the beat, our ancestors are keeping time, echoing in traffic. Pumping our chests, arching our backs, we get low low low so we can burst up & out like uncapped hydrants, flow out into these streets until the water seeps in, seeps down & we out.

Radio Water

Francine Witte

Every morning that June, we would watch Ralphie dip into the lake behind our summer house. Ralphie came from nuclear country and told us the lake was radioactive.

Radio water, he called it. He never told us much about where he came from so we didn't know if it was a bomb or what. He would just point to the hairless patch above his right ear. He did say that whatever had happened left him mostly immune to further radiation, and that's why he could swim, untouched, in the lake. My little brother told us he didn't believe Ralphie. Said he saw him through the window one day with a razor and shaving cream.

~

Father had told us that this would be our final summer at the lake. He said he would be leaving us for good to live with the other family he made when my mother wasn't watching him every goddamn minute, which was how my mother would later describe it. My parents didn't speak to each other anymore. She wouldn't even look in his direction. Not when he burned hamburgers on the grill or when he zoomed his car away each night after supper.

~

One morning, late in July, we were watching Ralphie like always. How he would dip his toe in, then up to his waist, finally knifing himself through the water to the other side where the rowboats knocked and swayed. Ralphie explained that the rowboats were also immune and that's why the water hadn't eaten them.

~

One other morning, my father showed us photos of his other family. All of us looking, except, of course, for my mother. Same number of kids in his other family. Two boys. Two girls. They were younger than us. Newer. They were swimming in a lake. They were eating perfect hamburgers.

~

Later, we went outside to see Ralphie coming out of the radio water and wrapping himself in a Spider-Man towel. He looked at us watching him and held up his right hand. Two fingers only. "Guess I'm not completely immune," he called over. Beads of radio water on his face and my little brother telling us that Ralphie was folding his other fingers back. Ralphie palmed the water off his face and walked over to my brother. "Listen, pipsqueak," he said, his chest glistening in the sunlight, glowing almost uranium, "I'd throw you in, but that water would fizz you up alive."

~

The next time my father showed us his new family, my little brother wandered outside, slapped the screen door closed behind him, and walked over to the water's edge. He just stood there looking at the spot where the boats sway.

~

I walked outside one night after supper. My father was sitting by the hammock that was always filled with mosquitoes from the rain. By this time, every other night, my father had driven off to his other family. But not that night. That night, he was sitting very still. Hands in his lap and looking down at the ground. We all went to bed and it wasn't till later when something woke me. I looked out the window to see my father loading up the car with all of his suitcases, along with a bundle of some kind, the exact shape of my little brother.

~

Ralphie told everyone the next day that my little brother must have wandered into the radio water and just fizzed away. "Like my fingers," he said holding up his hand, "like my hair." I thought back to my little brother doubting everything Ralphie said. I thought back to last night watching my brother disappearing into my father's other family.

~

Now that my mother didn't have my father to ignore, she became chatty and younger somehow. We never talked about my little brother anymore. Ralphie's story seemed to be enough for her. It's like my brother fizzing away in the radio water was an easier thing to believe.

~

End of August and my mother told us we would be coming back next summer. She had fallen in love with the nearby hiking trails and woke us up at six each morning for a run. She ignored the men who came to examine the lake, who told her the water was safe to swim in. Ignored Ralphie even when his hair grew in and she could see his fingers plain as day. Ignored the photo my father sent with my little brother seated on his knee, and smiling as if for the first time in his life. My mother waved it away and said, That's a boy who looks like your brother. That doesn't make him your brother. When she said it, she looked off across the lake at the boats still swaying and knocking. The boats that maybe even only looked like boats.

An Alternate Theory Regarding Natural Disasters, As Posited by the Teenage Girls of Clove County, Kansas

Myna Chang

IT WAS THE SUMMER THE tornado ripped through town, peeling the roof off the Crossroads Diner and powdering the big front windows, hurling the deep fat fryer through the windshield of a Ford Ranger in the parking lot, and spinning the silverware bin so fast it embedded seven coffee spoons into the wooden door of the Lucky Dog Tavern across the road.

It was the summer of jagged hailstones and flattened wheat crops, of immature seed heads pulped into the flash-mud that baked dry again before lunchtime the next day. There were no jobs for farmhands that year, but plenty of work at the Windfall Roofing Company, so the high school boys labored in town, hammering shingles and sweeping boiled tar across the flat roofs of the laundromat and the Two Dudes Enchilada Hut. They cursed and shimmered shirtless in the heat for us girls to assess as we sat in Delfa Cargill's car on the vacant lot that used be the Crossroads Diner, sipping cool vodka lemonade and passing judgment.

It was the summer Crystal Toynbee tied her drunk husband up in a bedsheet and beat him with the cast-iron skillet until he pleaded for mercy, but she knew how his bare-knuckle mercy worked, so she kept swinging until her muscles burned with fatigue and hope, leaving everyone in town marveling at how a tornado could render a man unable to speak or eat or piss without a straw.

It was the summer Worthington Cargill left his wife and daughter, taking the insurance money from his hail-damaged farmhouse and his dented Ford Ranger, and drove all the way to Telluride to bet his life's cash on a pair of jacks with a group of players who knew how to handle. a yahoo who insisted they call him "Worthy."

It was the summer Jim McCross fell bare-assed on the floor of the men's room at the Lucky Dog after a surprise weasel launched out of the toilet, the animal misplaced and traumatized by the storm, the man misplaced and traumatized by the loss of the diner his father had built, leaving Jim staggering more from the sudden absence of patrimonial obligation than from intoxication or rodent-fueled adrenaline.

It was the first summer in ten years we saw Delfa Cargill's mother smile. Mrs. Cargill used her husband's life insurance payout to go into business for herself, finding that a decade of marital disappointment had honed her knack for sizing up unemployed farmhands and stray local boys. She put them to work slopping hot tar, while teaching Delfa how to keep the books and structure an insurance policy and size up a man.

It was the summer we watched Crystal Toynbee and Jim McCross fall in love over a platter of cheesy poblanos at the Two Dudes Enchilada Hut. Filled with spice and newfound freedom, they ran off to

Telluride to open a T-shirt shop with a two-for-the-price-of-one sales policy and a wildcat poker game in the back that more than offset their loss on bargain-priced Van Halen tees. The loft above the shop came with a half-size refrigerator and a king-size bed where they slept until noon, whenever they wanted, and no one could give them any shit about it.

It was the last summer of acquiescence, when convention spun free in a ferocious whirl of wind and consequence, and though our fathers argued we didn't yet understand, we decided that sometimes a tornado is just what a town needs.

Pounds Across America

Meg Pokrass

ON TUESDAY AFTERNOON I LINE UP with other petite brunette actresses, silently, our eyes underlined with dark liner. When it's my turn to walk onstage, the assistant casting director asks me to smile, inspects my teeth for flaws. She has purple hair, a nose ring, and a T-shirt that says 2nd Butch Bitch. She looks me over—back to front to back. Says they'll call if I make the cut.

I work in the fringes of Midtown Manhattan on the night shift, which allows me days to audition. My coworkers are mainly out-of-work actors. Our job is calling people who've ordered our diet product from a TV infomercial.

The floor manager creates a sales contest to motivate us, calls it POUNDS ACROSS AMERICA! We're all nervous, fluttering and bullying each other. I pile Three Musketeers bars next to my coffee. A bite, then a sip, then a call. I wave at Jeremy, who's been on the night shift the last month.

The prize is Broadway show tickets for two. I dial, opening my
Three Musketeers.

"Yep?" a tired female voice says.

"Hi. Is this Janet?"

"Depends," she says.

"This is Martha Tiffany with Dr. Feldman's weight loss system!
Congratulations, Janet! We've shipped your trial order and you should
be receiving it anytime!"

"Jingle-jangle-jesus!" says Janet D. Higgins, 190 pounds, in Racine.

"Janet, Dr. Feldman is having us call every customer individually
so we can design your unique program. How many pounds do you
need to lose?"

I can't help reaching for my Three Musketeers bar. I hear the pop
of a fart from the young recruit behind me.

"Fifty," she says, followed by a puff of air.

"Great. How fast would you like to do that, Janet?" I ask, tonguing
the caramel nougat.

"Three weeks? Heh!"

"Let's see, I'm just looking at the chart," I say.

I turn to see what's happening. Dawn (who started when I did)
is doing her shtick for a group in the back, saying, "Pee—niss," in a
Mickey Mouse voice. "Pee-niss, pee-niss, pee-niss!"

Janet screams, "Mommy needs a little time-out too, honey."

"Janet, we're looking at . . . (here the script suggests to impro-
vise) . . . two to three to four months if you follow the easy step
system!"

I look over at Jeremy, his new haircut. He just did a national soda
commercial—knows he's hot. He's rolling a joint under his desk, not
really caring if he gets caught.

"I got to try something," Janet says. I hear a child yelling.

"Let me get to the other reason I called . . . and this has to do with what we just talked about. We care about your success as much as you do, Janet, and we don't want you to have a gap in your continuation—an important concept in weight loss. We're real backed up here, Janet! People are waiting for months to receive orders because of the success they're achieving."

The script says, WAIT NOW FOR REACTION.

"Oh," she says. "I guess that's good then. Was your name Martha Tif-ney?"

"Martha Tiffany Reynolds," I say.

I wave at Jeremy near the window grid flipping me off like he always does. I stick out my tongue and he gives me his rat face. We spent last weekend in bed and he's probably bored already.

Janet tells me in a hushed tone that I sound like *a super, no B.S. gal*.

"You do too, sweetheart—we love you here," I say.

She says she's a waitress. Her husband died on the way home from work one-and-a-half years ago, crushed by a semi. She has a toddler named Trevor. He's a handful, and needs a good preschool. She hopes to be able to afford one soon.

Sweat is forming under my breasts and pits even though the air-conditioning is blasting. I say the last line of the script a bit early, feeling my full bladder, pressing it with my hand to make it worse. "You. Deserve. Success."

She gives me her credit card number, saying, *Shit yes!* to the Supreme Success Package (the most expensive).

"I bet you're pretty and thin, Martha Tifney!" she says before she hangs up.

~

After work I bring Janet's order sheet home under my shirt. I read off each name as I tear the sheets into bits: Kelly, Nita, Jen, Marla, Iris,

Nancy, and Janet. They will be mystified when there's no charge on their statements and they receive nothing else.

I take off my clothes and stand naked in front of the bathroom mirror. Look at myself from different angles. The way a casting director would.

Beethoven's Fifth in C Minor

Pete Stevens

M Y HUSBAND DOESN'T LISTEN TO the voice from my lungs or the nuance of my protest, only the music of California wine and Beethoven's Fifth in C minor. He says it has to be the Fifth. He has rules, my husband. It was Beethoven at our wedding. It was Beethoven on the beach for our honeymoon. He says the Fifth is a cave to crawl into, that with each listen new cracks and gems are exposed. Now, tonight, he says it must be the Fifth when the other couple comes over. We are what they call hosts. We are to be sophisticated in our debauchery. We prepare our bodies with scented soaps and limbs shaved smooth. James walks from room to room with wineglass in hand, a Sonoma merlot, the Fifth following with him as he goes.

This is our first time opening ourselves to others. The couple on their way is experienced in manners of the flesh and with sharing, and they assured us that everything will be fine, without worry, a night of new beginnings. I am not so sure. And is it my fault? Probably yes.

The song of my disdain was sung too softly, the notes discarded by my husband in a wash of wine and drips from his chin.

The lights have been dimmed, the second bottle ready on the table. My eyes say no. My heart sings unheard. I cannot say what I want to say to a husband who will not listen, who is convinced of his ways and of his decisions. Yes, it is true that a spark has been lost to the night. Yes, it is true that what we once had was fresh with possibility. Yet, how can the answer be my husband inside another woman while I watch? How can the answer be my lips pressed to a man I do not know?

The couple, younger, in their late twenties, is soon to arrive and my husband goes to the stereo and raises the volume. Beethoven fills the house like smoke from a fire. There is no escape. I suggest other music, maybe jazz. I say to James that jazz is sexy, mood music, that yes, Miles Davis, his trumpet is sex. My husband says jazz. He says please. He says that Beethoven's Fifth is sex and life and death. He says the Fifth is perfect for our night, that the crescendo of strings will stoke the flames of our lust.

I hear a knock at the door through the music and my husband goes to answer. The couple waits, expecting, on the doorstep. They enter and bring with them the smells of foreign skin. This couple, they are not shy. They remove their coats with bright smiles and laughter, suggesting it should be more than coats coming off. Together we sit at angles along the couch in the living room. My husband pours wine and speaks in hushed tones. The woman, her skirt riding higher, tells James to be quiet. The Fifth gains speed. I watch as she stands before my husband, as she lifts her skirt to show him her lace. She looks to me for approval and I shift in my seat, restless. I am not sure of my place or my role. I have no desire to dance for this other man, to show him inside. I stand with bottleneck in hand and continue to watch. The man removes his shirt, his chest thick with black hair. The woman straddles James and lowers her lips to his neck. I turn and walk away. None of the bodies on the couch notice my absence or my advance toward the stereo. The Fifth still climbs, ever higher, and I end it. I turn the knob until the thump of electronic dance music erupts from the speakers. I turn it up and up and up. The bass drums kick and snap with the pounding of my heart. I close my eyes and begin to dance, my hips rocking with the beat. It is then that my husband listens. It is then that he comes to me with palms upturned.

The Kiss

Pamela Painter

N̲o ONE CAN GUESS so she finally tells us.

Actually Mona doesn't tell, she sticks out her tongue at us and there it is—a gold ball the size of a small pea, sitting in the creased rose lap of her glistening tongue.

We all lean forward from our pillows on the floor, seven of us, the wrung-out remnants of a grad party in the low-candle stage. Inge asks Mona where she got it done (Cambridge as an undergrad), Raphi our host asks her why (she likes something in her mouth), my boyfriend wants to know what it tastes like (no taste). We're still peering into her mouth so she lifts her tongue slowly, the rosy tip pointing up toward her nose. There on the silky downward slope is another gold ball.

"A bah—bell," she says, her tongue still showing off.

And it is. A tiny gold barbell piercing her tongue.

We settle back into our pillows and she closes her mouth.

My boyfriend, a chef at Valentino's, is probably wondering which taste buds sit in the middle of the tongue and if they are affected and how. Inge, the etymologist, is mouthing the word tongue, no doubt marveling at how the tongue loves to say that word. I can tell we're all wondering something. Our tongues feel heavy in our mouths, empty except for the privileged gold fillings and ivory bondings of the middle class.

It occurs to me that Mona's not able to enjoy her barbell. Enjoy the way the tip of my tongue visits a rough molar, soothes a canker sore moistly healing on its own, or wetly licks the hairy friction of chapped lips.

I say I wonder what it's like to kiss her?

Everyone shifts and nods as if they were wondering the exact same thing. We turn to the man Mona came with, who shrugs and says he doesn't know. They just met three hours ago at Huddle's Pub.

Well, who's going to kiss her? Inge says.

We all look first to the man she came with and then at the other eligible male. No one counts mine, which disappoints him and he lets it show. The man she came with weighs thirteenth century Inca bones after reducing them to ashes in an autoclave the size of a toaster. Raphi, our host, is a religion major—the Hellenistic culture—who thinks the world is fast approaching a non-religious end. "I'll kiss her," he offers, then defers to the man she came with.

"Wait a minute. Maybe not," Jorie says, holding up her hand. She and I are in gender studies. "Don't you think we should run it by Mona first?"

We all turn belatedly to Mona.

"Oh," she says, "It's all right with me." The gold ball doesn't show when she talks. I wonder if it makes a dent in the roof of her mouth.

The man she came with says, "I'll kiss her." Neither man is looking at Mona.

"You choose," Inge says to Mona.

Mona shrugs and points to Raphi. "You offered first."

He grins.

In perfect sync, they both stand up.

"No, do it here," we all say, "here in front of us." But we needn't have worried; they had no intention of leaving.

Mona and Raphi face each other above us. They are the same height. Mona's hands rest on the hips of her black jeans, her elbows jut out, claiming space to equal Raphi's greater weight. He has his hands deep in his pockets. We are all aware of his hands in his pockets.

They stand inches apart—two inches apart. She tilts toward him first, just her shoulders and head, and then he catches her tilt, catches her mouth with his mouth. They kiss. They kiss tenderly and well for two people who have just met. Their heads glide with their mouths and their shoulders move ever so slightly. I imagine his tongue filling her mouth, sliding toward the ball, searching, pressing, perhaps turning it, rolling it; her tongue letting him. I imagine their hands aching to touch the other person but refraining as if to abide by some set of rules. No one looks away.

Minutes, but probably seconds, later they stop. "It's pretty far back," Raphi says, and we all swallow with him.

Mona turns and sticks out her tongue to show us she thinks not, and we see it's not so far, really. Perhaps an inch and a half.

She turns back to Raphi and they kiss again and we all watch them kiss, even better the second time: harder, deeper, her tongue and his tongue, her generously letting him, that slight tilt, their scrupulous hands.

They pull away. We have all been holding our breath.

Well?

They settle themselves cross-legged and facing each other. I imagine another night such as this for them, moving away from the kiss toward the questions and answers of getting to know someone, and that moment when they invite their hands to join their kiss.

We listen as Raphi describes to Mona the amazingly hard muscle of her tongue, the cool surprise of the tiny gold ball, the flick past the ball underneath. They tilt toward each other.

Raphi's hands talk.

Mona is smiling that smile. She's got what she wanted.

The man she came with leaves first.

My boyfriend leaves with me, but we go home separately. We all go home with something missing on our tongue.

Amelia

Aubrey Hirsch

A MELIA HATES IT WHEN PEOPLE call her Amy. Amy is her mother's name, she tells them, and her grandmother's name. And she is nothing like them. She is educated. She is a career woman. She wears pants and a leather jacket and has short hair because she is a flier. And Amy and Amy? They are helpless wives of alcoholics, dragging their children behind them like designer luggage through the clatter of empty whiskey bottles.

She also does not want to be called Meeley anymore. It is an unfortunate nickname. It conjures images of undercooked oatmeal and apples that have sat too long in the blue bowl on the kitchen counter. It reminds her of the time she rode her sled off the roof of the farmhouse. She spent a moment on the ramp, angled toward the clouds. Then a long beat in the air—flying! It was the same stomach-dropping feeling as being at the top of her arc on the swing set, the moment when the chains go slack and you just fall. And then the hard smack of the ground. Her dress torn, her elbow bleeding, her molar turned to powder in her mouth. She shifted it around with her tongue. Rubbed it against the roof of her mouth. Mealy.

The students in her class called her "the girl in brown who walks alone." That's what they printed under her photo in the yearbook. Maybe she wouldn't have been alone so much if any one of them had had half a brain. Or even a quarter of a brain. A quarter of a brain she could work with. But the girls at school were mindless idiots. They were just looking to get out of high school, get married, have baby after baby until they get a boy to carry on the family name, and die having learned nothing more than they knew in high school. Amelia filled a binder with images of women doing men's jobs and doing them well: scientists, doctors, a mayor in New Jersey, a pilot. And look at her now. Ten world records under her belt. Now she is attempting her biggest stunt yet. The papers say she is the first woman to attempt to fly around the world. But she knows better. She is looking for more than good press.

Amelia really doesn't like being called Mrs. Putnam. She'd rather be called anything else, including almost all of the cuss words. When the reporter from the *New York Times* captioned her photo, "Mrs. Putnam," she was so mad she couldn't see straight. George smiled a wide, beaming smile. "What do you think about that, Mrs. Putnam?" he said. She would have pitied him if not for the searing heat suddenly cloying at her brain. "I don't know, Mr. Earhart," she spit back. He struck her, the only time he ever did. She knew then she'd have to leave him. She rubbed her flushed left cheek. It would happen soon. She would board the Electra and never look back.

A.E. she doesn't mind so much. She could make a fuss about society reducing her whole being to two letters, but she doesn't. She concentrates instead on her flying. It is her escape. She takes Canary, her yellow biplane, up to eight thousand feet where even the air she breathes feels different. Up there her busted sinuses magically clear and her headaches evaporate like dew in hot sun. No one is as fast as she. No one can follow her up this high. This is where she gets away. This is how she will get away.

Amelia is what she really wants to be called. Fred Noonan, her navigator, calls her Amelia. "Amelia," he says, "we should start sending the signals now. We're about three hundred miles out." She nods at him, takes his hand. He calls in their coordinates as if they are heading for Howland Island. But they are not. They are flying toward Gardner Island. It will be lonely there but beautiful. Fred is a marine man. He can make them shelter and find them food, fishing in the island's big lagoon. She has nurse's training. She will keep them safe and healthy. Her hair will get long. Fred will grow a beard. There will be no whiskey and no stupid girls and no grandmother telling her to wear a dress like a lady. Every morning she will wake up, naked as the day God made her, to the feeling of warm wind on her face and Fred's sweet voice in her ear whispering, "Amelia."

23 Men

Grant Faulkner

I SEE JACQUES HOLDING A CIGARETTE to the back of his hand and watching it singe his skin, then asking me if he can burn the butt on my stomach. I see Vincent putting on his virtual reality goggles and saying, "I wish we could be in this world together." I see Peter accidently breaking a wineglass in the kitchen and leaving the shards of glass on the floor as he leads me to his bedroom.

It's odd that anyone has a one-night stand. You join this creature in the most vulnerable of acts, a creature who might as well be a stray cat, and you don't even know if they're petty thieves or petty sadists. You just want a little warm flesh to lie alongside, a few touches of tenderness to get you through the darkness. An adventure.

I was in between relationships, in between jobs, a new girl in the big city. It was my year of sleeping around, or not caring too much who I slept with, or just wanting something different. I often though of a Jane Austen quote: "Seven years would be insufficient to make some people acquainted with each other, and seven days are more than enough for others." Seven minutes could suffice for me, Jane.

I'm a light sleeper, especially if I'm not in my own bed, and I never brought anyone home with me because then I couldn't leave. When I woke up in the middle of the night, I'd lie as still as I could, listening to the rhythms of breaths, trying to trace dreams in the shrill inhales. A gasp. A breath taken in but not released. Even the most macho man becomes a child when he sleeps, defenseless, vulnerable. Sleep sweeps you away, erases you. You're not guilty of anything.

One morning, as the dawn's light snuck through a gape in the drapes, I stared at the way a boy named Justin's thick black curls fell upon his neck, how his freckles sprinkled across the pale skin of his shoulder blade. He'd given me bourbon in a chipped mug. He'd traced his finger along my jaw before kissing me. He'd told me he once made eggnog with rum from scratch at Christmas. These are the kinds of things one knows after a single encounter. My phone lay on the floor next to the bed, so I took a photo of him, a memento of our night together.

I dressed and snuck out the door, imagining him rising later and wondering where I'd gone. Would he be relieved? Had he hoped for morning sex? Would he check to see if I'd stolen something?

I started sneaking photos of every man I slept with. The photos became my own private accounting, a journal of my "nights abroad," as I liked to call them. These men had moved inside me. They'd held me like they loved me. They'd revealed something true about themselves, even if just for a moment. I owned a little piece of each of them now, swatches of pretend love. They took nothing from me, but they'd be forever mine.

Tristan, the aspiring holy man who didn't believe in God. He once spent a month alone in a cabin reading the *Bhagavad Gita*. He bragged that he'd fasted for a week. A row of Buddhist statues lined his window-sill, a boy's spiritual toys. I took a picture of him sleeping on his back, as if he were lying in a casket. I stole the smallest statue, a laughing Buddha not much bigger than a cockroach. My way of helping him not be attached to the things of this world.

Ian was a dandy, a man who indulged in the puffery of life. He said things like, "It's beaucoup fantastic," or "It's mucho delicioso," so pleased with himself. He giggled after he ejaculated, his face breaking into ripples of laughter. His neck was like a swan's. His shoulder blades were as sharp and angular as a teenager's. He would have said "Ciao" when I left the next morning if he'd had the chance.

Shane's cheeks were hollow, tinged with an unhealthy sallowness. His eyes, teardrops. "Somewhere, there's a person who was killed by a falling suicide," he said. He mumbled that he had to get up early the next morning for a doctor's appointment. I took a photo of his lips quivering to a dream, his pillow stained with a pool of saliva.

I knew I'd eventually get caught. As I photographed Kyle's chest rising with his breaths, I accidently dropped my phone. I sat on the floor, leaning over his futon, my legs bent underneath me. "What are you doing?" he asked. "Your chest, it's so beautiful," I said. He smiled in a way that defined the word "beatific" for me, and then he took off the sheet so that I could photograph him fully nude. We all have a secret desire to be seen.

They weren't all so poetic, though. There was Manuel, the athlete. His hands never stopped moving, his eyes filled with hunger. Sex was just another form of cardio, it seemed. He took a shower afterward, but he didn't invite me to join him. I opened a drawer of his bureau. A mess of underwear, a box of condoms, a pocketknife, a cigar. I kicked a pile of gym shorts on the floor. I took a photo of him scrubbing his chest in the steam of the shower, but he didn't even notice me.

My friend Maya asked me why I did it. I shrugged my shoulders. I'd always liked things that came apart easily, I said. I liked roller coasters, the way you fall, then come back to life. I liked being the one who accepted the dare. When I was a girl, I wondered if it was possible to bomb a rainbow.

"Parts of the universe break apart from time to time," I said. "It's funny how we try to find them and put them back together again."

Varieties of Disturbance

Lydia Davis

I HAVE BEEN HEARING WHAT my mother says for over forty years and I have been hearing what my husband says for only about five years, and I have often thought she was right and he was not right, but now more often I think he is right, especially on a day like today when I have just had a long conversation on the phone with my mother about my brother and my father and then a shorter conversation on the phone with my husband about the conversation I had with my mother.

My mother was worried because she hurt my brother's feelings when he told her over the phone that he wanted to take some of his vacation time to come help them since my mother had just gotten out of the hospital. She said, though she was not telling the truth, that he shouldn't come because she couldn't really have anyone in the house since she would feel she had to prepare meals, for instance, though having difficulty enough with her crutches. He argued against that, saying "That wouldn't be the *point*!" and now he doesn't answer his phone. She's afraid something has happened to him and I tell her I don't believe that. He has probably taken the vacation time he had set aside for them and gone away for a few days by himself. She forgets he is a man of nearly fifty, though I'm sorry they had to hurt his feelings like that. A short time after she hangs up I call my husband and repeat all this to him.

My mother hurt my brother's feelings while protecting certain particular feelings of my father's by claiming certain other feelings of her own, and while it was hard for me to deny my father's particular feelings, which are well known to me, it was also hard for me not to think there was not a way to do things differently so that my brother's offer of help would not be declined and he would not be hurt.

She hurt my brother's feelings as she was protecting my father from certain feelings of disturbance anticipated by him if my brother were to come, by claiming to my brother certain feelings of disturbance of her own, slightly different. Now my brother, by not answering his phone, has caused new feelings of disturbance in my mother and father both, feelings that are the same or close to the same in them but different from the feelings of disturbance anticipated by my father and those falsely claimed by my mother to my brother. Now in her disturbance my mother has called to tell me of her and my father's feelings of disturbance over my brother, and in doing this she has caused in me feelings of disturbance also, though fainter than and different from the feelings experienced now by her and my father and those anticipated by my father and falsely claimed by my mother.

When I describe this conversation to my husband, I cause in him feelings of disturbance also, stronger than mine and different in kind from those in my mother, in my father, and respectively claimed and anticipated by them. My husband is disturbed by my mother's refusing my brother's help and thus causing disturbance in him, and by her telling me of her disturbance and thus causing disturbance in me greater, he says, than I realize, but also more generally by the disturbance caused more generally not only in my brother by her but also in me by her greater than I realize, and more often than I realize, and when he points this out, it causes in me yet another disturbance different in kind and in degree from that caused in me by what my mother has told me, for this disturbance is not only for myself and my brother, and not only for my father in his anticipated and his present disturbance, but also and most of all for my mother herself, who has now, and has generally, caused so much disturbance, as my husband rightly says, but is herself disturbed by only a small part of it.

High on the Divide

Chauna Craig

T HE MEN ARE DESCENDED FROM hard-rock miners, their lungs gone to granite, their hearts chunks of ore. "On the rocks," they say when they order their bourbon. The bar is O'Sullivan's. The city is Butte. They call me Angel of Mercy because they're Catholic and can never remember my name, not when their eyes mist with memory. Not when they cry. You can cry at O'Sullivan's. In a city where the Bulldogs are Double-A wrestling champs year after year and the jail fills on St. Paddy's by noon, there are still places where grown men can cry.

I refill their glasses and leave extra napkins, and they whisper, "You're the Angel of Mercy. Sent by the Lord." Sometimes, when it's someone with a sense of humor—Dylan Downey or Old Man McClure—I say, "I was hired by Liam, and he's not the Lord."

"Yes, Angel, we know that. But who will tell Liam and break his old heart?"

"You can't break his heart," says another. "It's stone."

And they all fall to silence, labored breathing, alcoholic fumes

I could light. Sometimes I imagine flicking a lighter and blasting another hole in this scarred mountain. New veins to explore, new work for this town.

The men, when they're sober, say go back to school. "Girl, that's the future. A college degree." And though none of their wives—first, second, third—had degrees, they want more for me, this future whose fingers they can touch.

When they're drunk, they say, "Angel. Don't leave. Take us into the next world. Angel. Mercy."

I've nowhere to go, so I stay their saint, serving up spirits, mopping those broken circles they leave under their drinks. Sometimes I imagine flicking that lighter and starting to smoke. My pink lungs will seize up, and I'll cough when I need to inhale. Sometimes I touch my wrists to remember the pulse. Michael Rourke sobbed one night—a sound like choking—because he couldn't find his pulse. He wept that he'd died and, since that one pope erased purgatory, he was surely in hell.

"So, I'm a demon, am I, Mikey?"

"Mercy, no," he said when he could breathe again. "I know I'm in hell because I can't touch you. You're miles away, up in the sky, holding Our Lord's punctured hand."

I clutched his thin wrist, pressed his finger to the groove below his thumb, and I counted with him. *One, two, three, four. You're not pounding on death's door.*

That night Liam couldn't drive him, so I walked him home, counting his heartbeats aloud on the steep mountain streets. *One, two, three, four, Mikey's heart ain't made of ore.*

"Unless it's gold," he whispered, stumbling at the threshold of his small, dark house. I wavered there in the doorway, unsure. Tuck him in? But I wasn't his mother, and I wasn't a saint. I shut the door on his cave, sealing him in. *Fool's gold*, I thought I heard him say, but the door was metal and warped and it could have been *whose gold* or *too cold* or so many other things.

One night the cowboy comes in, and I feel for my pulse. Thumping, thumping for escape. I think of that lighter under the bar, this place sky-high in a shower of flame, my blood rushing out of me, my heart set free. I crouch low to the bar, swish my hair in my face, and Danny Riordan says, "Angel, you okay?" And one by one, these men still on their bourbons but ready for Coke walk to me. Wobbly as toddlers. "Is she sick?" "Is she hiding?" "Is her heart broke?"

Silence. Then someone, not me, says, "An angel's heart can't break."

And someone else, the cowboy, says, "No, it just flies away."

No one here entertains strangers, so none of them like how he steps through their words. They grumble as if they are young men with strong hearts, strong lungs, strong fists.

No stranger to me, this cowboy. He's held to my finger a circle so perfect that I fled all my dreams of riding over the plains into the setting sun. I came back to this place high on the Divide where whole generations believe the sun is lit on the end of a wick a mile underground.

The men cluster tight like they can save me. But they're the ones drowning in bourbon and rum, in memory shafts they've cut with too little air.

"You could cry here," I say. "You could pour out a bottle and, depending on which side of this mountain you chose, it might join the Pacific. Or head to the Gulf."

The cowboy knows. He studies the men, how they clutch their drinks and stare. Later, he will say *stony stares.*

That night I think of gold. Golden rings, golden plains, his bare golden arms, those golden sunsets melting through our golden years.

I let the lighter decide. Flame on the first try mean "yes." And it lights like a tiny sun. I inhale this air soaked with bourbon and the sour breath of old men. Nothing explodes. I flick the lighter again, and it glows in the dark bar. Circles of light on every man's glass. Extinguished as soon as I raise my thumb.

I flick it again and again, but that night the lighter is constant. The cowboy waits just beyond the glow.

So I leave these men descended from miners. Without mercy. I unlace my angel wings, reckless as I abandon what they know of copper, what they've taught me of gold. Broken rock, all that broken rock.

Willing

Jennifer Wortman

ONE OF THE MEN I love is pointing a gun—stainless steel, ecru handle—at his temple, and I tell him I'll do anything if he puts down that gun. This is the man I'm not leaving my husband for. But now I tell him I'm leaving my husband. I call my husband, so the man can hear, and tell my husband I'm leaving him. My husband isn't surprised, but he's pissed. He knows about this man, because we have the kind of marriage where I can tell him about this man, and because we have that kind of marriage, I wasn't going to leave him for this man. But now it turns out I'm leaving him for this man, because this man has a gun to his head, which is like putting a gun to my head, because I love him that much. I love the kind of man who will put a gun to his own head, and therefore, by implication, my head. My husband, though pissed, will not put a gun to his head over any of this, and I also love the kind of man who will not put a gun to his head over any of this. But it turns out the gun wins. I tell my husband we'll talk later. I hang up and hold out my hand, into which the man places the gun, gently, like a pet newly dead.

I love this man, and I love my husband, but I also love this gun.
I open the chamber and eject the bullets, just in case I start loving it
too much. Because of guns' obvious phallic properties, no one speaks
of their feminine beauty, their curves and holes. I don't speak of their
feminine beauty. Instead, I say to the man I love, "You should fuck me
with this gun." We have never fucked, because I love my husband. We
have never even kissed. Then I say, "Just kidding. I'd never fuck a gun.
Unless it was loaded, with the hammer cocked."

When I was a girl, my dad would take me shooting. I was a terrible
shot, but my dad praised my skills, because I went shooting with him,
and my willingness to do so was skill enough.

My willingness has limits. I don't own a gun. The man I love's
willingness knows no bounds. Life is easier that way, when you are
willing to shoot people to protect yourself or shoot yourself to protect
other people. When you're willing to leave the husband you love for
the man you love or willing to leave the man you love for the husband
you love. But now I love this man extra, because his gun released my
willingness, a wildcat fresh from the cage. And I love him because
when I say things like, "I'd never fuck a gun. Unless it was loaded, with
the hammer cocked," and laugh until I cry, he holds me and strokes my
hair but doesn't kiss me or cop a feel, even though he could. Even now,
after I've left my husband, he holds me and strokes my hair, nothing
more. And I hold him and stroke the bristles where his hair would be if
he hadn't shaved it off, a practical move that nonetheless looks, with his
sad face, like mourning. I love his sad face, and my husband's sad face,
and, come to think of it, my dead dad's sad face. But I hate my sad face.

Before this man put a gun to his head, I'd sent him photos of my
saddest face. I wanted him to see me as I am, not just sad, but ugly,
shorn of makeup and hygiene and youth and sleep: photos reeking
of bad breath and funked armpits and cellular rot. I looked that way

because I wasn't leaving my husband for this man, and we were saying goodbye. I took pictures of myself looking that way because it was the closest I could get to shooting myself. This man saw the pictures and put a gun to his head: my hero.

He strokes my sad face and says, "Shhh. It's okay." He strokes my hair. "We're together now, right?"

His eyes are ovens, burning dark.

"Forever," I say.

The word tastes like cold steel.

I smile.

Misty Blue Waters

Darlin' Neal

A T SCHOOL SHE WAS Bitchy Boo Hoo. She was Slut Eyes. She was Fucking So Very Grave. Girls gawked and turned their backs and whispered and laughed when she passed. Kids said, "Your name is Redgrave, not Waters." They were so stupid. They didn't know anything. She was a freak and proud of it. Her daddy was a rock 'n' roll star. Her name was Misty Blue Waters and all that needed to be changed on the birth certificate was the last name, if she decided to make it legal. What the stupid asses didn't check were the CD covers with her dad's last name, Waters, on each and every single one. They lived in Memphis and they didn't know shit about music. *They* couldn't get in to a show just by saying their dad's last name. She didn't even have to say his name anymore, all she had to do was show up with her face. One day they would be a little older and they would *wish*.

She wouldn't have even gone to school that day but it was the deal she made with her mother, go and then you can spend the weekend with your dad. So she went and after school she took her time and got dressed for her date with Daddy and headed for the Young Avenue Deli. She couldn't stand to wait so many hours for the night to come in that house with no one to talk to. She was way too excited. At the Deli, everyone knew her. They said, Hey, Misty Blue, look at you! Look at your hair! Where'd you get that skirt? They loved the glitter on her eyes. She'd bleached her hair blond with a tinge of pink dye on the ends. She found a poodle skirt at a vintage store. After all, he was taking her to meet a '50s retro band. She wore fishnet hose because to be a little sexy was important for a girl. She had been preparing for this weekend for two months. At least.

A stripper friend of her dad's, Crescent City Delilah, joined her at the bar.

CC Delilah said, "Misty Blue, you shouldn't be smoking." She shook her head and smiled.

Then she said, "What can I say, I started smoking at twelve. But I wish I hadn't. You'll wish you hadn't."

And, "What are you, all dressed up with nowhere to go?"

"Are you crazy?" Misty Blue said. "Dad's taking me to a show in Nashville. In a limousine."

CCD's face lit up with a smile and she adjusted Misty Blue's low-cut sweater a little. "Look at you growing up," she said. "And girl, you're going to be one of the lucky ones." Misty Blue knew what she meant and the compliment was a great one, coming from someone so endowed as CCD, and with all that great skin. CCD aimed her long fake lashes behind Misty Blue.

Wanda came in with a crooked, shiny walking stick and all that red hair and sat on the other side of her. She put her hand on Misty Blue's, who could have sworn the mood ring she wore turned from black to red at the touch.

"Hey, pretty girl," Wanda said. "I'm making ads for my restaurant.

I want you to come and be in the photo shoot. Wear something wild."
They talked about it for a while, but Misty Blue couldn't keep anything
in, she was thinking about the night. The musicians would stare at her.
Her dad would be so proud. She wrote the date of the shoot on her arm
to remember.

She stared at Wanda dreaming. Wanda was old, but she was still
so mysteriously beautiful. A lot of people thought Wanda had magic
powers. Everyone talked to her with respect. She wore a black hat with
a peacock feather in it. Behind Wanda, strips of shiny gold shimmered
from ceiling to floor all across the empty stage.

The bartender brought Misty Blue a charred hamburger and a
plate of spicy fries.

"God, I wish I could still eat like that," CCD said.

"Well, do, then," Wanda said.

Misty Blue took a twenty out of her purse and offered it to the
bartender. Wanda grabbed her wrist and reached inside her own silver
purse. The bartender winked and shook his head at them both. She
slid her near-empty plate away. She jumped down from the barstool
and kissed CCD and then Wanda. Wanda squeezed her inside all that
warmth and all those wonderful scents and gave her a big smack on the
cheek. Not until she was out of sight of the bar windows did she wipe
the lipstick off.

At home she waited on the steps with the phone in her hand. She
had on a gorgeous white fake-fur jacket. She had painted her shoes silver with bottles of nail polish.

She went in to check the time. She put her jacket on a hanger. She
really didn't need it. She decided to have a beer, to pour it in a glass like
a lady, but she knocked the glass off the counter and it shattered. She
swept shards into a dustpan and took her beer outside. She waited for
the limousine and she waited for a very long time, even though it didn't

take long before she started saying to herself, "You knew better, stupid. This happens every time."

Last time, when her dad promised to make it up to her, he'd apologized and said he'd run into some strippers. Who could blame him? Strippers or a kid? Misty Blue blamed it on the drugs. She vowed to never do drugs.

In her mother's room was a long oval mirror. Misty Blue went in there and teased an imaginary audience. She wisped a scarf between her legs. She took her clothes off slowly, seeing the picture she made with each piece she removed, because this was art. She danced to no music. She wanted to keep listening for a limousine, just in case.

Emmy vs. the Bellies

Meghan Phillips

EMMY WAS PISSED ABOUT the bellies. I mean, we all were to some degree. They were ugly and heavy and covered up our new school clothes. The letter to the parents said they were supposed to help us understand the weight of our decisions. Cam said she was more confused than anything. She hadn't gotten her period yet, so how could she even? Gabi said that at least we knew the school hadn't started monitoring our cycles. Yet.

So yeah, none of us were happy about the bellies, but Emmy was *pissed*. She said it was stupid that the school used grant money to buy fake pregnant bellies for all the freshman girls. They could have reopened the arts wing or hired an actual health teacher *to teach actual health*. She said it was even more stupid—so stupid *and* unfair—that all the boys had to do was watch the Lifetime original movie *Too Young to Be a Dad* in the auditorium and do a worksheet.

Emmy said that she would not rest until she got rid of the bellies. She slammed her fist into her palm to emphasize "rest." When Gabi asked how, she said sabotage, wrapping her mouth around each sylla-ble like a hard candy. She said, the less you know, the better. Plausible deniability. Emmy had always been the bravest of us. The loudest, the bossiest, the one who knew things the rest of us didn't. When she said she was going to do something, we believed her.

We'd only been wearing the bellies a few days when Stephen Coo-per's mom created a petition to make us wear something over them. Mrs. Cooper said the boys should not have to be confronted with our lumpy cotton-stuffed bellies and sandbaggy breasts in bio lab and lan-guage arts and Algebra II. Poor guys couldn't concentrate on their schoolwork. She posted her petition in the Panther Parents Facebook group. It took less than forty-eight hours for an email to go out man-dating that girls had to find shirts that would cover them or they would be forced to use their study hall to sew maternity tops. It took Emmy less than twenty minutes to ride her bike to Community Aid and find us all XL T-shirts. "I Survived the Sooper Dooper Looper" shirt for Cam, a green "Girls on the Run" 5K shirt for Gabi, and for me, a shirt from the "Spend the Night with Alice Cooper" tour. She kept the bright pink "I Stand with Planned Parenthood" shirt for herself. She served out a week of detentions for inappropriate attire. Cam left a note in my locker: is this the plan? I wrote back: idk??!!

Emmy was pissed about the boys and the petition and detention. She was pissed because the bellies made it hard to do sprints. But then we got used to the weight. After the first month of running drills with the bellies, the whole team was pulling six-minute miles. Emmy said they were the best thing to happen to the Eastern High Lady Panthers JV field hockey team since Playtex Sport tampons. Coach said that if Emmy kept it up, she'd make varsity next year. All of us would.

Emmy seemed less pissed about the bellies the more seconds she shaved off her mile. Cam thought maybe she liked the bellies now? I said it was hard to tell with Emmy. Gabi thought maybe she'd given up on her plan? I said maybe a monkey would fly out of my butt.

Our bodies were changing under the bellies, *because* of the bellies. Our round little bellies, our actual bellies, were firmer, flatter without the baby fat. Legs felt longer, stretched by new muscles. Our arms were lean, but biceps bulged when we picked up our backpacks or closed our lockers or tackle-hugged when Gabi scored her fifth goal in three games. We were getting stronger, and it felt like a secret. We were getting boobs and hips and pubic hair. That felt like a secret too.

When Emmy started mixing buckshot into the stuffing of her belly, claiming it was to increase resistance, I thought, This is it. When she gut-checked Central's forward in the last five minutes of the game, I thought, Here it is. When the athletic trainers were strapping the girl to a stretcher and Emmy, who was suspended for the rest of the game and probably the season, yelled over her shoulder "I stopped the fuck-ing game-tying goal!"—I tried to beam it into Cam and Gabi's brains: The plan.

Coach wouldn't let us talk to Emmy after the game. He made her sit in his office while the rest of us showered and changed and helped each other back into our bellies. There was a message from her that night in the group chat that said, "no bellies tomorrow, the plan worked xoxo."

We texted back "yayayayayay!!!!!!" and "get it girl!!" and heart emo-jis and popping champagne emojis and the smiley face wearing a party hat emoji. Cam messaged just me, "what are we going to do now???" I texted back, "idk." Gabi texted, "i'm gonna miss my belly, don't tell Emmy." I texted, "so will i, bb." I texted, "don't worry i won't." I texted, "i have a plan."

The One-Eyed Bat!

Yalitza Ferreras

THE GUY I'M DATING IN Ann Arbor is The One-Eyed Bat! He wrestles with a mask over one eye. He's from a *Mayflower* family in Massachusetts, and he goes to Mexico to wrestle Lucha Libre–style. He jumps from the ropes onto his opponents and ensnares them with his black velvet bat wings. It's an art thing.

When he drives us to Detroit, to photograph urban ruins, we pass this wiener sign outside the factory where they make them on Holbrook Street. The wiener is in big red neon, disproportionate in size to the building it is attached to by a giant skewer. The first time I saw the sign, I gasped and screamed out, A big red wiener! and he just nodded as the wiener cast its shadow on us, didn't even crack a smile. The wiener sign says "Kowalski" and is in the city of Hamtramck, just outside of Detroit. Has there ever been a more delightful name for a city? H-A-M-T-R-A-M-C-K. It needs more vowels. I think about the missing vowels, and phonemes and epenthesis, and I think that Hamtramck seems like enough when you say the name, but not when you see the word. Sometimes he takes my left hand in his and blows warmth into it as we drive on ice-covered streets, and I feel happy. The first time he took me to Ypsilanti for another art thing, and we approached the city's old water tower, named the Word's Most Phallic Building by entities that declare such things, I didn't say anything as we drove by its girthy base on Summit Street, the highest point in the city. He was talking about the themes of masculinity in his Lucha Libre project. Summit Street! I was hoping he would notice the delight on my face, but he didn't. Okay, so I try to engage with his work, I say, uropatagium instead of fixating on penis. We talk about studies on how bats use their uropatagia in flight thrust, but when I call the membrane their bat butts, I lose him. So anyway, what scientists are saying is that wings are obvious, but bat butts are important, too.

And then we get to Detroit, and he makes art. I wander around the decay of these abandoned buildings, and I politely ease out of his frame, spinning on split floorboards, risking my life on tippy-toes. He takes these photographs that make the desolation look like a movie set built just for him to explore themes of loss of industry and people. After elegiac pronouncements, he lights the shot, makes use of something that was once useful. Then, we fuck.

I am supposed to be writing. He is a multi-medium artist. I don't mean multi-media. He sings and plays guitar and dances and takes pictures, and he mentioned something about a unicycle once, and he makes films, and this wrestling thing, too. He must've exhausted his parents. My mother says that I was sometimes so quiet she had to poke me to make sure I was okay.

I walk around. I don't understand why everyone is in love with these ruins. I prefer the parts of Detroit with people in them. All these places look like my childhood memories of burned-out squats in Bushwick, where I was born brown like everyone around me, you know, before Bushwick was cool. Detroit feels familiar, but this is not my city, these are not my ruins. He is photographing a heap of books with mushrooms growing out of them. These dead books are my worst nightmare. I am standing off to the side under an art-deco archway, its red, blue, and orange tiles fallen off and strewn at my feet. A faint light glows through a hole in the floor. I take a step forward, and a loud clanging echoes through the space. He looks up and tells me to be careful, and I think about pressing down harder. I want to make an offering to this place. I picture my congealed guts dangling off the jagged entrails of the building. I slide down carefully instead. I put down a knee. Other knee. Head tilts. I slowly uncoil my scarf from around my neck. I call him over.

Afterward, we go to the gallery in Detroit where he's showing the photographs of himself soaring above Mexicans in his flappy wings, black shorts and Lucha Libre mask. In one image, he stands on the ropes of a makeshift boxing ring outdoors in a field or what looks like someone's backyard. He is gritting his teeth, stomach muscles bulging. He is beautiful. His tousled white-blond hair is peeking out of the half-face head mask that makes him The One-Eyed Bat! His body looks like a classical statue looming over his opponents.

They say that bats see better than humans. What I see is the torso from a David about to topple on all these smaller, rounder, browner men, but I don't say it. I start waving my hands around the space. I tell him what I think about the lighting, how to arrange the photographs, not what I think about white bodies coming down on brown bodies in their own backyards. The gallery owner comes over and smiles at me like, You guys are such a great couple. I just keep trying to make some arrangement out of the pieces and pointing at the walls.

Theo & Annie

Randall Brown

I WALK THE DOGS ALONG THE nature trail, past the duck pond, through the campus and its stretch of green and trees in the midst of the Philadelphia Main Line. A tiny tricolored Coton and a bigger white Bichon, the boy. I could feel old among the students, but I don't. "How cute," they say, and I can imagine they are talking about me.

We leave the trail for the sidewalk, around buildings. A tiny man runs out to me. "Are they married?" he says. I like the urgency of the question and his run, set against the nature and trails and buildings that stand as still as can be.

"The dogs! The dogs! Are they married?"

He is at me now. The dogs sniff his pants, move on. The Bichon licks the Coton's ears, inside and out. "I don't know," I say. "I guess not."

"We will marry them. I'm a wedding photographer. Was! How I forget."

There is a long middle section here, when he explains a valve operation, missing a course on digital photography, having to take a job at the college involving new students and parents and maybe they ask him to take a picture now and then. Then there is a part about Italy, a cornfield, a girl he chased around and around, that ends with the exclamation, "She knew. Oh, she knew." And how they fight, he tells me, even now, but that's better than, and here, he cannot find the word. He sputters, looks to me for the answer.

"Indifference," I say.

"Yes. Not to be noticed. How miserable."

He tells me not to move and off he goes. I sit down in the grass by the sidewalk. It is August and the parents look bewildered, and the kids look as if they want to take off in a sprint. My wife is on a vacation alone. I think she's searching for a way to tell me she doesn't love me anymore.

The Bichon lies down first, the Coton next to him, in the curve of his belly. He continues to lick her ears. And oh my, here comes the wedding photographer, a tripod banging against the ground, his leg, the bag of cameras and lenses pulling him to one side. And a woman behind him, as in the fairy tales, the woodsman and his wife who lived far away from everyone else. Maybe that is sexist. I don't know. I love them right off, and it's odd how that can happen sometimes.

"My wife! Lydia! Come, come. You will say something I hope."

Lydia has wild white hair. She comes over and takes my hand. I can't wear a ring because it gives me a rash. "Paulo, he tells me you are all alone."

"I don't remember saying that to Paulo."

She turns my hand over. There's a scar from college, I explain, when I tried to lengthen my lifeline with a filet knife. She smiles and says one must be careful about asking for such things, unless one wants a loneliness that goes on and on. She whispers into my ear, "You are an angel for doing this for my Paulo. See how excited he is!"

He is. Setting things up. Moving here and there, putting together this and that, wiping lenses. The dogs remain indifferent, except to ears and tongues and tails that wag in unison.

"Ready!" Paulo says. "Now you will say your words."

I stand facing Paulo. I've spent hours with the dogs, training them. Finding the voice that, as the trainer advised, is like one has when giving directions to someone. Rewarding each iteration of the desired behavior. Ignoring the mistakes. Shaping for the complex movements, a treat for the movement toward the object, for touching it with a nose, for picking it up, for dropping it. So that's a long explanation of why they sit, facing each other, still, eyes on me, waiting for the treat.

"Something nice," Lydia says. "Something beautiful." She stands next to Paulo, her arm around his waist. He doesn't seem to notice.

"Theo and Annie," I say. Some people have stopped, the deer-like parents, the fawn-like kids on restless legs. "We have gathered here to marry—" I stop to give them each a treat. They take it so gently. I am so sad. I didn't realize that until now. I wish love would last. It's a silly thing to want, to say, but there it is. "—to marry Theo and Annie—" There's Paulo, too, moving his camera to the horizontal, to the vertical, twisting it, clicking it, repeating yes, yes, that one, yes.

"And I think they are going to make it," I say. "These two kids, because all Theo wants to do in the world is lick Annie's ears and all Annie wants is to have her ears licked and I think that's enough, I really do."

Lydia removes her arm and claps. So does the tiny crowd, then they scatter slowly. There's more. More pictures. More talk with Lydia. The writing down of address and phone numbers for me to pick up the pictures. I will bring them something, since they won't hear of taking money. I imagine I will see them often, maybe we'll move in together, the three of us, maybe we will go into business for dog weddings. I don't think dogs fall out of love. I've never heard of it, at least.

There's another thing maybe. When she comes home and mumbles those words, or maybe before she has the chance, I will show her Theo's and Annie's wedding album. I will give it to her. I will say I understand. I will say look at the way she looks at him. That's what I want. What everyone wants. Don't you?

Walking on Ice

Arlene Eisenberg

He polished my toenails red. He blew short, cool puffs from side to side, from the biggest piggy to the littlest one. But that's not all he did. First he massaged my calves, rubbing baby oil into them, kneading with his fingers and the heel of his hand. Then he attended to my feet, bending the toes in his palm, pressing his knuckles into the soles. He tugged my toes one at a time and stretched my arches, sliding my feet through his warm, buttery hands. Then he polished my toenails.

But that's not what really happened. He didn't do any of those things. Actually, he hardly touched me at all before he took my hand and placed it on himself. And soon, too soon, he was on top of me, pushing, until my head knocked against the headboard. Not a hard knock, but a knock just the same, again and again, until I whispered, "Move down a little, I'm banging my head." And we went on like that for a while and I liked it, I honestly did. And that's what really happened.

I was walking on ice. The other side of the frozen lake seemed unreachable. Sleet pelted my face and loose scarf threads stuck to my mouth. It was very, very cold. The tips of my nose and fingers went numb, although I wore thick mittens. When I finally reached the other side (because I feared I might not make it) dirty heaps of frozen snow and ice rested where the plows shoved it, and I crunched deep holes with my boots (the snow piled above my knees), to get to the front door. This was a dream, and it ended at the front door.

It rains all winter in Los Angeles. Many people don't know this, and those who live here say it's not so. But it rains, and torrents carve petroglyphs into bare hillsides, and throngs of weeds, dandelions and foxtails, sprout between the lavender and sage. And spiders. The city is besieged by spiders. Not big furry ones like in horror movies, but those with fine, long legs that break if you try to rescue them. They live in the bathtub and dance up the walls.

A bird flew into my chimney once and trapped itself in the fireplace. It flapped and flapped like mad, caged by the screen. It terrified me, so I fled. When I returned it was gone—flown out the way it flew in.

He came by again last night. Not the bird, but you know, him. Half-moons dampened under his arms and he smelled somewhat sour. Not too bad, but even so. When he took off his shirt and let it drop to the floor I thought, *Oh, the dog's going to love that.* And he didn't polish my toenails or massage my feet. What he did was pretty much the same as the last time, and it was okay. Not great, but okay.

When the sun shines and he's looking a certain way, specks of orange shimmer in his eyes. I can't look away, trying to discern the depth of those amber crystals. Are they on the surface, like paint, or do they sprout at the core and pierce the iris? I squint for focus.

"What are you staring at?" he asks.

"Your eyes," I say, "I'm looking at your eyes."

He grins bashfully and turns away. For a moment I feel love for him. Not a great love, but love all the same.

He sits on one end of the couch, I nestle in the other. When he's not here, I read. Books about people, mostly; books they wrote about themselves. And short stories. The ones that tell what happens in a few hours, or maybe a few days. Not those that jump from year to year, or decade to decade, explaining the time between with a sentence or two. The space left out is too wide. My dream about the icy lake is the beginning of a story that ends in less than a day, inside the house, on a sofa facing the fire. And I am sitting there alone.

I plant cuttings and seeds in my garden. I like to watch them change as they grow, become confident, independent. To see them rise up after pelts of rain knock them about, or when the gardener's heavy boots crush them. He (you know, the guy who didn't really paint my toenails) sliced pieces of succulents from neighbors' lawns with the knife he carries on his key chain. He presents them to me, green juice dripping onto his palm. (The part of his hand he kneaded my calves with, but not really. He never did that.)

He waits for me to return home. I am out with friends and we talk about him. But that's not all we talk about. He smiles as I open the door and turns from the TV. I join him on the couch: he's on his side and I'm on mine. My toes inch under him, but he stares at the screen as if he doesn't feel them. Then my feet slide in—to the warm crease where denim meets upholstery.

"Did you see that left shot?" he asks.

Water cascades down the boxer's face which is already oozing with sweat and blood. Giant hands shove the mouthpiece around and set it back in place.

"Look at this, you've got to see this," he says. A head is pummeled.

Brown hands separate them and they collapse on stools: one in his corner, the other in his. Soon they are holding each other like lovers.

Wildflowers bloom in the vacant lot across the street from the school. They are yellow and white. I sever the stems with my brother's knife, but by the time I get home they've wilted. Even water won't rouse them. So he brings me roses. A dozen violet roses and I say, "Where did you get them? How did you know?"

He smiles shyly and turns away, sunlight filtering through his lashes. I place the roses in a crystal vase and set it on the table. We eat dinner by candlelight, and then we make love.

No, that's not what really happened. Nothing like that happened at all.

All Your Fragile History

Jasmine Sawers

I GOT THIS DNA TEST FOR my dog because he looks like a cloud and he looks like a luck dragon and he looks like something your lint roller picked up when you banged it around under the couch for the first time in three years and I was sick of people asking sick of having no answer when they did so I followed all the directions on the packet I got him up first thing in the morning before he could take a sip of water before he could go lick the other dog's eyeball before he could root around the other dog's asshole with his tender pink snoot I got him and I swabbed his gums while he jerked to and fro like a malfunctioning Furby and I stuck the Q-tip in the test tube and sent it back to New Jersey postage paid no problem and I sat back to wait the appropriate amount of time for some labcoats to put his elementals into a centrifuge and spin it around until they could draw out all the threads of him and look at his heritage as if it were a map as if they could build him his own family tree as if they could slot him into some ongoing canine narrative and say, "His people left France in

1647 and roved across the English countryside before boarding a ship to Mexico it all makes sense now how he makes that weirdo monkey sound how he howls and shakes when he's excited how he shrieks when you approach the door to leave him," and anyway it took two weeks exactly and I woke up to an email telling me he was not half cumulus half cryptid but half rat terrier a quarter miniature poodle a quarter Chihuahua and I looked at him and I said, "Huckleberry Finn you have never caught a rat in your life," and he looked at me and didn't say anything I assume because he was ashamed of his failures as a vermin exterminator and I assume because he wanted to make a point about my hypocrisy walking around with this face and not getting a DNA test myself but let me tell you white people love to take DNA tests white people love to parcel out what kind of white they are white people love discovering "<1% Sub-Saharan African" or "3% Native American" on their rainbow pie graph summaries white people love to tell other white people that they come in all different shades and they can portion out their blood in riveting fractions but when they ask me what I am and it's a day I happen to answer it's always, "Thailand? I hope you get liberated from China soon," or, "No, you're Indian, don't lie," or, "Ugh I'm so jealous you never have to go tanning," and wouldn't you know it's worse when I tell them I too am cobbled together of fractions I too am white enough to want to spit into a beaker to find out if I'm one-quarter Irish or two-fifths French wouldn't you know it's worse when they say, "Oh you *do* look white you're actually really pretty," or "You're so *dark* for only being half" or "Are you *sure* you're not Indian," wouldn't you know it's worse to fear you will be unmoored should you spit into that beaker only for a stranger to be spat back out shouting, "Italian!" "Indonesian!" "Greek!" "Vietnamese!" "Swedish!" waving a flag you don't recognize singing a language your tongue can't curve around loosing the tether to all your fragile history as if a single

PDF has the power to cleave you from the memory of the burst of mangosteen across your tongue the touch of your grandma's hand as she helped you whisk the German chocolate cake batter the way Thai and English merge in your mouth to crack out interlingual puns the way your mother decorated the Christmas tree with garlands of jasmine blossoms and a slender Buddha up top the way your eyes glint green in a certain light the way your grandma said "davenport" and saved used Ziploc bags the way your grandpa said, "I just want to help someone," and let you hammer nails into blocks in his woodshop the way you slipped between buildings and under scaffolding to find a bustling halal restaurant cooking khao mok in a wok the size of a bathtub the way the street vendor in Bangkok asked your mother, "Is that child half white," only to jack up the price when the answer was yes the way your brother hid his birth name from the kids at school because if they'd known it they would have run around chanting, "Ching chong ching chong," the way you've been called a "nigger" and a "chink" and a "gook" and a "slant" and a "spic" the way you've been called "the perfect Asian student" the way you've been told to go home the way you used to scrub your skin until you were one big livid pink abrasion hoping the color would rub off with the blood the way you look for evidence of belonging the way you look in the mirror the way you look.

Hatched

Nicole Rivas

Lily AGREED TO HAVE DINNER with me in my car. She wanted to see how I lived, and I wanted to see if she could handle it. When she arrived, I was checking my eyeliner in the rearview mirror. She knocked on the passenger's side window with the blunt edges of her painted fingernails. In the crook of her arm was a wooden bowl covered in plastic cling wrap. I unlocked the door, reached across the passenger's seat, and let her in.

"I love hatchbacks," she said, placing the bowl on top of the dashboard. "I used to have one for a while in college."

"It's surprisingly comfortable to sleep in," I said.

"I slept in mine a couple times. Too wasted to drive home after parties, I think. If I'm remembering correctly," she continued, "I wouldn't describe it as 'comfortable.' "

"Fair," I said.

Lily poked me in the arm. She wanted me to lighten up.

"Is that salad?" I asked, pointing to her wooden bowl.

"Greek," she said.

"Great. I'll put some music on," I said, and reached for my phone with my sweaty hands. I scrolled aimlessly, unsure of what Lily would want to listen to. Superficially, she seemed much different than me. She was nine years my senior, grew up in Ohio, and worked as a graphic designer. I knew nothing about Ohio or graphic design. I'd met her at a coffee shop three weeks ago. Unlike me, Lily was an over-sharer. She told me she'd dated lots of women throughout her life, but also some men. She'd given a baby up for adoption when she was in college. Said she still thought a lot about the child, who was now a teenager living somewhere in Minnesota.

"Where do you keep all your stuff?" she asked. She shifted her body to peer into the backseat. All that was there was a Tupperware container filled with paper plates, plastic spoons, and plastic cups. She seemed to expect piles of clothing, books, toiletries. The sorts of things that make people human.

"In the back," I said. Then, acknowledging my half lie, I continued, "Also, under the car. Well, when I have guests. There's a lot of clutter, otherwise."

She smiled. "And what's for dinner?" she asked.

I observed her smile. It reminded me of my mother's mouth when she also sat in the passenger's seat—cracked and drained of life. Part of Lily's discomfort, I knew, was her frustration with my reticence. I hadn't told her what college was like, wasn't eager to share anything about exes or family or traumatic experiences. These things didn't make me feel any closer to people. In fact, they made me feel more alone than ever.

"Macaroni and cheese," I said.

"How do you make that in a car?" Lily asked.

"I make it outside on a camping stove," I said. "It's easy when it's not windy."

"Wow," she said.

"Yes," I said. I opened my car door, walked to the backseat, and removed the bowl of macaroni and cheese.

"Do you have tongs?" Lily asked, watching me. "Something to serve the salad? I forgot to bring anything."

I looked at Lily and she looked at me. Her eyes seemed to narrow, harden, shrink.

"I think I have something under the car," I said. "But it's under the car."

"We can look," she said.

"No, you don't have to—"

"To what?" Lily asked.

"You know what I mean," I said.

"I don't," she said.

"The car. Everything," I said.

"I mean, we can look," she said, opening the passenger's side door.

I placed the macaroni and cheese on the dashboard. Outside, Lily was already on her hands and knees, pulling Tupperware containers out from beneath us. A duet of scraping and sighs as she maneuvered around on the cold ground. Lily wasn't even close to where a pair of tongs would be. I told her so. But she continued. She was in a box of socks and underwear, in a small bag of knitting yarn, in a Ziploc baggie of egg remnants from the one chick I'd seen hatch on my grandfather's farm. Then she was reaching into a cookie tin filled with photos of old lovers. She pulled out a Polaroid photo of breasts I hadn't seen in person in three years, tossed it aside.

"Stop—" I said.

But she didn't stop. Next were my lucky coins, my childhood stamp collection, a series of state-themed magnets for the fantasy version of myself that owned a house with a kitchen and a refrigerator. Then another bin: my dead dog's collar, expired acne prescriptions, a vibrator the shape and color of a skyscraper. She tried to turn it on, but the batteries were dead. And still further, an older container: one box of journals from the past ten years, a suicide note no one but me had ever read, a stack of therapists' business cards with numbers I'd never called, and so on. She scanned the letter, nodded, and placed it aside. Kept digging.

I shivered and got back in the car. I could see Lily's calves and shoes protruding from beneath me. I pressed the car horn. She sprang up, dusted herself off, put her hands up as if to say, What gives?

But my foot was already heavy on the gas pedal by then. The sound of crunching over boxes filled with trinkets and paper, etc. In a brief moment of regret, I glanced at Lily's form in the rearview mirror. She had found the tongs after all. She was already using them to sift through what little remained of me.

Lobster

Robert Shapard

E DDIE SAID TO SEND THE lobster first-class or whatever it took to
get it to Wyoming alive and reasonably happy so they could boil it
to death there. He made her smile, talking like that.

She'd fallen in with him yesterday afternoon at the fundraiser, on
probably the largest private lawn on Cape Cod. He said he was crazy
about her, she said why, and he said because you are endearingly geeky.
Then he offered her a job with the campaign, though it wasn't clear he
had the power to do so.

The party went on into the night and at last they found a room, in
the gable of a house, bumping heads on the slanted ceiling, first him on
top then her, grappling in the single bed. Afterward, Eddie dropped—
more like *imploded*—into sleep, and she tried the same but was fitful.
She groped her way down a dark hall to a bathroom feeling fraudulent
because she'd pretended to know more than she really did about social
media strategy. Really she was just a humble second-year law student.

Eddie had been with the presidential campaign since June. He had already passed the bar.

In the morning when she woke, because he was bumping around getting dressed, he told her, Don't get up, it'll be so great if you can make it to Wyoming, but it's hugely important to send the lobster. He bent over the covers but she shrank away. You might want to rethink me, she said. No, I will not rethink you, he said. Speaking from beneath the comforter she said, How do I send it? I'm maxed out on my credit card. He wrote instructions on a scrap of paper and was gone.

Two hours later she strode into town with her weekender bag and a headache, trying to feel confident. The fisherman said yes, he had her lobster. She watched him put it in a battered grapefruit box, lined with a garbage bag and wet seaweed, Cape Cod's best, he grinned. She understood this was going to burnish Eddie's reputation for ingenuity in filling odd requests by presidential aides. Possibly it could help earn him a place in Washington after the election. She lugged the box and her bag across the road to a dark bar where men were downing shots and had coffee and a Danish then took the town's only taxi to the airport.

On the way the Cape seemed empty, almost haunted—it was so crowded only a few days ago—now it was September, cool with a front coming in, winds gusting this way and that. She felt disconnected— literally because her phone was dead and she'd lost her charger. If only she could fly to Wyoming like Eddie said. Nancy Rossi had urged her to, her friend on the law review who invited her to the party, because it was history and exciting—how often did a presidential campaign happen? But Nancy wasn't broke, she had money, it was easy for her.

Coming over the dunes in the taxi it became obvious—she could borrow the money. But not from Nancy, then who?

The airport terminal was a single-wide mobile home with two wooden steps to a passenger lounge with a small electric heater and half a dozen people seated in plastic chairs. A man behind the ticket counter was chatting to someone in his headset. She waved to get his attention and asked if she could charge her phone. She said she needed to send a lobster.

He said, You want a ticket for Bob?

She said, No, not Bob, a lobster, it has to go on the next flight.

Not unless you want to buy him a seat, he said.

His mic distracted him for a moment, then he said to her with a kind look, There's no cargo space and almost no luggage space left. She followed his glance at the window—speckled a bit with rain—to the plane outside, parked on an irregular patch of asphalt. It looked tiny—a seven-seater. I can take him in the copilot seat, he said, but I'll have to charge regular passenger fare.

He shrugged, as if to say people do this sometimes, then listened to his headset again.

That left so much to decide. Her parents would never loan her money to fly a lobster somewhere, they would want her to return to school. Auntie Lynne might back her—she was her childhood hero, a lawyer in Vermont who handled prenups, wills, trusts, divorces, all the most important things in people's lives. Now she was more like a friend—usually harried like last summer, hair straying across her face as she talked a volunteer out of Dunkin' Donuts to her office to witness a signing, then picked up the kids, and between other clients called the Geek Squad to come fix a computer disaster. Meanwhile Uncle Jack was off hiking. He thinks he's Robert Redford, she said, and that's okay.

The man behind the counter announced to the passenger lounge, We'll start boarding in a few minutes.

People stirred. Damn, she thought, forcing herself to be calm, looking at the lobster in his box—she couldn't help but think of him as Bob now—weighing options, (1) Send Bob in the copilot seat to Boston to connect to Wyoming and his eventual death, (2) Dump Bob, because it ran against her grain to buy a seat for a lobster instead of a human being, herself, and there were subsets, (2b) It was reasonable to return to law school but she dreaded it because as she admitted, now, she wasn't the greatest student, (2c) Hurry up and call Aunt Lynne to charge both her and Bob's flight all the way to Wyoming because Eddie *did* want to see her, she *did* want to be with him, she did know about social media strategy, anyway more than a lot of people . . . she would have to make the argument to Auntie Lynne in one sentence—she remembered her saying the law was full of impossible choices.

The man behind the counter stood and pulled on his pilot cap and jacket.

She looked out the window and realized the runway was like one of those long driveways through the dunes to cottages she saw coming up the Cape from Wellfleet almost lost in the coastal grass rolling in the breeze this way and that, and she realized all her choices were right and how beautiful it was, how beautiful it all was.

David Hasselhoff Is from Baltimore

Kara Vernor

YOU ARRIVE FINALLY ON THE California coast, and even though this is northern California, you're expecting tan, leggy blondes and barrel-chested surfers. You're expecting red swimsuits and life-guard stations and blinding white sand. You've brought your own red swimsuit and you're expecting California to deliver.

Here's what you get instead: jagged cliffs covered in seagull shit. You get wet wind. You get big-armed bearded men who ride Har-leys, and tie-dyed, wrinkled women who smell like lavender. You get a runny nose and damp feet and an icy ocean that couldn't care less about red swimsuits. It says fuck you red swimsuit, I am busy tearing at land. I will tear until I reach the Atlantic.

This is the news after 1,062 quiet miles—after one divorce, two yard sales, four months of double shifts, and a spate of Coors Light hangovers. With no idea how many hours' drive it is to palm trees, you stop at the roadhouse and get a room upstairs, #7, with a lighthouse quilt. You get shared bathrooms at the end of the hall with a basket of toiletries from previous guests. This is better than standing in a Walmart in Montana choosing a brand of hair spray. Which is least likely to catch fire? You are happy not to have to decide. You are happy for leftover Aqua Net.

As a girl you stood in that Walmart in Montana pulling at your mother's skirt. You watched as she set a box of Life back on the shelf, shut her eyes, and breathed out, "California." You let go and tried to catch the word in your hands, tried to hold it between you like it was something you could share.

Downstairs at the bar you find a book of matches with "Mike" and a phone number penciled inside the flap. You head outside and use one of the matches to light a cigarette, a Virginia Slim, which you feel you deserve for having come a long way. You dial Mike and when he answers you say, "Convertibles."

He says, "Hello? Who's this?"

You say, "I see cars but no convertibles. I see a chapel and a feed store and a community center and three teenagers walking to the cliffs, and not a one of them is rollerblading."

He says, "You're still at the bar. Stay there, I'm coming."

He arrives and he is handsome. Blue eyes, black hair. He is a big-armed, bearded man, and he is looking for someone else. You show him the matches and ask if you'll do.

"Let's walk," he says, and the two of you head out through a field to the edge of the ocean. You tell him you are not trying to find your mother, and he shrugs like it's not for him to say. He says, "What I know is this: the bartender, from Nebraska, will let you smoke inside during the Tuesday night pool tournaments. The cook, from Kentucky, will make grits on cold days even though they're not on the menu. The taxi driver, from South Dakota, drives drunk after seven p.m. And I," he says, "don't know dick about surfboards, but I can mix you a margarita. I can shine your shoulders with oil."

"Nebraska?" you say. "Kentucky? South Dakota?" You say, "I'm trying to find California."

He scratches his beard. "Which is what?" he says. "Hollywood? David Hasselhoff? How about you ask him where he's from."

The non-rollerblading teenagers begin setting off fireworks, and you try to remember if today is a holiday. Mike's face turns orange, purple, white as he watches. You tell yourself you'll kiss him when the number of explosions reaches 101, the highway you're to take south in the morning. You're counting 84, 85, 86, and you're smoking faster and laughing harder and he's daring you to strip down and wade in. "Go all the way," you say, and you unbutton and unzip, push down and pull off. Mike whistles as you tramp over sand that might as well be snow, your body illuminating under the bursts. You push into that angry ocean, the cold whipping your thighs, cementing your lungs, your mouth sucking the night for air. An oncoming wave readies to bury your head, and your arms butterfly forward, your feet kick free of land.

Sketches of the School Staff in Winesburg, Indiana

Michael Martone

CARL FRANKENSTEIN, CUSTODIAN

I am a big man, a big man with an unfortunate name. The embroidery on my uniform stretches way beyond the pocket, over-sews the placket. An ugly man who lives alone. A man who will not unlist his home phone number. A man who answers every phone call each night. "Franken-stein," I answer. I hear the murmuring laughs. At halftime of the basketball games, I lumber onto the hardwood with my wide furry mop, up and down the court. The students mob the stands, heave trash into my path. I circle, shaking my fists at the throng in the shadows of the bleachers, the monster that I am. Their monster. After the game, I walk home. I want to mop up the puddles of light cast by the streetlights, sop up the shadows the moon spills in the gutters. At home, I listen to WOWO radio. There are all the scores of all the basketball games in the state that night. I read the phone book by the fire, chanting those numbers. And before I go to bed, I rip out the stitches of my name from my uniform. Every last thread. I open that old incision over my heart.

CAROL APP, TRUANCY SECRETARY

All day, I make the calls. I check on the absences. The rolls come in from the homerooms right after the first bell, collected by dedicated student aides, circulating through the contagious corridors and hallways. The stairwell sings and sewers. Names of the absent. The never-made-it-ins. I contact the contact numbers. I push the number buttons with the eraser on my pencil. No one is home. No one is ever home. Or, no, I imagine them at home in bed, the situation dire. So sick, so stricken that no one can reach the jangling phone on the table next to the sickbed. It rings and rings. Sometimes there are ghostly recordings, ghosts in the machine. "We can't make it to the phone right now . . ." I see them wasting away, sweaty in soiled sheets. The stench. The pestilence. Chronic illness is chronic. I put a checkmark next to the names, a vector indicating that I will call them back. I call them back. I call them back. Receive the stutter of the persistent ring. Percussive pertussis. A buzz like a biting sting. Allergic to my ear. I am, sad to say, the only one who will receive, in the next hopeful spring, a certificate, one I will make myself, recognizing perfect perfect attendance.

LESLIE SANGUINE, CAFETERIA CASHIER

I believe everyone in the school, including the teachers, receives a free or reduced lunch. I am for show, running the old mechanical NCR register, registering the chits ringing up the dimes. Afterwards, I wipe the tables down, restore the order to the condiments, turning the catsup bottles into hourglasses, dripping what's left of one bottle into the leavings of the other. Gravity works, okay? I sweep up the litter of each day's notes that the kids' moms have packed with their cold lunches, little scraps of paper with messages, instructions, prayers. Half-baked home-baked sentiments, fortune cookie scribbles slipped in the pails and sacks. "Try to have a good enough day, Tim!" "Don't fret too much!" "Hope you do a better job in math." "Don't embarrass yourself or us!!!" Or sometimes just a penciled face. One big O with three little o's inside. Oh, oh, oh, oh. My other job—we all work other jobs—is restocking the greeting cards concessions in town. The rack at Blister's Pharmacy downtown. Rumi's Cigar Store. Rupp and Otting's Market, the Five and Dime, the newsstand in the courthouse run by the blind. I've noticed that the birthday cards, the ones for weddings, new births, anniversaries languish, while the get-well ones and the cards of sympathy and bereavement fly out the doors. I work on commission. Pennies a card. After hours, on my hands and knees, I count out from the cartons the somber cards and their dour envelopes and count them into their predetermined slots on the racks. It is like another cafeteria line. Here you go. All the grief you can eat. One more fresh smorgasbord of sad sadnesses.

HOWARD JUNKER, FACILITIES ENGINEER

My friends call me "How." "How, how you do this?" I get asked all the time. I always know how. How to tape and mud the drywall. How to build a header and shim a doorframe. How to wire and plumb. How to snap a plumb line. How to fire the boilers, move the steam. How to make the clocks run on time. My workshop is a shack I built on the roof I roofed. There on my workbench all the guts of the appliances are spread out on the Masonite table I built from scratch. My tools, a silver Milky Way on pegboard. Coffee cans of fasteners. Tupperware tubs of fuses, switches, drawer pulls. I know how to maintain. Look! Do you hear that? This mechanical calculator I salvaged from Mr. Rice's physics lab thirty years ago is still running. Big as a bread box, studded and stuttering with gears and ratchets and armatures and levers, it has been sawing away all that time. Long ago, I told the machine to perform an impossible task. I divided a whole number by zero and the contraption's workings have been searching all this time (in the toothed flanges, greased widgets, stripped screws) for the mechanical expression of infinity. The machine makes a racket as it calibrates, clucking and clunking, at any moment on the edge of entropy, unengineering itself, a twitching pile of junk. But it goes on and on. How does it do it? I maintain it. I tend to it. It will keep looking for infinity forever. Forever forever. It is a little engine that asks how how how how. How's time machine telling time.

How to Write a Hardship Letter

Nicole Simonsen

IF YOU REALLY WANT TO save your house, do not tell the people at the loan workout team that your soon-to-be ex-husband has renounced all material pursuits or that he is living in the back of the revival movie theater in exchange for running the projector and sweeping up the popcorn. They are in the middle of an F. W. Murnau retrospective. He invites you to come to the next screening of *Sunrise*, but you just don't have it in you to watch the lovers reunite. He seems to have stepped into these old movies, to have turned into a black-and-white version of himself. He wears a black overcoat with an upturned collar, and a ridiculous fedora that sits low over his forehead to hide bloodshot eyes. You will have to admit that he doesn't have a job, but do not tell the bank that he quit. And do not tell them what he told you the day he left, when you stood outside the house, the sunlight slicing your eyes like a razor, that he would never work again, that the nine-to-five life was killing him. He didn't need much to be happy; he could live like a monk. You didn't believe him, but when you stop by the movie theater because you are lonely and miss the old talks, he will show you his makeshift cot behind the screen. He has a pillow, a mat, and a crate with a change of clothes and a copy of *Don Quixote* and *Les Misérables*, the only things he has kept from your life together. The rest he has rejected. You don't know him anymore. He might never work again or pay his fair share, but don't tell the people at the bank.

If you want to avoid the filing cabinet of hopeless cases, do not tell them that your three-year-old son is on the spectrum, that he doesn't make eye contact, that his speech is delayed, and that at night when he is finally sleeping, you wish you could slip your fingers inside his skull and massage those neurons into the right places so that in the morning the two of you could have breakfast together and have a silly conversation about who would win in a fight—a killer whale or a great white, or why Santa Claus doesn't visit the children of China, or why some birds eat other birds—and then when you drop him off at his expensive school and hug him tight and whisper in his ear that you love him, he will say the words back. That is something money will never fix.

Do not tell them about the other morning when you went to the river to collect water samples. You used to enjoy tracking pollutants because they were identifiable and measurable and could be contained in your tiny vials. But there, at the edge of the river, the water cold and fast and higher than usual, it all seemed a pointless exercise, the mere naming of things and nothing more. You noticed a lone seal, its black head bobbing on the surface. It seemed to implore you with its oily eyes; it had a message if you could just get to it. You thought that if you walked into the water you might slip out of your skin and become a seal, too, and that you would like that life, swimming up and down the river, dining on small fish, no mortgage, no job, letting the current take you where it may. You tried to summon your old childhood belief in shape-shifters, but, as usual, you hesitated a moment too long. Your boss found you and wanted to know why you only had three samples—*What have you been doing this whole time?*—and you realized the spell was over, the opportunity lost.

Above all, do not tell them about your newly ambiguous feelings toward the house you claim you want to save. Do not tell them that you have considered packing whatever will fit in your car and driving to Mexico or even farther south to Chile or Peru where you could live in a hut with your son. Do not tell them that the house has become a jail, that it requires you to work for it like someone on a chain gang, like a modern form of indentured servitude, or that in French the word mortgage means *death pledge*. Ambiguity makes these people uncomfortable. They are bankers, after all. They like numbers and money and for things to add up.

Strike up a friendship with whomever answers the special 1-800 number the bank has set up for people like you. The woman with the Southern accent is a good listener. Get her extension. Call her often. You can tell by the timbre of her voice that she is a smoker and has a good twenty years on you, that's why it's okay for her to call you "honey," which she does often, followed with optimistic platitudes. Coming from anyone else, these pithy sayings would drive you crazy, but from her they are oddly reassuring. She knows, she's been there. In 1982, her house was destroyed by a tornado, in 1993 a flood. Real biblical stuff, she says. Right now, you need stories about people who rebuild their lives from the rubble.

Remember to be brief. These people do not have time for your life story, nor are they literary critics, so you may use the occasional cliché—"I will get back on my feet"—you can write. There are conventions to this genre, and they expect you to follow the formula, not get too inventive or creative. That might signal an instability.

Don't forget to sign your name. And for fun, because nothing about this has been fun, use the wild, fake signature you practiced in junior high when you were sure you were going to be famous one day.

Gloria

K-Ming Chang

GLORIA GAO WAS THE FIRST GIRL I ever hurt. I punched her in the face for calling my family a bunch of dirty mainlanders. I was Taiwanese like her too, but just half, on my mother's side, which meant the other half of my family must be made up of organ sellers, gutter spitters, and serial gamblers. It was true that I had an uncle who stabbed another man twice during a card game in the basement of a pet store; it was true my grandfather won my grandmother in a game of mahjong, along with a flute that he demonstrated how to play by prodding the mouth-tip into his ass and farting into it.

Gloria was a church girl. She thought she was better than us because she had dime-sized nipples and an almost-new navy Honda. She prayed every day, and her tongue must have been tuned into the right frequency, because her prayers always came true. She prayed for her own pocket-radio when she was nine and the next day they were growing from the sycamores like silver-skinned fruit, batteries falling out of the sky in a gunmetal rain. Then there was the time she prayed for the moles on her nose to be evicted from her skin, and the next day they fled her face as horseflies.

My grandfather went to the temple twice in his life. Once to pray for the lottery numbers to arrive as the number of birds in the sky. Once to pray I'd be born a boy. Both prayers were returned to sender. After he died, we pickled his ashes in a jar of rice vinegar and left him there as a lantern.

Gloria Gao wore a jade cross and skirts with overlapping layers like the bell of a tulip, and she was so thin I could see her bones go stealth beneath her skin. She had a mouth like a Ming Dynasty poem, weaned off cream and perfectly circular, and when she prayed—which was all the time, wherever she was—she lowered her head and muttered, forcing us all to watch her fold. The neighborhood girls and I joked to her once that she probably kneeled more than a prostitute. There were things we did to bend her faith like a fishbone, like stealing the side-view mirrors off her Honda while she was at church or sending her a text that read 666 every day for a month, but she remained above us all, a self-appointed saint. She was pristine as an apple and we all wanted to skin her.

I've never seen the inside of a church, but I imagine it's swollen with light—nothing like the temple where I went once to visit my grandfather. His name was pasted to the wall for the first one hundred days after death. Inside the temple, it was dark and damp, like the inside of a plum, the pit pulsing down my throat. I couldn't look at his last name, the one he gave me, the one I didn't say, the one Gloria called dirty. In the back of the room was a Buddha sitting cross-legged, shoulders slumped, face shedding gold paint, a chipped nose that reminded me of the time I punched Gloria, the sap of blood on my knuckles, the sweet. Her bottom lip unzipped against my fist. Her knees ducked to the street. *Take this, take this from me*, I wanted to say. Pray for me to stop. I'll answer to my name in your mouth.

Gloria got a chaste boyfriend, a church boy. The neighborhood girls and I planted thirty-one dollars in his pocket, along with a note urging him to get it in her and bring us proof when he did. *God designed you to do this*, we wrote, and he obeyed, bringing us her underwear dangling from his maw like a dog. We were disappointed by the plainness of them, no lace waistband to tattle on, no little satin bow, not even a pattern of cherries or hearts. They looked unworn, the kind of white that meant her mother owned a washing machine and didn't scrub the family's underwear in the sink with a stone shaped like a fist, the way our mothers did. We knew then that we would never dirty her.

I saw her alone once, in the parking lot of the church. It was true I was following her, true that I thought of kidnapping her family's beagle so that I'd see her again on her knees, searching for something. But I knew she was the kind to leash her losses and walk them down the street like shining beasts, so I left the dog alone. In the parking lot of the church, I saw her sit in the driver's seat of her almost-new Honda, put her hands on the wheel, and go nowhere. It was dark and no one knew where she was. The light was on in her backseat. I wanted to wear that light, so I knocked on the car window. She rolled it down and told me to go away, but instead I got in beside her, told her it was dangerous to sit in an unlocked car. Her glovebox was open and inside I could see the sweet beads of a rosary, and something that glistened behind it—a gun. She saw me looking and said it was for protection, that when her father first came to America he worked on a farm and shot pigs and strung them up, unbuttoning their skin. I told her there weren't any pigs here. I didn't know her mouth was capable of making that word, pig, and I pulled it from the air like a pin.

That night, she tried to teach me the word of God. She asked if I had ever felt his love. But all I could think about was her father with a pig slung across his shoulders, the satin shawl of its blood. In the backseat, she straddled my face, came in my mouth, knotted my wrists with ribbons of salt. I saw her nipples and they were ordinary, not currency, no faces minted into them. I hated how perfectly plotted her spine was, her symmetrical shadow, how she rummaged light from the whites of my eyes, how faithful I was to the taste of her.

Chew

Venita Blackburn

WE CHEW IN OUR FAMILY. It's our God-given freedom to chew what and when we want. I chewed the legs off my grandmother's piano. It keeled over and crushed her thirteen-year-old Bichon Frise, Gingersnap. My granddaddy laughed his ass off. Me and my brothers used to chew shapes into things all the time. We turned straws into palm trees. I made a lily out of a milk carton for my brother's girlfriend. I had to be careful around the seams and not use too much saliva or it would've turned to oatmeal. He busted my lip for that one. My boy is just like us, can't keep his teeth off things. He chewed a plastic coin into a funny shape and supposedly threw it at some girl. They suspended him for two days for a plastic coin. I had to sit in front of the superintendent with his blood-red hangnails while he read off a statement from a teacher. "Because of the zero tolerance policy, suspension was warranted after the disruption caused by the object. The student chewed a coin made of plastic until it resembled a bullet and threw it" yada yada "while yelling bang, bang" blah blah "repeatedly until the situation escalated" or some garbage. I had to sit there for thirty-nine minutes looking at that shitstorm of a desk. It was metal and the color of every dull memory I ever had, just covered in papers, papers, papers. He held his palms above the papers and patted the air as if disgusted, as if afraid to touch anything because he knew it all linked to him somehow. One wrong move would topple it, and he'd be late for some god-awful appointment or something. I told him to let's just get right down to it. He sighed like he'd heard the story a few too many times, from the teacher, from the principal, from that big-haired news anchor, and his own bosses probably. Still he needed to hear the story right from my boy. So that's what happened. My boy told the truth of it. I told my boy to be out with it, and he stayed quiet because kids don't know what to say without a question. What happened? I asked. "I chewed a shape the teacher thought was bad. She made me go to the principal, then she brought all my stuff and called you, Dad, to come get me." That's what he said. The superintendent dared to look at me like I coached him, like my boy is just so acutely aware of my breathing and knew every inhale and internal body gurgle and could tell the good from the bad. How is he supposed to know what gesture meant certain doom and which meant good job, son? But he said it right anyhow, "I never threw it at no one." My boy told me about that crooked-eared girl who teased him all the time about his dirty cuffs. I told him never wash your cuffs for a girl. If she can't love your grease and grit, she can't love you. Well, he washed his damn cuffs and got more teasing for the trouble. That's when he chewed that shape into the coin and supposedly threw it. I knew he wasn't trying to make a bullet and pretend to kill that girl. That's crazy. I told him to tell that pudgy superintendent what he was really trying to chew into that fake money. "I was trying to make a rocket. I chew rocket ships and I like guns and tanks and I was just trying to draw a rocket but it turned out to look more small like a bullet than like a rocket, and the teacher just thought it was a bullet." The teacher just thought it was a bullet. Boys that age chew all kinds of things. I must've chewed a cock into the side of a cereal box a hundred times before I knew what it was for. Boys just celebrate themselves, you know. It's human. But the superintendent didn't get it. He just sat there on his secretary's wide wood chair thinking, "*Your boy is an unholy wretch that will grow up to hurt people. The world is going to have to kill him someday. He'll embarrass you and drive you indoors for good. You are an enabler. You think you're helping, but you're reinforcing terrible behavior. There are volumes of books written, studies done, talk shows even, about you and your boy. There will be nowhere safe to drive to except hills with no life on them.*" The superintendent blinked. He looked at the stacks of pink and yellow papers, folded and crinkled, some thin as spit, and blinked. What right did he or anybody have to judge me and mine? They call it enabling. I'm enabling my son to keep on with his bad behavior. They just don't understand our lives. Maybe he did chew a bullet on purpose, and throw it, and push her down, and kick her until she cried. We all chew to survive in this world. My granddaddy chewed, up until his last days on this earth, a little foil applesauce lid. He made a teacup for my grandmother. I heard she told him to swallow it for being such a mean bastard all his life, but that's just how they loved each other. Everybody else can't know what it's like to put something in your mouth and have something different come out, what it means, the power. They just want to take it from us, keep us docile like starved dogs. They don't know anything about how we live, love, and die. My boy is innocent. My boy is gifted.

Tall Grass

Ann Pancake

S HE IS BORN IN TALL GRASS there between the apple trees, them like crippled old people looking on, and the bugs looting heavy after she comes. Timothy beards sloppy with it. Their seed a dry seed. Mother fourteen years old and this when it is mostly white men work the orchard, only a few Puerto Ricans for the dirtiest jobs and no blacks, but her grandaddy watches her close, though she grows up rust-colored like the rest. A rust-speckled enamel. Sweat bees, bottle flies, wheeling away from the mess in the grass with her birth on the bottoms of their feet.

Fried sour apples and canned meat she remembers earliest, the shanty a kerosene throat gob of a winter. Come summer, she plays in the peach rot in the corner of the packing shed while her mother bags, winesaps rumbling the antiquated conveyor belt, and the women laughing full from their throats. Let's get it in high gear, this from Mister, but the women just crow, and it is only Ervin, locust husk on a high stool, who mutters and bulls. There she learns bees. Her lip stung and her crying obliterated in the ungreased gears and the apple chutter and the hoots of the women, her lip ballooning to fill the rafters. Busting past those to rub the clouds. Later, in early winter, she will squat whole afternoons in a forgotten crate along one of the orchard rows. Frost smoking mysterious off petrified grass, the grass, she sees, in clumps thrown forward, like women with fresh-washed hair, forward thrown in clumps. Heaved like that. And the deer in the distance trodding this hair tender.

Teenage 1970s and the migrants, Puerto Ricans and Jamaicans, African big-bundled heads walking rigid-backed the shoulders of the county road under the drench of an Appalachian August night sky. The brown people get shanties like hers, but the black ones are put up in abandoned school buses, and the scent from the dining hall a foreign breeze so much more complicated than salt, black pepper, and pork. She stands the edge of the lot, breathes it before heading home. Thirteen, she is packing now, and Angelino rides to the shed on the flatbed behind Mister's tractor, Angelino pulling the crates, ball-muscled in his arms, and flinging fruit on the line.

Conceived, then born, she reconceives in tall grass, her Angelino kneading her between the legs, speaking surf in her face, rolls out and sprays. He has come, he tells her, across an ocean, and an ocean is something she will never see. This on Sunday afternoons, her grandaddy not letting her out after dark. Unromantic dog day sun, the grass bleached and the bees bad in their wet. Her creeping to the little creek in the hollow seam after it's done, lying full-length in knee-deep water and glad to take stones in her back. And she reworks it in her head until she reaches a point between a weeping and a come, which she will know no better than the ocean.

Her mother a grandma at twenty-seven, her own a great at forty-two. Her grandaddy has raised two generations, but balks at three, and the old man, Ervin, agrees to marry her with a television thrown in. Shocking handsome by three years old, her son is dark, curly-headed, looks like none of her people, and she calls him Angelino, but the old man calls him Karl. The old man rubs his infant skin at night with Ivory soap, wishful at making it lighter.

In the early eighties, the orchard bankrupts and the shanties are empty year-round except those of the whites who have no place to leave to. Lush apple waste, the trees untended, unthinned, but still sapping, budding, blooming, swelling, to shrivel knot-hard on branches or rot and smear in the grass. Deer ranging bold, and the yellow jackets, delirious. Her mother by now has taken up with a chicken catcher a county over and appears on holidays to straddle the front stoop and cuss the out-of-state tags driving dirt in the shanty as they pass up the hill to their new weekend homes.

The other children come rust-haired and speckled like herself. Her forced to sleep between the old man and the wall, a familiar old-people odor of stalish urine and a yeast unwashed. And her life a weight, thrown again and again, against that wall. One weekday in January she must escape the house, the little ones intolerable fussy and the woodstove stoked like Satan. She bundles them and goes, Angelino with the three-year-old by the hand and the baby smashed across her chest, riding sidesaddle the fourth in her belly. The cloud cover is a patchy flannel, and the sun, straining from the far south, falls through in tired pieces. Above, the weekend homes castle the ridge among acres of uprooted fruit trees pitched in heaps to die. She drives her children ahead of her to an interruption in the grass. The tall grass, winter-blond and humped, abruptly close-cropped and brittle. A lawn. Mama, can we see inside?

Finding a chunk of limestone smaller than her fist, she shatters a rear window, bloodying her knuckles a bit. Works out the shards with her coat doubled over her arm, and then she boosts her Angelino through. He meets them at the front door and every footfall on the plush rug is a gasp, a pleasure, under a gallery of self-photographs the second-homers have hung. The chocolate pie they discover in the refrigerator is missing only one piece. She feeds them from a single spoon, deciding dirtying more would be bad manners, while each weekend face beams from the wall. And between turns, her babies wallow, luxurious, in the cream carpet.

How to Be a Conqueror

Matthew Salesses

1. In 1956, John Wayne played Genghis Khan in *The Conqueror*. It was a Howard Hughes film, shot, epic-scale, in the deserts of Utah. Susan Hayward was a Tartar princess, stolen away to the Mongolian Steppes. The last line was: "From forth their loins sprang a race of conquerors."

2. Utah had been a successful nuclear test site three years earlier. Of the 220 Hollywooders involved with *The Conqueror*, 91 were eventually diagnosed with cancer. Susan Hayward died of complications in 1975, and John Wayne followed four years later. Under normal circumstances, maybe 30 of the 220 *should have* expected cancer.

3. Barry watched the movie knowing these facts. He liked to come home from teaching to a movie. He ate dinner in front of the TV. This had been his routine since his girlfriend had left him in May. Now it

was December, and the wind carried the cold from pocket to pocket. He stuffed his hands into his pajamas as if to hoard up all his warmth.

4. The movies he liked best were the ones in which white people played Asian leads. Since his girlfriend had left, that had seemed to become more of a fact. He took pleasure in watching *The Conqueror*, knowing who would get it and who wouldn't.

5. Barry taught his fifth-grade class that Genghis Khan was not terrible. Genghis Khan *had* murdered, but he had also united his people. Genghis Khan's real name was Temüjin. As Khan of Mongolia, he had established a meritocracy, disallowed racism and religious prejudice, and enforced women's rights.

6. In *The Conqueror*, John Wayne said, "There are moments for wisdom and moments when I listen to my blood; my blood says, take this Tartar woman."

7. Barry had trouble suspending his disbelief. His girlfriend had left a list of what to work on for his next relationship. Suspending his disbelief followed one bullet. "•Do not doubt yourself," she had written. Not being so serious followed another.

8. As he watched, he began to wonder which scene had given which actor his fatal dose of radiation. The film was really about life and death.

9. Rereading his girlfriend's letter, she hadn't said anything about race. She had said, in the strangest line that seemed a little less strange, "We never fought."

10. After Genghis Khan defeated the Jin Dynasty, he told the Khitan prince, Chu'Tsai, that the prince's forefathers had been avenged. Chu'Tsai's father had worked under the Jin regime that had overthrown the Khitan. The prince replied that his father had served the Dynasty well, and he did not consider his father his enemy, so revenge did not apply. Genghis Khan left him in charge of much of Mongolia.

11. Barry watched the yellow-faced actor with empathy.

12. Genghis Khan once wrote to a Taoist monk: "I, living in the northern wilderness, have not inordinate passions."

13. John Wayne said: "I stole you. I will keep you. Before the sun sets, you will come willingly to my arms."

The Solution to Brian's Problem

Bonnie Jo Campbell

SOLUTION #1

Connie said she was going out to the store to buy formula and diapers. While she's gone, load up the truck with the surround-sound-home-entertainment system and your excellent collection of power tools, put the baby boy in the car seat, and drive away from this home you built with your own hands. Expect that after you leave, she will break all the windows in this living room, including the big picture window, as well as the big mirror over the fireplace, which you've already replaced twice. The furnace will run and run. Then she will go to your mother's looking for you, and when she does not find you, she will curse at your mother and possibly attempt to burn your mother's house down. Connie has long admired the old three-story farmhouse for its west-facing dining room with window seats and the cupola with a view for miles around. You and Connie have discussed living there someday.

SOLUTION #2

Wait until Connie comes back from the "store," distract her with the baby, and then cut her meth with Drano, so that when she shoots it up, she dies.

SOLUTION #3

Put the baby boy to bed in his crib and sit on the living room couch until Connie comes home. Before she has a chance to lie about where she's been, grab her hair and knock her head hard into the fireplace that you built from granite blocks that came from the old chimney of the house your great-grandfather built when your family first came to this country from Finland—blocks you gathered from the old foundation in the woods. Don't look at the wedding photos on the mantel. Don't look at Connie's wide wedding-day smile, or the way her head tilts back in an ecstasy that seems to have nothing to do with drugs. Don't let the blood stop you from hitting her one final time to make sure you have cracked her skull. Put her meth and her bag of syringes and blood-smeared needles in her hand so the cops find them when they arrive. You will tell them it was an accident, that you were arguing and the argument escalated because she threatened to shoot meth into your baby.

SOLUTION #4

Just go. Head south where it's warm. After a few hours, pull over at a truck stop and call your mother to warn her to call the cops if she sees Connie. After that, pretend not to have a wife and baby boy. When put to the test, Connie might well rise to the occasion of motherhood. Contact the union about getting a job with another local. Resist taking any photographs along with you, especially the photographs of your baby at every age. Wipe your mind clear of memories, especially the memory of your wife first telling you she was pregnant and how that pregnancy and her promise to stay clean made everything seem possible. Do not remember how the two of you kept holding hands that night, how you couldn't stop reaching for each other, even in your sleep. She lost that baby, and the next one, and although you suspected the reason, you kept on trying.

SOLUTION #5

Blow your head off with the twelve-gauge you keep behind the seat of your truck. Load the shotgun with shells, put the butt against the floor, rest your chin on the barrel, and pull the trigger. Let your wife find your bloody, headless corpse in the living room; let her scrape your brain from these walls. Maybe that will shock her into straightening up her act. Let her figure out how to pay the mortgage and the power bill.

SOLUTION #6

Call a help line, talk to a counselor, explain that last week your wife stabbed you in the chest while you were sleeping, that she punches you, too, giving you black eyes that you have to explain to the guys at work. Explain that you're in danger of losing your job, your house, your baby. Tell her Connie has sold your mountain bike and some of your excellent power tools already, that you have been locking the remainder in your truck, which you park a few blocks away from the house now. Try to be patient when the counselor seems awkward in her responses, when she inadvertently expresses surprise at the nature of your distress, especially when you admit that Connie's only five-foot-three. Expect the counselor to be even less supportive when you say, hell yes, you hit her back. Tell the counselor that it's the little things, too, that at least once a week Connie rearranges things in the house, not only the furniture, but your financial files and the food, all of which last week she moved to the basement, including the milk and meat, which you then had to throw away. Then realize that the counselor probably has caller ID. Hope that the counselor doesn't call Social Services, because a baby needs his momma. Assure the counselor that Connie is a good momma, that she's good with the baby, that the baby is in no danger.

SOLUTION #7

Make dinner for yourself and your wife with the hamburger in the fridge. Sloppy joes, maybe, or goulash with the stewed tomatoes your mother canned, your mother who, like the rest of the family, thinks your wife is just moody. You haven't told them the truth, because it's too much to explain, and it's too much to explain that, yes, you knew she had this history when you married her, when she got pregnant, but you thought you could kick it together, you thought that love could mend all broken things—wasn't that the whole business of love? Mix up some bottles of formula for later tonight, when you will be sitting in the living room feeding the baby, watching the door of the bathroom, behind which your wife will be searching for a place in her vein that has not hardened or collapsed. When she finally comes out, brush her hair back from her face, and try to get her to eat something.

Never-Never Time

Justin Torres

WE ALL THREE SAT AT the kitchen table in our raincoats, and
Joel smashed tomatoes with a small rubber mallet. We had
seen it on TV: a man with an untamed mustache and a mallet slaugh-
tering vegetables, and people in clear plastic ponchos soaking up the
mess, having the time of their lives. We aimed to smile like that. We
felt the pop and smack of tomato guts exploding; the guts dripped
down the walls and landed on our cheeks and foreheads and congealed
in our hair. When we ran out of tomatoes, we went into the bathroom
and pulled out tubes of our mother's lotions from under the sink. We
took off our raincoats and positioned ourselves so that when the mallet
slammed down and forced out the white cream, it would get everywhere, the creases of our shut-tight eyes and the folds of our ears.

Our mother came into the kitchen, pulling her robe shut and rubbing her eyes, saying, "Man oh man, what time is it?" We told her it
was eight-fifteen, and she said fuck, still keeping her eyes closed, just
rubbing them harder, and then she said fuck again, louder, and picked

up the teakettle and slammed it down on the stove and screamed, "Why aren't you in school?"

It was eight-fifteen at night, and besides, it was a Sunday, but no one told Ma that. She worked graveyard shifts at the brewery up the hill from our house, and sometimes she got confused. She would wake randomly, mixed up, mistaking one day for another, one hour for the next, order us to brush our teeth and get into PJs and lie in bed in the middle of the day; or when we came into the kitchen in the morning, half asleep, she'd be pulling a meat loaf out of the oven, saying, "What is wrong with you boys? I been calling and calling for dinner."

We had learned not to correct her or try to pull her out of the confusion; it only made things worse. Once, before we'd known better, Joel refused to go to the neighbors and ask for a stick of butter. It was nearly midnight and she was baking a cake for Manny.

"Ma, you're crazy," Joel said. "Everyone's sleeping, and it's not even his birthday."

She studied the clock for a good while, shook her head quickly back and forth, and then focused on Joel; she bored deep in his eyes as if she was looking past his eyeballs, into the lower part of his brain. Her mascara was all smudged and her hair was stiff and thick, curling black around her face and matted down in the back. She looked like a raccoon caught digging in the trash: surprised, dangerous.

"I hate my life," she said.

That made Joel cry, and Manny punched him hard on the back of the head.

"Nice one, asswipe," he hissed. "It was going to be my fucking birthday."

After that, we went along with whatever she came up with; we lived in dreamtime. Some nights Ma piled us into the car and drove out to the grocery store, the laundromat, the bank. We stood behind her, giggling, when she pulled at the locked doors, or when she shook the heavy security grating and cursed.

She gasped now, finally noticing the tomato and lotion streaking down our faces. She opened her eyes wide and then squinted. She called us to her side and gently ran a finger across each of our cheeks, cutting through the grease and sludge. She gasped again.

"That's what you looked like when you slid out of me," she whispered. "Just like that."

We all groaned, but she kept on talking about it, about how slimy we were coming out, about how Manny was born with a full head of hair and it shocked her. The first thing she did with each one of us was to count our fingers and toes. "I wanted to make sure they hadn't left any in there," she said, and sent us into a fit of pretend barfing noises.

"Do it to me."

"What?" we asked.

"Make me born."

"We're out of tomatoes," Manny said.

"Use ketchup."

We gave her my raincoat because it was the cleanest, and we warned her no matter what not to open her eyes until we said it was OK. She got down on her knees and rested her chin on the table. Joel raised the mallet above his head, and Manny squared the neck of the ketchup bottle between her eyes.

"On the count of three," we said, and we each took a number—my number was last. We all took the deepest, longest breath we could, sucking the air through our teeth. Everyone had his face all clenched up, his hands squeezed into fists. We sucked in a little more air, and our chests swelled. The room felt like a balloon must, when you're blowing and blowing and blowing, right before it pops.

"Three!"

And the mallet swung through the air. Our mother yelped and slid to the floor and stayed there, her eyes wide open and ketchup everywhere, looking like she had been shot in the back of the head.

"It's a mom!" we screamed. "Congratulations!" We ran to the cupboards and pulled out the biggest pots and heaviest ladles and clanged them as loud as we could, dancing around our mother's body, shouting, "Happy Birthday! . . . Happy New Year! . . . It's zero o'clock . . . It's never-never time! . . . It's the time of your life!"

AFTERWORD

I T IS TRUE THAT THE TITLE *Flash Fiction* was occasioned by a freak winter lightning storm in Ohio, over three decades ago. It struck at the precise time that the editors needed to come up with a name for a short story form that sounded more urgent than *Sudden*, which had been used a few years before.

When the book came out, the very short stories fell like spring rain on the literary landscape. Readers found the form refreshing and accessible. Brevity was key, and some critics attributed *Flash Fiction*'s success to the shortening of the American attention span. So much so that *Publishers Weekly* referred to the book as "good subway reading," and starred it.

Poets pointed to the latent energy of the words left out and the power of the voice that remained. Artists talked about minimalism and magic, texture and light, canvases implicit and explicit at the same time. Journalists noted the form's sharp edges, words boxed in and insistent to be heard, right now. Literary critics cheered but held their breath.

But it was among writers and readers themselves that the form took hold. Here suddenly was an entire volume of uniquely whole stories, each of them only a few pages long. A feast to devour. Both teachers and students sat down to the table and fell in love with the possibilities. Fewer words led to an unexpected freedom. It seemed the writer could take a deep breath and exhale meaningfully onto the page. Making more out of less.

This was all before the internet. Finding the stories for that first *Flash Fiction* meant many visits to many libraries, maneuvering through the stacks to find literary magazines and books in print, and others on microfiche in a separate room. Computer programs were a lot of trouble and there weren't so many MFA programs. Email was a hassle and writers didn't know much about one another. That was thirty years ago.

The new century changed everything. Cell phones proliferated, GPS steered us around, search engines explicated literary history and shed light on writers. Online magazines popped up and their stories were free to read. Libraries flung open their doors and independent publishers showcased new authors. Books ordered online arrived on your porch before you knew it. When it came time to make *Flash Fiction Forward* in 2008 the databases were humming and could be spun into reliable research.

Those early online magazines defined the genre through example and spread the word. *SmokeLong Quarterly* came on the scene in 2003, waving the thousand-word flag, and illuminating the stories by interviewing the authors. With this and other congenial magazines and inviting websites, a sort of open forum developed where authors started exchanging gossip and news of each other's publications, often offering criticism. *The Rose Metal Press Field Guide to Writing Flash Fiction*, edited by Tara Lynn Masih, was a watershed for practitioners when it was published in 2009. By this time there were university course offerings, conference panel discussions, networks and workshops, and organized reading series nationwide.

Flash Fiction Forward followed a generation of technological development to a place where time and space seemed to collide and new story shapes emerged. It was an easy book to carry around, good for coffee shop reading and making mental notes, prompting friendly arguments about character interaction and unfolding events. Narrative.

Then readers realized that flash wasn't just a U.S. phenomenon but had spread all over the world. It seemed that people in far-ranging places were interested in eavesdropping on their cross-border neighbors, window-peeping into other people's business and hearing their stories, real and surreal, told quickly. It was natural that a good number of those stories, some of the most deftly told ones, would find their way into another anthology, *Flash Fiction International*, published in 2015.

But it seemed that as soon as that book had set sail to favorable reviews and worldwide attention, it was time to return to America, where the form's popularity had rocketed and in 2017 *The New Yorker* came online with its "Flash Fiction Summer Series," expanding the audience and increasing the form's legitimacy. If *Flash Fiction International* showed the wide variety of stories being told today in many different cultures around the globe, *Flash Fiction America* speaks to the diversity of voices heard here now. Much has changed over thirty years. The geography is the same but the light has changed, the landscape is more vibrant.

Technology has everything to do with it. Media channels have transformed how we receive narrative, and news is filtered and delivered to us in ever smaller packets. Highly charged language pulls us in and pushes us away. And since writers are loud, their stories fly out from every platform, fiction on the wing. But some stories land on the printed page, touch down on the truth, and there are more books being published today than ever before.

Flash Fiction America is democratic. The book is a house with many small windows, but a door big enough to let everyone in. The stories are told in many different ways and through multiple voices, and that's the point, it is noisy. The book was made to entertain, but also edify, with new writers in mind. It is full of narrative strategies, new ways of telling truths that will break the fall, resonate with meaning. The words on the page will show you the way in and show you the way out, with a ticket to ride, all the way home.

—*James Thomas*

BOOKS BY THE AUTHORS

Christopher Allen ("When Chase Prays Chocolate"): *Other Household Toxins* (Matter Press, 2018).

Jensen Beach ("Family"): *Swallowed by the Cold* (Graywolf Press, 2016); *For Out of the Heart Proceed* (Dark Sky Books, 2012).

Aimee Bender ("Origin Lessons"): *The Butterfly Lampshade: A Novel* (Anchor, 2020); *The Color Master: Stories* (Anchor, 2013); *The Particular Sadness of Lemon Cake* (Anchor, 2010); *The Girl in the Flammable Skirt: Stories* (Anchor, 1998).

Venita Blackburn ("Chew"): *How to Wrestle a Girl: Stories* (MCD x FSG Originals, 2021); *Black Jesus and Other Superheroes: Stories* (University of Nebraska Press, 2017).

Randall Brown ("Theo & Annie"): *This Is How He Learned to Love* (Sonder Press, 2019); *How Long Is Forever* (Running Wild Press, 2018); *I Might Never Learn* (Finishing Line Press, 2018); *Mad to Live* (PS Books, 2011).

Bonnie Jo Campbell ("The Solution to Brian's Problem"): *Mothers, Tell Your Daughters: Stories* (W. W. Norton, 2016); *Once Upon River* (W. W. Norton, 2012); *American Salvage* (W. W. Norton, 2009).

Joy Castro ("A Notion I Took"): *Flight Risk: A Novel* (Lake Union Publishing, 2021); *How Winter Began: Stories* (University of Nebraska Press, 2015); *Nearer Home: A Novel* (Thomas Dunne Books, 2013); *Island of Bones: Essays* (University of Nebraska Press, 2012).

K-Ming Chang ("Gloria"): *Gods of Want: Stories* (One World, 2022); *Bestiary: A Novel* (One World, 2021); *Bone House* (chapbook, Bull City Press, 2021).

Rita Zoey Chin ("Solo"): *The Strange Inheritance of Leah Fern: A Novel* (Melville House, 2022); *Let the Tornado Come: A Memoir* (Simon & Schuster, 2014).

Tyrese L. Coleman ("Dear Nnamdi"): *How to Sit: A Memoir in Stories and Essays* (Mason Jar Press, 2018).

Desiree Cooper ("Something Falls in the Night"): *Know the Mother* (Wayne State University Press, 2016).

Chauna Craig ("High on the Divide"): *Wings and Other Things* (Press 53, 2022); *The Widow's Guide to Edible Mushrooms* (Press 53, 2017).

Lydia Davis ("Varieties of Disturbance"): *Essays Two: On Proust, Translation, Foreign Languages, and the City of Arles* (Farrar, Straus and Giroux, 2021); *Essays One* (Picador, 2020); *Can't and Won't: Stories* (Picador, 2015); *The Collected Stories of Lydia Davis* (Picador, 2010); *Varieties of Disturbance: Stories* (Picador, 2007).

Natalie Diaz ("The Gospel of Guy No-Horse"): *Postcolonial Love Poem* (Graywolf, 2020); *When My Brother Was an Aztec* (Copper Canyon Press, 2012).

Steven Dunn ("At the Taxidermy Museum of Military Heroes"): *Water & Power* (Tarpaulin Sky Press, 2018); *Potted Meat* (Tarpaulin Sky Press, 2016).

Stuart Dybek ("Bruise"): *The Start of Something: The Selected Stories of Stuart Dybek* (Vintage, 2017); *Ecstatic Cahoots: Fifty Short Stories* (Farrar, Straus and Giroux, 2014); *Paper Lantern: Love Stories* (Farrar, Straus and Giroux, 2014); *I Sailed with Magellan: Stories* (Farrar, Straus and Giroux, 2003).

Grant Faulkner ("23 Men"): *All the Comfort Sin Can Provide* (Black Lawrence Press, 2021); *Nothing Short of 100* (Outpost19, 2019); *Pep Talks for Writers* (Chronicle Books, 2017); *Fissures: One Hundred 100-Word Stories* (Press 53, 2015).

Kathy Fish ("Some Hard, Hot Places"): *Wild Life: Collected Works* (Matter Press, 2018); *Rift* (with Robert Vaughan, Unknown Press, 2015); *Together We Can Bury It* (The Lit Pub LLC, 2012).

Stefanie Freele ("James Brown Is Alive and Doing Laundry in South Lake Tahoe"): *Surrounded by Water* (Press 53, 2012); *Feeding Strays: Short Stories* (Lost Horse Press, 2011).

Molly Giles ("My X") *Wife with Knife* (Leapfrog Press, 2021); *All the Wrong Places* (Lost Horse Press, 2015); *Three for the Road: Stories* (SheBooks, 2014); *Iron Shoes: A Novel* (Simon & Schuster, 2001).

Amy Hempel ("Beach Town"): *Sing to It: Stories* (Scribner, 2019); *The Dog of the Marriage: Stories* (RiverRun, 2009); *The Collected Stories of Amy Hempel* (Scribner, 2007); *Tumble Home: A Novella and Short Stories* (Scribner, 1998).

Justin Herrmann ("Dimetrodon"): *Highway One: Antarctica* (MadHat Press, 2014).

Aubrey Hirsch ("Amelia"): *Why We Never Talk About Sugar* (Braddock Avenue Books, 2013); *This Will Be His Legacy* (Lettered Streets Press, 2014).

Dave Housley ("The Combat Photographer"): *The Other Ones: A Novel* (Alan Squire Publishing, 2022); *Howard and Charles at the Factory* (Outpost19, 2020); *If I Knew the Way, I Would Take You Home* (Dzanc Books, 2015); *Ryan Seacrest is Famous* (Impetus Press, 2008).

Randa Jarrar ("A Sailor"): *Love Is an Ex-Country* (Catapult, 2021); *Him, Me, Muhammed Ali* (Sarabande Books, 2016); *A Map of Home: A Novel* (Penguin Books, 2009).

Gwen E. Kirby ("Shit Cassandra Saw That She Didn't Tell the Trojans Because at That Point Fuck Them Anyway"): *Shit Casandra Saw: Stories* (Penguin Books, 2022).

Juan Martinez ("Customer Service at the Karaoke Don Quixote"): *Best Worst American: Stories* (Small Beer Press, 2017).

Michael Martone ("Sketches of the School Staff in Winesburg, Indiana"): *Plain Air:*

Sketches from Winesburg, Indiana (Baobob Press, 2022); *The Complete Writings of Art Smith, the Bird Boy of Fort Wayne, Edited by Michael Martone* (BOA Editions, 2020); *The Moon Over Wapakoneta: Fiction and Science Fictions from Indiana and Beyond* (Fiction Collective 2, 2018); *Four for a Quarter: Fictions* (Fiction Collective 2, 2011).

Dantiel W. Moniz ("Exotics"): *Milk Blood Heat* (Grove Press, 2021).

Darlin' Neal ("Misty Blue Waters"): *Elegant Punk* (Press 53, 2012); *Rattlesnakes & the Moon* (Press 53, 2010).

Pamela Painter ("The Kiss"): *Fabrications: New and Selected* Stories (John Hopkins University Press, 2020); *Ways to Spend the Night: Stories* (Engine Books, 2016); *Wouldn't You Like to Know: Very Short Stories* (Carnegie University Press, 2010); *Getting to Know the Weather* (Carnegie Mellon University Press, 2008).

Ann Pancake ("Tall Grass"): *Me and My Daddy Listen to Bob Marley* (Counterpoint Press, 2016); *Strange as This Weather Has Been* (Counterpoint Press, 2007); *Given Ground* (University Press of New England, 2001).

Kimberly King Parsons ("The Touch"): *Black Light* (Vintage, 2019).

Deesha Philyaw ("Not Daniel"): *The Secret Lives of Church Ladies* (West Virginia University Press, 2020).

Meg Pokrass ("Pounds Across America"): *Spinning to Mars* (Blue Light Press, 2021); *The Dog Seated Next to Me* (Pelekinesis, 2020); *The Dog Looks Happy Upside Down* (Etruscan Press, 2016); *Damn Sure Right* (Press 53, 2011).

Nicole Rivas ("Hatched"): *A Bright and Pleading Dagger* (Rose Metal Press, 2018).

Michelle Ross ("The Pregnancy Game"): *They Kept Running* (University of North Texas, 2022); *Shapeshifting* (Stillhouse Press, 2021); *There's So Much They Haven't Told You* (Moon City Press, 2017).

Maurice Carlos Ruffin ("Bigsby"): *The Ones Who Don't Say They Love You: Stories* (One World, 2021); *We Cast a Shadow: A Novel* (One World, 2019).

Matthew Salesses ("How to Be a Conqueror"): *Craft in the Real World: Rethinking Fiction Writing and Workshopping* (Catapult, 2021); *Disappear Doppelgänger Disappear* (Little A, 2020); *The Hundred-Year Flood* (Little A, 2015); *I'm Not Saying, I'm Just Saying* (Civil Coping Mechanisms, 2013).

Joshunda Sanders ("Rhythm"): *I Can Write the World* (picture book with Charley Palmer, Six Foot Press, 2019); *The Beautiful Darkness: A Handbook for Orphans* (CreateSpace, 2016); *How Racism and Sexism Killed Traditional Media: Why the Future of Journalism Depends on Women and People of Color* (Praeger, 2015).

Robert Scotellaro ("Nothing Is Ever One Thing"): *Ways to Read the World: Stories in Triptych* (Scantic Books, 2022); *What Are the Chances* (Press 53, 2020); *Nothing Is Ever One Thing* (Blue Light Press, 2019); *New Micro: Exceptionally Short Fiction* (with James Thomas, W. W. Norton, 2018); *What We Know So Far* (Blue Light Press, 2015).

Rion Amilcar Scott ("Boxing Day"): *The World Doesn't Require You: Stories* (Liveright, 2020); *Insurrections: Stories* (University Press of Kentucky, 2017).

Sejal Shah ("Skin"): *This Is One Way to Dance: Essays* (University of Georgia Press, 2020).

Robert Shapard ("Lobster"): *Flash Fiction International: Very Short Stories from Around the World* (with James Thomas and Christopher Merrill, W. W. Norton, 2015); *Flash Fiction Forward: 80 Very Short Stories* (with James Thomas, W. W. Norton, 2006); *Motel and Other Stories* (Predator Press, 2005); *Stories in the Stepmother Tongue* (with Josip Novakovich, White Pine Press, 2000).

Sadia Quraeshi Shepard ("Monsters"): *The Girl from Foreign: A Memoir* (Penguin Books, 2009).

Amber Sparks ("The Logic of the Loaded Heart"): *And I Do Not Forgive You: Stories and Other Revenges* (Liveright, 2021); *The Unfinished World: And Other Stories* (Liveright, 2016); *May We Shed These Human Bodies* (Curbside Splendor, 2012).

Pete Stevens ("Beethoven's Fifth in C Minor"): *Tomorrow Music* (Map Literary, 2021).

Terese Svoboda ("Seconds"): *Great American Desert* (Mad Creek Books, 2019); *Professor Harriman's Airship* (Eyewear Publishing, 2016); *When the Next Big War Blows Down the Valley* (Anhunga Press, 2015); *A Drink Called Paradise* (Dzanc Books, 2014); *Tin God* (University of Nebraska Press, 2006), *Trailer Girl and Other Stories* (Counterpoint, 2001).

Lisa Teasley ("Why I Could Never Be Boogie"): *Heat Signature: A Novel* (Bloomsbury, 2006); *Dive: A Novel* (Bloomsbury, 2006); *Glow in the Dark* (Cune Press, 2002); *FLUID, stories* (Cune Press, 2023).

Justin Torres ("Never-Never Time"): *We the Animals: A Novel* (Mariner Books, 2012).

Luis Alberto Urrea ("The White Girl"): *The House of Broken Angels* (Back Bay Books, 2019); *The Water Museum: Stories* (Back Bay Books, 2016); *Queen of America: A Novel* (Back Bay Books, 2012); *Into the Beautiful North: A Novel* (Back Bay Books, 2010); *The Hummingbird's Daughter* (Little, Brown and Company, 2005).

Kara Vernor ("David Hasselhoff Is from Baltimore"): *Because I Wanted to Write You a Pop Song: Stories* (Split/Lip Press, 2016).

Bryan Washington ("How Many"): *Lot: Stories* (Riverhead Books, 2020); *Memorial: A Novel* (Riverhead Books, 2020).

Diane Williams ("The Beauty and the Bat"): *How High? That High* (Soho Press, 2021); *The Collected Stories of Diane Williams* (Soho Press, 2019); *Fine, Fine, Fine, Fine, Fine* (McSweeney's Publishing, 2016); *Vicky Swanky Is a Beauty* (McSweeney's Publishing, 2012); *It Was Like My Trying to Have a Tender-Hearted Nature: A Novella and Stories* (Fiction Collective 2, 2007).

Kate Wisel ("I'm Exaggerating"): *Driving in Cars with Homeless Men: Stories* (University of Pittsburgh Press, 2020).

Francine Witte ("Radio Water"): *The Way of the Wind* (Ad Hoc Fiction, 2020); *Dressed All Wrong for This* (Blue Light Press, 2019).

Jennifer Wortman ("Willing"): This. This. This. Is. Love. Love. Love. (Split/Lip Press, 2019).

Tessa Yang ("The Weatherman's Heart"): *The Runaway Restaurant* (7.13 Books, 2022)

CREDITS

Grant Faulkner, "23 Men," from *All the Comfort Sin Can Provide*, Black Lawrence Press 2021, copyright Grant Faulkner. Reprinted by permission of Black Lawrence Press.

Yalitza Ferreras, "The One-Eyed Bat!," from *Aster(ix) Journal* October 2019, copyright Yalitza Ferreras. Reprinted by permission of Yalitza Ferreras.

Kathy Fish, "Some Hard, Hot Places," from *Ploughshares* Summer 2021, copyright Kathy Fish. Reprinted by permission of Kathy Fish.

Stefanie Freele, "James Brown Is Alive and Doing Laundry in South Lake Tahoe," from *Feeding Strays*, Lost Horse Press 2009, copyright Stefanie Freele. Reprinted by permission of Lost Horse Press.

Molly Giles, "My X," from *Wife with Knife*, Leapfrog Press 2021, copyright Molly Giles. Reprinted by permission of Leapfrog Press.

Amy Hempel, "Beach Town," From *The Dog of the Marriage* by Amy Hempel. Copyright 2005 by Amy Hempel. Reprinted with the permission of Scribner, a division of Simon & Schuster, Inc. All rights reserved. From *The Collected Stories of Amy Hempel* (Scribner, 2006) and originally published by Tin House. Copyright © 1999 by Amy Hempel. All rights reserved. Used with permission.

Justin Herrmann, "Dimetrodon," from *Washington Square Review* 2012, copyright Justin Herrmann. Reprinted by permission of Justin Herrmann.

Aubrey Hirsch, "Amelia," from *SmokeLong Quarterly* October 2010, copyright Aubrey Hirsch. Reprinted by permission of Aubrey Hirsch.

Dave Housley, "The Combat Photographer," first published in *Hobart*, from *Ryan Seacrest is Famous*, Impetus Press 2007, copyright Dave Housley. Reprinted by permission of Dave Housley.

Randa Jarrar, "A Sailor," from *Him, Me, Muhammad Ali: A Memoir*, copyright 2021 by Randa Jarrar. Reprinted with permission of The Permissions Company, LLC, on behalf of Sarabande Books, www.sarabandebooks.org.

Gwen E. Kirby, "Shit Cassandra Saw That She Didn't Tell the Trojans Because at that Point Fuck Them Anyway," from *Shit Cassandra Saw: Stories*, copyright 2022 by Gwen E. Kirby. Used by permission of Penguin Books, an imprint of Penguin Publishing Group, a division of Penguin Random House LLC. All rights reserved.

Honor Levy, "Good Boys," from *The New Yorker* July 23, 2020, copyright Honor Levy. Reprinted by permission of Honor Levy.

Juan Martinez, "Customer Service at the Karaoke Don Quixote," copyright 2000 by Juan Martinez. First published in *McSweeney's* and reprinted in W. W. Norton's *Sudden*

EDITORS' NOTE

THE EDITORS ARE INDEBTED TO the many wonderful people who have helped make this book a reality: The authors who have graciously allowed us to bring together their stories in these pages, the editors and publishers, big and small, who first printed the work, our editor Amy Cherry, editorial assistant Huneeya Siddiqui, Nat Sobel, Adia Wright, Dave Cole, Danielle Evans, and Lisa Robinson. We would also like to thank Cindy Chinelly and Rick Schweikert for their patience and encouragement.

ABOUT THE EDITORS

James Thomas has received a Wallace Stegner Fellowship from Stanford University, a Michener Grant from the University of Iowa, and two NEA grants. He founded *Quarterly West* magazine and directed the Writers at Work Conference. He has co-edited all nine of the *Flash*, *Sudden*, and *Micro* anthologies. He has taught at the University of Utah and Wright State University. He lives in Xenia, Ohio.

Sherrie Flick is the author of a novel and two short story collections. She has received fellowships from the Sewanee Writers' Conference, the Pennsylvania Council on the Arts, and the Creative Nonfiction Foundation. She is a senior editor at *SmokeLong Quarterly* and a series editor for *The Best Small Fictions 2018*. She served as co-director of the Chautauqua Writers' Festival. She teaches in the MFA program at Chatham University in Pittsburgh.

John Dufresne has written two story collections and six novels, including *Louisiana Power & Light* and *Love Warps the Mind a Little*, both *New York Times* Notable Books of the Year. He has also written four books on writing, two plays, *Liv & Di* and *Trailerville*, and has co-written two feature films. His stories have twice been named Best American Mystery Stories. He is a Guggenheim Fellow and teaches creative writing at Florida International University in Miami.